ART SHULMAN

The Billy Chronicles

*A whimsical tale of lovers
who had to face life head on*

ASH & CREED
PRESS
Bold Stories. Sacred Questions.

Contents

Why I Wrote The Billy Chronicles

I've written a lot over the years—novels, a self-help relationship book, an illustrated kids book, a best-seller book about childhood recollections, plenty of published plays, and stories that wander into the odd corners of human behavior. If you look me up on Amazon, you'll find book titles like *A Kid Grows in Brooklyn*; *Tyrus Carson's Ride*; *I'm Wrong. I'm Sorry. I Love You*, and *Barnaby Brain*. Most of my work leans toward humor, because that's how I make sense of the world. People are funny. Life is funny. And if you pay attention long enough, you'll see that even the serious moments have a comic edge.

The Billy Chronicles grew out of that same instinct. Based partially on experience raising five kids, and trying to grow up myself, Billy showed up in my imagination as a kid who doesn't quite fit the mold—curious, thoughtful, and often just a step or two away from trouble. He's not trying to be funny, but he is. He's not trying to be profound, but sometimes he lands there anyway. I'm told by early readers that the story reminded them of their childhood—the way childhood actually feels: confusing, surprising, and full of moments that make more sense years later.

What I enjoyed most was letting Billy tell the truth as he sees it. Kids have a way of cutting through adult nonsense without realizing they're doing it. They ask the questions we've stopped asking. They notice things we've learned to ignore. Or notice them in a different way. Billy does all of that, and he does it with a kind of sideways honesty that made me chuckle as I wrote.

The Billy Chronicles carries pieces of the world I grew up in—neighborhoods, characters, and oddball situations that stuck with me long after I moved on. If you've read my other books, you'll recognize the same mix of humor and heart. If you're new to my writing, this tale about Billy is a good place to start. He's got a lot to say, and he says it in a voice that's entirely his own.

I'm grateful to readers who take a chance on a story about a kid faced with a serious problem who's just trying to figure things out.

Aren't we all?

Art Shulman

August 2026

Thanks!

This book could not have been written without my having lived with two groups of children who grew up right before my eyes. First were my biological children: Jennifer and Kerrie. Each of them has made me a grandfather.

Then, years later, after Jennifer and Kerrie became adults, were three kids—the children of my new wife, Rebecca, who became my stepchildren—Carrick, Ersson, and John, all of whom have grown into successful adults despite having to live with me for many years.

The characters in this book are unlike any of these kids, but events in their lives inspired its contents, as did actual events in my own life while growing up that I somehow managed to recall.

Special thanks to Peter Faur for his sage advice, diligent editing, and patience in dealing with me in the journey of preparing the manuscript for publication. And doing it all with a timeless natural smile, which was always comforting.

Most of all, thank you to Rebecca Westberg, my gifted, supportive spouse. She edited drafts, advised me on lots of decisions, and encouraged me throughout.

Whoopsie-Doopsie!

Lately, my life had been only updings and blessings. That week I'd been voted by schoolmates as most popular boy in the class, though, honestly, I'd have preferred most likely to succeed. Earlier in the day I'd found I scored in the top one percent nationally on the college boards. Flowers bloomed brilliantly all over Cedar Glen, like the world itself was showing off for me. And I had a new pair of Swazi loafers, with tassels.

Even better, I had a warm spring date with Joannie, with prospects of ending up under the stars on Moonlight Bluffs. I felt vibrant, tingly, almost buzzing, in my prosperity. I was delighted by how things were going, oblivious to misfortune, eager to romp and cuddle with my adorable steady, as I pulled nifty Jake's Spirit curbside to pick her up.

But from the second Joannie got in the car I knew something was off. The part in her silky brown hair wasn't quite straight, and strands stuck up, highly unusual for my normally meticulous girlfriend. Usually, after she sat, she reached over to pull the latch on my side. This time she stared straight ahead, hands in her lap.

Then, on the way to the multiplex, when I offered a choice of two movies, she blankly said she didn't care and I could choose. She said this even knowing that Crypt Tales IV was scary and gory, the type she usually avoided, while The Singing Bishop, the third movie in the series (after The Singing Imam and The Singing Rabbi), was a musical comedy, the type she enjoyed.

But before we reached the multiplex, she asked me to pull over. "I have something quite important we need to discuss," she said.

It turned out to be something very important. Well, gigenormously important!

"I'm pregnant," she announced after a deep breath.

"What?!! Whoopsie-Doopsie!!!"

She looked down at her sweatshirt like she expected to see a baby bump.

Wham! My pupils must have swelled huge and intense. My heart pounded. Joannie was pregnant! That meant she was expecting a baby. My baby. There was little question I was responsible. Partly responsible, that is. I couldn't be totally responsible, since Joannie was a willing participant and had given much thought to mattressing. In fact, as she'd told me six months ago, she'd talked with her mom about mattressing before we did it. Her mom had told her how proud she was about having a daughter who felt close and comfortable enough to seek her advice. Then, naturally, her mom went on to recommend against it, citing the usual reasons—venereal disease, loss of self-esteem, placing too much importance on a relationship at such an early age, pregnancy. That kind of stuff.

But then she assured Joannie it was her decision. "You're a big girl now," her mother declared.

"Just like I'd have handled it, if it was a child of mine," I thought at first. "Treating her like an adult."

Then I thought more clearly and realized that maybe she wasn't at all treating Joannie like an adult. If she was talking to a real adult, she'd have told the adult in no uncertain terms not to do it, to wait. So, she was being tricky, a typical understanding mother of a teenager, trying to outsmart her daughter by holding back, assuming her daughter was no more than a defiant adolescent who'd rebel against whatever she was told not to do.

Then I reversed myself again by concluding, "I suppose if it were my child I'd be tricky too. So, I guess Joannie's mom's as good a mom as any."

I thought that the next time I visited Joannie's house, even though I'd always been made to feel comfortable there, I'd feel crummy and embarrassed, sensing, maybe imagining, the pressure of Mrs. Gold's ferocious censuring eyes as she was thinking, "So this is the boy who wants to mattress with my little Joannie!"

"How could you be pregnant, Joannie? You were on birth control pills."

Joannie's dermatologist had started her on birth control pills for a broken-out face. We'd been discussing the possibility of mattressing, and once she'd been on the pills a few weeks, we realized one of our concerns—the terrible peril of pregnancy—had been eliminated. The pills, in effect, had given us permission to mattress.

"I was. I still am! Except for once or twice when I forgot, I've taken them almost every day," she asserted. "But they didn't work! And now you've got a pregnant girlfriend on your hands, getting tubbier by the day."

Unable to observe any bulging or widening of her slender shape, she didn't look at all pregnant. Then I realized it wasn't a fair judgment, since her baggy Save The Animals sweatshirt extended over her jeans below her hips. And, equally as relevant, I recognized my perception might be a result of wishful denial.

"How long has it been?" I asked.

"About a month and a half," she answered.

"What are we going to do?" I asked, chiding myself after the words were out for mouthing such a feeble question. She didn't answer, except to slide her face to my shoulder.

"Do your parents know?" I asked.

"No, I haven't said a thing to anyone."

"Do you know for sure you're pregnant?"

"The test strip lines from the kit said so and, then this morning the doctor who examined me was very certain about it."

We both were silent. Then, elevatoring her eyelids, she suggested, "I could get an abortion."

Whoopsie-Doopsie! Was she testing me? Did she really want an abortion? Did I? No! This could not be happening to Billy Harrington, high school junior, popular boy, college bound! Careful! Well, usually careful! Now, my life totally screwed!

The shock of her news was so threatening, my inability to comprehend and manage the implications of it so severe, it was essential to postpone further talk. "Why don't we think about it!" I suggested. "You think about it, if you really want one. And I'll think about it. And then we'll make a decision."

I was slightly relieved, putting off the inevitable decision, when she nodded. We hugged, and I softly rubbed the sweatshirt over her belly. I asked myself whether I was comforting her or searching for bumpy signs of a baby.

"Let's just go to the movies," she suggested, brushing away a tear.

I drove slowly, in keeping with the dampened mood—also, possibly, I thought, because impending fatherhood and the baby inside Joannie meant I now had to be even more responsible than usual. In a few minutes we arrived at the multiplex, where, being too late for the other movie, we saw Crypt Tales IV, with its tense predatory music score, involving a creepy psychopath, creaks and wails, sudden ambushes, detached body parts, and raw brains. Normally, when we went to a scary movie, I'd bring along a glove as a shield to prevent a frightened Joannie from drawing my blood as she clawed her nails into the back of my hand. But I hadn't brought along any hand protection this time. I thought, "This movie is so scary it should be a two-glover. Yet zoned-out Joannie is sitting dreamlike and isn't attacking me at all."

When I peeked over, her eyes were directed at the screen, but it was obvious she was paying attention to something other than the frightening images. She noticed me peeking at her and shot a glancing smile, then slunk down in her seat.

Needless to say, we didn't visit Moonlight Bluffs. An even greater void was Joannie making no comment about my new loafers. I wondered if she hadn't noticed or simply decided not to mention them. Not that loafers were significant in the grand scheme. Just that we'd always seemed to notice special things about each other and remark about them. This hit different.

We left each other with everything unresolved, except that we'd each think on it more and talk the next day. It wasn't as if something had to be done right away. Yet, as Joannie's news sunk in, and I recognized its helpless hopeless implications, I spiraled down dizzily in anxious depression.

Sharp dawn light, at odds with my mood, invaded the room through unturned blind slats as I laid subdued in my bed, immobilized. A father at seventeen? My eyes fluctuated between staring blankly at the ceiling and being shut tight while I sluggishly rocked my head from side to side, as if denying something. All night I'd been alternating between fitful sleep and lying awake like this, thoughts flitting by without my being able to still them for examination, unsuccessfully trying to sort things out. I felt infinitely more defeated than I'd felt after my team had lost in the Huckle Buckle championship tournament years ago, when I was so, so much younger.

Now, I was ashamed, and guilty, and angry, and inept, and cornered. "I'm a real mess," I thought. I'd never been in such a mess before, and normally extremely capable of handling even big messes, I had no idea how to handle this one. My plans, my self-image, and my stability had abruptly been recast. I no longer lived in a hopeful world. Instead of mostly good happening, instead of me being the winner most everyone seemed to respect, my personal universe was altering, not slowly modifying, but toppling down on me.

Toppling Down

No longer being a baby was just fine with Billy, whose second birthday was today! Not everybody agreed he was no longer a baby. But he knew they were wrong.

Now, he could tell his mom and dad what he wanted to eat or drink, rather than rely on their whims. Tell them he wanted meelk, rather than appie chuse or wadder. Or he might want gapefoot chuse! Just this morning, he'd told his mom he wanted a beckfist of seewee-o, towss, and yeggs.

Grown-ups and older kids were less scary-looking now that they weren't quite as big as they'd been before. And he could get around without falling on his behind.

He could even go in the back yard all by himself, as long as he let someone know where he was going. If he wanted to go somewhere, he could just toddle over, rather than rely on someone to wheel or carry him, or crawl like a baby. He could play with all those grown-up toys in the kitchen cabinets, like soap powder, pots and pans, cans of food, and hammers. He especially liked to bang the drum his mom stole to make spaghetti sauce.

He knew many colors, such as wed, gween, boo, or, his favorite, yeyow! He could even do some counting … un, fee, sis, fi, sebum. And soon he'd know which numbers followed which.

He knew he was a boy, and not a girl, though he wasn't sure just why. What made him a boy rather than a girl? He knew his mom was a girl, and so was his older sister Susie, and his dad was a boy, and so was that other person. He was sure he looked more like his dad than his mom. He couldn't understand how some people could say he looked at all like his mom. What does a nose have to do with looking like someone? Especially if they're a girl! And how could your nose look like the nose of someone much bigger, who naturally has a much bigger nose?

He could play all day, although these days his mom sometimes made him wait to play with her, since there was that new person in the house, who couldn't feed himself, and couldn't walk, and couldn't count, and couldn't do all of the things he, Billy Harrington, could do. It wasn't fair when his mom had to stop in the middle of playing because the stupid baby was crying.

He found out he could say "No" if he didn't want to do something, and sometimes his mom and dad listened to him, though not all the time. They especially listened if he yelled "NO!" really really loud, and said it many times in a row, "NO! NO! NO! NO! NO!"

But even then, he still had to do some things because his mom and dad told him so.

He knew some of the words to a few songs. Tinkle-tinkle was a song about a star. Hunty Dunty was about a boy with a really big tummy. He knew because he saw a picture of Hunty Dunty—who fell down and broke himself. Hunty Dunty should have been carefuller.

He loved to sing, and even when he didn't know the words, he'd hum. He had a wonderful voice, he thought, and he just knew his mom and dad, and especially Susie, loved to hear him sing all those tunes he could just make up in his head.

He knew songs were different from lullabies, though he didn't exactly know why. Actually, he did know why. It was "because," which was the answer to many questions that started with "why." His mom still sang him a lullaby when he went to bed at night. He really liked the one about the angels in heaven, which his mom told him was up high, even higher than the ceiling or even the attic. But he didn't like that scary rocketby baby one where the cradle fell down with the baby in it. He also didn't like the sad one about the little boy who had a busy day because his wed wagon was stolen, someone ate his jellybeans, and he fell down and got a big ow-wee on his knee.

He didn't have to take a nap in the afternoon now, unless he felt tired. Most afternoons, after playing all morning and following lunch, he felt tired, so he decided to take his nap. Sometimes he was so tired he fell asleep before deciding it was time to take his nap. Sometimes he woke up in his crib without remembering getting into it!

He liked his baths now. He splashed and sailed his boats and ducks across the tub. He remembered when he was a baby, he cried when they put him in the bath. Now he got mad if they took him out of the water too soon. Billy told his mom, "I come out when my boat sink." Billy thought it was very funny indeed when his mom held a boat under the water, telling him it sunk, and then the boat jumped out of the water when she let it go and made a splash! He laughed a lot. But he stopped laughing when his mom took him up out of the water.

He liked feeling warm when they wrapped a towel around him after they took him from the water. But he hated it when they rubbed too hard to dry him off. And he couldn't move his arms.

And he had lots and lots of toys. The shelves in his closet were full of toys. Almost no more toys could fit, though he wished his mom and dad would get rid of some of those stupid clothes so even more toys could fit in.

But, Billy, to be sure, didn't find life perfect!

Like just before, when he heard his mom sing *his* lullabies to that little pest. Why couldn't the brat have his own lullabies? The stupid baby couldn't understand what she was singing anyway! He didn't know *any* words. Why didn't his mom just hum him the tune?

Billy loved his mom, although he wished she was fat again, like she was before she went away to get the baby. When she first brought the baby home, she said it came from Babyland. But yesterday she told him the baby came out of her belly, and that was why she got skinny. He wondered how the baby could get out of his mom's belly. Even though the baby was small, he still was much too big to fit through her bellybutton.

And why would his mom first tell him Babyland? Hmm.

Anyhow, he thought, "I wish she would put it back where it came from!"

Now that he had places he wanted to go, he hated being in the playpen or his crib when he wanted to get out. He had to scream when his mom and dad were in another room. Just wait until he got older and could climb better! But climbing wasn't safe yet, even though he certainly was strong enough. He had muscles, all right. His dad was always feeling his arm and saying something about his muscles. He remembered some of the words: "You've got big muscles, Billy. Muscles are very important, for they allow us to control our movements so we can manipulate the world according to our needs. Next to our words, muscles are our most important possessions. Why when we lose our muscle control, we might as well be infants."

Billy was good at memorizing words people said, even if he didn't know what they meant. So, he didn't understand most of what his father told him, other than letting him know that big muscles were good. But that was the important part!

Nowadays, his mom and dad seemed to be disappointed when he did some of the very same things he did when he was a baby. Like, they made such a big deal when he had what they called a mess in his pants. Why did they call it a mess? What did they expect him to do anyway? And besides it made him comfortable to have warm stuff in his pants. He wondered whether to believe it when his dad told him he had muscles down there, muscles he could control. Billy knew his muscles were in his arms. Whenever someone came over and asked him to make a muscle, they felt his arm, not his butt, didn't they?

He also wondered why his parents didn't let him sit in a regular chair at the table, instead of the highchair. He was big enough. He felt trapped in that highchair, with the tray locking him in his seat. Maybe he did spill things from time to time, but it wasn't his fault. The cups and glasses and dishes were always in the wrong place in his way! And what was the big deal about food slobbering out of his mouth onto the tray of the highchair? Food is slippery! And he put most of it back in his mouth, didn't he?

His mom and dad smiled and told him how cute he was in that stupid chair. But he wanted to be treated like a growed-up, not a baby. Why couldn't the new baby sit in the highchair?

The new baby! The new baby! Susie held the new baby, and made stupid noises at it, some of the same stupid noises she used to make at him. His mom and dad spent more time with the new baby than with him. What for? The new baby couldn't do anything! It wasn't even cute, not as cute as he knew he himself was when he was that little.

Oh! His parents had told him how lucky he was to have a baby brother who he could play Huckle Buckle with when the two of them were older. But he doubted the new baby would ever be able to play Huckle Buckle! After all, he couldn't even hold a wattle!

He wished his baby brother wouldn't be invited to his birthday party that afternoon. The nuisance would get all the attention, even though it was his own birthday. Maybe they could lock the baby up in the bedroom the two of them shared. That was another thing. Before, he had his own room. Now he had to share one.

Later in the day Billy saw his mom and dad blowing up all different colors of balloons. It looked like a lot of fun. He tried to blow up some balloons. Although he made very loud spritzing sounds, showing how hard he was trying, he couldn't do it. His mom explained he didn't have enough air in him, but when he grew up, he would. Then his mom and dad hung the balloons in the kitchen, living room, and dining room. He proudly helped out by doing the job they gave him of telling them whether they hung the balloons in the right place. Usually they did, but sometimes they put one in a wrong place and he had to tell them, "No, no, no, no, NO!" and tell them the right place.

After the balloons were up, his mom and dad hung colored crinkly paper between different walls and put two tablecloths on the dining room table. One of them was made of material like some of his shirts were made of and was pink. The other one, which they placed on top, was made of paper. It was white and had all sorts of colors on it. He was glad they placed that one on top, to cover up the pink. Pink was a girl's color.

Susie wore a pink dress and had her blond hair combed, with a pink wibbon in it. His mom had a bright red wibbon in her hair. His dad, as always, had his hair combed with a smart part down one side of his head and didn't have any wibbon in his hair. But he never wore any wibbon in his hair. Wibbons were something that girls used in their hair, but not boys. That was another big difference between boys and girls. Billy knew he didn't want anybody putting any wibbon in his hair, ever! Billy let his mom comb his hair, but warned her, "No wibbon! I not a girl!"

Billy was glad they left the sleeping baby in the bedroom during the party.

Some neighbors and friends of his mom and dad came over, and they put on pointed hats, just like the ones his family wore. Billy overheard one of them say during the party, "I haven't had as much fun since New Year's Eve."

Billy wondered whether this was the same Eve as the one in the Bible his dad had told him about who lived in a garden and ate ribs and talked with snakes. He'd ask later, if he remembered.

On top of the tablecloth his mom and dad placed bowls of ships and petzels, samwishes, tato salad, dishes filled with candies, and a long plate of carrots, coocumpers and corryfower. Why would anybody want to eat from that long plate if they didn't have to?

His dad took from the refrigerator a big glass bowl filled with a pink water, and as he set it down in the middle of the table, he informed Billy, "And here's the party punch."

Billy began to sob.

"What's wrong?" his mom asked.

"That girl's punch!" he informed her.

"Why is it girl's punch?" she wondered.

"Ess pink!" he told her.

"Oh, I see!" his mom noted, and he followed her as she went to the refrigerator, opened up a jar of purple chuse with pictures of gwapes on it, and poured it into the punch bowl, turning the stuff in it more wed. Wed was a very different color than pink, Billy knew.

He giggled and finished in one long swig the punch his mom poured for him. She wiped his mouth. "You can't have a mustache for your birthday party!"

Billy was patted on the head by a lot of the grown-ups. He did not like this. He thought, "I'd like to bop them all over their heads on their birthdays."

Some grown-ups brought their children, and a few of them wanted to open his gifts, which were piled in the living room. He felt like bopping them over the head too!

"No, no. Go away. These mine," he let know a bratty little girl he hardly knew named Joannie. The little girl rubbed her eyes and then started crying. Out loud. Very out loud. "What a baby!" thought Billy. "Just like that little brat who has to be in my room!"

Soon, Billy's dad took his hand and strode him to the dining room table. Billy felt himself being picked up and sat down, his dad stating, "Billy, you go in the seat of honor," which was the chair his dad usually sat in at mealtime. Billy knew that if anyone asked a question, he'd have to tell the truth as long as he was in that seat. That was what being on your honor was about! Billy knew it was special to be in the seat of honor. But, on the other hand, if there was any day you should be able to make up something and not tell the truth, it was your birthday.

Billy wondered why his dad usually got to sit in the seat of honor. Why didn't his mom sit there once in a while? Did she tell the truth less often than his dad? Maybe that was another difference between boys and girls he didn't know about yet.

Then he heard his dad call everyone over, "Time for birthday cake." Pretty soon everyone was in a circle around Billy. His dad asked his mom to turn down the lights. Then his dad went into the kitchen and came out carrying a big birthday cake with brown and white writing on it. The cake had two lit candles because Billy was turning two.

"Wow!" thought Billy. Then everybody began to sing, as his dad placed the cake on the table.

"Happy Birthday to you!
Happy Birthday to you!
Happy Birthday, dear Billy!
Happy Birthday to you!"

Billy thought, "What a fine song." And he giggled as they sang.

"OK, Billy, bwow out the candles," his dad said, lifting Billy up to stand on the chair. "But before you bwow them out, make a wish."

Billy thought he knew what a wish was—the very same noise he'd make when he blew out the candles. But he wondered why his dad said to make a wish before he made a wish. Sometimes his dad puzzled him. Sometimes his dad didn't make any sense at all.

Billy pulled in his breath, puffed out his little pink cheeks, and blew the air out as hard as he could, moving his head from side to side. The flames in the candles went out. Some people started to clap and say "Hooray yippee!" But they stopped when the flames came on again.

"Try again, Billy," his dad encouraged.

He blew out air again, and again the candles went out. And then they came on again.

People laughed, but Billy didn't think it was funny. What kind of a boy was he if he couldn't even bwow out candles? With everyone looking too!

"Oh, Gordon," went his mom, like she sometimes did when his dad did something silly.

"OK Billy, let's take out those candles from the cake and instead, put in these candles," his dad said. Then he lit the new candles. This time, when Billy bwew out the candles, they didn't go on again, and everybody hoorayed and yippied. Billy was thankful to his dad for putting the easy candles on the cake. His dad was always helping him out!

"I bwowed it out," he bragged.

After people ate birthday cake, it was time to open presents. There were lots of them, and Billy sat on the floor as his mom handed them to him one by one. The presents were in color paper and wibbons and came with cards on them. The wibbons were very skinny, and Billy couldn't understand why he couldn't tear them. What was wrong with them? It was like they wanted to keep the wrapping paper on so he couldn't get his presents. His mom had to cut them for him with a scissors. "Wibbons are not my pals," he decided.

Once the wibbon was off it was really fun to rip the paper. He liked the crinkly noise of ripping paper. He liked making a mess of ripped paper. But once the paper was all ripped off, he didn't care very much about it. He knew ripped wapping paper and wibbons were garbage. Another sign of growing up into a little boy!

Billy liked some presents more than others. For instance, he liked all of the toys and none of the clothes. After opening all his presents, Billy now had the movie Bimbo, about a deer animal. Also, there were some new shirts and pants, a story book, a coloring book, a jigsaw puzzle of a farm, a big box of blocks to build things, a lawnmower with color balls, and a fashlight that really worked. If he got scared by something in the night, he could put on his fashlight.

When he was done, the paper, wibbons, and gifts were in a pile all over the living room carpet. Billy knew it looked like a big mess. He saw some guests began to leave and his mom and dad were saying goodbye. So, he thought he'd just show them what a big boy he was by starting to clean up!

He took an armload of wapping paper and wibbons and walked to the trash can in the kitchen, making sure he wasn't knocked over or run over by any grown-ups who weren't watching out. He was getting pretty big, but he wasn't that big yet, and grown-ups were still much bigger. The can was already filled with used paper plates, cups, and knives, forks, and spoons that people just threw away. So, he ditched the wapping paper and wibbons on the kitchen floor and left them there. Well, at least it was out of the living room!

He went back into the living room and picked up some gifts. He lugged them to his bedroom and put them on the floor of his walk-in closet. He stood on his little red chair, reached up as far as his arms would go, and one by one put the stuff on the second shelf. There wasn't much room, but he managed to stick them all in so they stayed.

Then he made another trip to the living room for more presents. Somehow, he squeezed them on the shelf too. Then he returned to the living room to get more stuff. The clothes he'd leave for last. Maybe he wouldn't take them at all. Those were presents for moms, not big boys. At least his mom seemed to like them much more than he did.

He trudged back to his closet carrying an armload of coloring books and story books. On the way he left a trail of some dropped books. Oh well, he'd pick them up later!

He stood on his little red chair again and tried to squish in some books on the same shelf he'd put things before. All of a sudden, Billy felt himself toppling! The whole shelf plunged. He was slammed flat to the floor. Something conked him on the head. Toys tumbled down on him. Clothes plummeted over him. He was covered by books and toys and games and clothes and things his mom used to take care of his baby brother.

He was really scared and began to cry. But no one came. Billy thought he might die, although he really wasn't very sure of what dying was, just that it was bad, and often happened to people who were in trouble. Or caught on fire! Or fell from a window! Or drank poison by accident! But why was dying so bad if people who did it went to heaven, which his mom and dad had told him was a beautiful place where they all would end up someday? He'd ask, if he remembered. And if he ever got out of this mess!

All of a sudden, he heard other crying. It was his baby brother, shrieking away. WAHHH! WAHHH! WAHHH!

Suddenly, Billy heard his mom rush into the room. She was cooing, "There there, little sweetkins baby," much like she used to say to him. Just hear her! It was as if she was just waiting for the baby to wake up. Then she comes in, just like that! Why didn't she pay as much attention to him, Billy?

He heard her stop cooing, then gasp. "Billy! What happened to you? Wow! What you have on your head. It must really hurt."

She looked at it carefully for a moment, and then reassured him, "It'll be fine. We'll just wash it up with soap and water."

Billy tried not to sob. But he couldn't help it.

"How did this happen, poor Billy?" she asked as she pushed aside the broken shelf, fallen clothes, toys, and games.

"The self bwoke," he told her, when suddenly his brother shrieked, WAHHH! WAHHH! He hoped his mom would not go to the bratty baby, would just forget that baby. And mostly, he hoped his mom would *not* tell him that if it wasn't for the baby, he, Billy, might be dead by now!

"Why didn't you ask me to help you?" she said, very calmly.

"Because," Billy explained meaningfully.

"My golly goodness! You must have been scared, really scared."

"No," he lied. He wished his mom wouldn't give the baby any credit at all for saving him. He himself was the one to deserve credit, anyway, for putting the toys away—at least three stars to go in his book.

"It must have seemed like such a long time to you, lying under all this stuff."

"Uh-huh," he choked out.

"Are you feeling all right?" she asked like she really cared.

"Yes," he replied, and they hugged each other.

Then Billy felt the comfort of being picked up by his mom and carried in her soft arms out of the closet, then into the bathroom, leaving the shrieking baby in his crib. She sat him near the sink and washed off his wound, covered it all with a bandage, and admired how brave he was. That made him feel special! He sniffled a little but did not cry.

Afterward, she carried him to his dad, who she told what happened. Then his mom and his dad and he all hugged each other at the same time, and everything was like old times. By now he was giggling from happiness.

That evening, after his mom had helped him brush his teeth, Billy was waiting for his dad to come in and tell him a story of what it was like in the olden days. Still wearing the band-aid covering the forehead bruise, he quietly tiptoed over to his brother's crib and said to the infant, who was awake, lying on his back, "Andew. Fank you for saving my yife."

Then, he stuck his small hand through the rungs of the crib and patted his little brother ever-so-gently on the head.

Andrew began to shriek!

A World Suddenly Changed

On the other side of the room, cocooned under a pillow and blankets, slept my snoring younger brother in his march toward adolescence. Andrew had only started to snore in the past year, and I was glad he muffled himself under his covers, muting his thunderous racket. We still shared the same room in the same house we'd always lived in. Over the years I'd grown comfortable with sharing my bedroom, and we'd become pals of sorts, although I didn't think my scampish brother would ever reach my level of maturity. Wait! How could I be so mature if I got into this new trouble?

I'd grown comfortable with all our endearing surroundings—our room cluttered with strewn clothing, and pennants and posters hung at odd angles. The sparkling, cheery kitchen with the tiny dining nook, which seemed so huge when I was little. The comfy dining room, dominated by the large, rugged oak table abundant with nicks and scratches. The immaculate bathrooms with the same light green tile that hadn't lost its sheen after all these years. The homey living room, where after dinner my dad sat lost in a book and my mom her magazines, the two sharing the flower print couch that camouflaged so many embedded stains and hid loose change and crumbs under the cushions. It was a used house, in the best sense; people lived there. I lived there.

Perhaps I began to turn nostalgic about the house because I realized that soon I might not live there, leaving it with the shadow of behind. Soon I might be sharing a different bedroom, with a new person. To override some of my gloominess, at least Joannie didn't snore. I hoped the inevitable, often mystical bodily changes that I'd heard often accompanied pregnancy didn't come with sonic side effects.

I was glad it was Saturday. Normally, once awake, I eagerly attacked each day. Now, possessed by a defeating fatigue, I had no desire to rise from my bed. It was so easy to drop back to sleep, although so difficult to stay asleep for very long. I wouldn't be running into Joannie at school where it would be hard to converse, fumbling in hallways or seemingly private areas where other students would interrupt us. We could have our discussion in privacy. Besides, how could I concentrate at school? And over the weekend my mom wouldn't be rousing me for breakfast, so I'd be on time for school. My mom still did that, sometimes treating me like an irresponsible teenager, or worse, like a baby.

A baby! Joannie was pregnant, and my mom still sometimes treated me like a baby, distrusting me to do responsible adult things like wake up in time. How could I have a baby if I myself was treated like a baby? Well, at least this situation proved I was more of an adult. Babies don't have babies!

What would I do with a baby? Play with it? Playing with babies was for girls! Mostly! Not to be sexist about it! It was just the way things were. Boys, no, men didn't want to spend their time changing diapers, speaking babble, and playing hootchie-kootchie. Maybe some men said they liked it, but if he was honest about it, what authentic man would prefer playing house to playing Huckle Buckle? I wasn't ready to be a father. I had other interests and plans for my future which would be wrecked by the demanding presence of a baby. I still needed to play with my pals, not rock back and forth and spoon mush into a tiny mouth. That was for girls!

If burly Ms. Hutchinson, my women's studies teacher, knew I had this viewpoint, she'd automatically flunk me! But why did they force boys to take women's studies classes? I didn't have to take a class in Afro-American studies, or Latino studies, or gay studies, so why was women's studies a requirement? Why were women so important anyway? Well, I knew several reasons why they were important, but why were they so important that they had to be studied as a separate group? With a required class of their own to boot! Why wasn't there a men's studies class? I didn't at all buy Ms. Hutchinson's argument that most of written history *was* men's studies!

But the world *was* remodeling itself by gender. Women globally were asserting themselves, battling for their rights, assuming functions traditional for men, grasping for equality. Women were mayors, governors, senators and justices. Other women made gains by discarding veils and even dresses, though not in the sense of being naked. And men were being forced to do things they'd never done before, like take classes in women's studies, and not whistle at pretty girls or face the threat of a sexual harassment lawsuit.

I was in favor of equal opportunity. "No one should be trod upon" was a motto of mine, one I believed I first saw imprinted on some currency, though it might have been on a box of cereal. Anyway, I didn't think someone who was whistled at was necessarily being trod upon.

My personal world was radically crumbling, erupting, disappearing. Even if events worked out such that Joannie wouldn't have the baby, I'd never be the same naïve youth, innocent of tragedy or of the injury of sudden radical events. My concerns of only yesterday, pre-Joannie meeting, now seemed so insignificant. Compared to having a baby, how important could an astronomy test be? Even a Huckle Buckle game. Soon, instead of making high grades, I might have to be concerned with making a living. My daily and long-term schedules could soon be forever altered. My once steady life, my regular activities, my expectations of daily events, were now wobbling, threatened, perhaps soon to be demolished and replaced with a terrible unknown.

First Day at School

Billy could hardly sit still. His mom had told him it was a very special day—his very first day of school. He smiled, hummed to himself, and played happily with the little toy cars in his plastic tub on the ride to Cedar Glen Nursery School. Every few seconds he let out a "ZOOOOOM," pretending a car was going very, very fast. He was proud his mom had told him, "You're just three years old, but you're certainly growing up fast!" His big sister Susie had a teacher—Susie was in the first grade—and now he'd have one, too.

He'd been quite happy staying at home. His mom was always around, except when she was playing with his little bratty brother Andrew. And even if she wasn't, there usually was something to do. He had lots of toys, and he could do puzzles, and crayon. He knew how to push the button to make the TV go on. And play games on the computer. But sometimes life wasn't very exciting. Like going shopping with his mom. Who cared about shopping, unless it was at the toy store? And more and more, he was being put in time-out for things he'd never been punished for before—like being too loud, or not cleaning up a mess, or calling someone "Dumbbell-head." So, Billy was thrilled when she told him he was now big enough to go to nursery school.

His mom parked the car, and Billy automatically put his arms in the air so she could take off his seat belt. She no longer had to ask him to raise his arms; he just knew it should be done. They held hands as they walked past the playground, moving through a gate with a latch so high up that only big people could reach up and open it. "This yard is much bigger than our yard," proclaimed Billy.

Then he and his mom walked into the very big, colorful Room 2, where his mom introduced him to his teacher, Miss Bonnie, who bent down, shook his hand like he was a little gentleman, and welcomed him with a sweet smile. She had a small red rose pinned to her blouse, which made Billy think Miss Bonnie was nice because flowers are happy, and 'wed' was his favorite color. Well, after yeyow. It wasn't a real red rose, but a jelwaree red rose, which Billy thought was smart because then she didn't have to water it.

"I'm happy to meet you, Billy. I'm glad you're coming to our school."

Billy hugged his mom's knee, shy to say anything to Miss Bonnie, though he could tell from her pudgy smiling face she was very kind.

While his mom was speaking with Miss Bonnie, Billy walked the room. There were lots of toys, and stuck on the walls were colored papers with paint or crayon on them. On the floor were wooden trains and big bright color blocks! A happy place with lots for a boy like him to do!

Miss Bonnie then showed Billy and his mom a cabinet without a door. "Look!" his excited mom exclaimed. "Your very own cubbyhole!" And she placed his little bag and blankie in it.

Miss Bonnie agreed, "This is Billy's cubbyhole." Billy beamed!

After a few minutes of further chit-chat with Miss Bonnie, his mom knelt and told Billy she was going to the school office but would be right back. After she left, Billy hummed happily to himself as he checked out the boy-sized tricycles and scooters in one corner of the room. School sure looked like so much fun.

His mom, Billy found out much later, went to the Main Office to drop off her Child Description Form with Miss Maplezewski, the school secretary, who sneezed three times just before taking the form. Mrs. Harrington noted that all the women working at the school were named "Miss," but some were Miss with a first name, like Miss Bonnie, and some were Miss with a last name, like Miss Maplezewski. She hoped Billy wouldn't get confused because it was a smidgen confusing to her! Why weren't they all Miss first name, or all Miss last name?

His mom returned shortly to Room 2, commenting, "This certainly is a fine place for you, Billy! You will learn a lot here!"

She stayed with him a little while, even going outside to romp in the playground. In her enthusiasm to show Billy what a fine time he'd have, his mom seemed to have even more fun than he did, until at the monkey bars she squeezed her head between two rails and got it stuck, finally managing to jerk it out at the cost of a broken earring. Both Billy and his mom were disappointed when Miss Bonnie coaxed his mom off the monkey bars so other kids could have their turn.

His mom left Billy with a big kiss on his cheek and a wish to have a wonderful day, which Billy knew was better than having a nice day. She'd pick him up later and give him thumbs up!

For the next bunch of minutes Billy played happily, mainly with Miss Bonnie and her assistant, Miss Wendy, but also with some of the other kids. Well, not actually *with* the other kids, but alongside them, for Billy didn't yet have a full set of skills for playing *with* other kids his age. Aside from taking turns. Billy did know it was important to take turns.

Miss Bonnie showed everybody how to make pizza by pasting scraps of yellow and red paper on a paper plate, and Billy thought that was very exciting, although he liked regular pizza pie better because you could eat it, and Miss Bonnie told them they shouldn't eat this pizza pie even if they were hungry. Later she had them ride scooters, climb on the monkey bars, play tag, and race. Billy really liked the Bunny Race, hopping on both feet from the front of the room to the back. He didn't know he could do that!

Miss Bonnie, an experienced teacher who really liked kids, nevertheless knew it was a good idea to wear out her pupils so there wouldn't be a problem later when it was nappy time. Besides, her troop of three- and four-year-olds was still much too young to be taught any of the three P's— penmanship, physics, and psychology—or any of the three R's—reading, writing, and rhythmic gymnastics. That was not what nursery school was about.

"I really like school. It's more fun than home," Billy marveled.

Billy's troubles began when Miss Maplezewski had to leave early because she was sick, telling Miss Bonnie, "I guess I've caught another cold from one of these little stinkers. I don't want to spread it, so I guess I'll go home."

On the one hand, Miss Bonnie thought Miss Maplezewski was right about not wanting to spread a cold. How often had she herself been mad at a parent for sending a child to school with sniffles? On the other hand, Miss Maplezewski had taken four weeks off since the beginning of January of this year because she didn't want to risk spreading colds. And this was only March.

Miss Maplezewski was supposed to give Miss Bonnie a copy of the Child Description Form Mrs. Harrington had filled out about Billy. But she forgot. Miss Maplezewski had what seemed to others a very messy desk, with papers upon papers, although she herself claimed she knew exactly where everything was. So, when Miss Bonnie went to Miss Maplezewski's desk for the form, she couldn't find it and was unable to locate certain key information about Billy. Like his words for going to the bathroom.

Over time, Miss Bonnie had heard scores of words three- and four-year-olds used for going to the bathroom. And later in the morning, knowing that Billy hadn't yet gone, she tried some of them on him. She asked him, "Billy, do you have to go ka-ka?"

Billy looked at her as if he had no idea what she was talking about.

So, she asked, "Billy, do you have to go doo-dee?"

This time Billy laughed. Doo-dee sounded like a funny joke she was telling him.

Miss Bonnie tried again. "Billy, do you have to go poo-poo?"

Poo-poo sounded even funnier than doo-dee, and he laughed even harder.

Miss Bonnie went through all the decent words she could think of. She asked if he had to go poop, poo, poo poop, number two, plop, ka-kee, boom boom, dah dah, and doo-dah. Miss Bonnie sure was a great teacher, telling all these fine jokes.

Miss Bonnie then pointed to her rear end. He thought that was the funniest thing she had done so far.

Finally, the stumped Miss Bonnie stopped being funny, maybe thinking, "Oh, well. When he has to go, he'll tell me."

But she was wrong. About a half hour later, Billy had gone to the bathroom. But not in the bathroom, just in his pants. Billy, who'd only recently become toilet trained, was too embarrassed to announce to Miss Bonnie, who he had only just met, after all, that he had to go. And since he didn't know where the bathroom was and didn't know any of the other kids well enough to ask "Where the bathroom is?" he just let it rip where he was playing.

An odor soon wafted over Miss Bonnie's Room 2, a familiar sort of smell. She now could make fine distinctions between the poop—as she herself called it—of different children, much as the Eskimos made fine distinctions between variations in snow. "Smells like corn flakes and prunes," she thought to herself.

Poop detective as she was, she sniffed out it was Billy who was responsible. She strode over to him, where he announced, "I just farted. I'm playing with this car," and started to push the car. ZOOOOM! But Miss Bonnie knew it was him, all right, not only from the odor, but because Billy was standing up while pushing the car, rather than driving sitting down, as he had been doing.

She thought "My goodness, used to be only four-year-olds would use the word 'fart.' Kids are getting more and more mature at a younger age."

Miss Bonnie knelt and chided softly, "Billy. You pooped in your pants."

"I did not!" Billy blurted. "I moved my bowels with my muscles."

"Well then, let's clean you up," Miss Bonnie announced, took his hand and walked to Billy's cubbyhole, where she reached for the bag with the spare set of clothes his mom had left "just in case." She steered him to the bathroom and opened the door. So that was where it was!

The bathroom was much, much different from any bathroom Billy had ever seen. Wow! Four toilet bowls lined up in a row! Billy had never been in a bathroom with more than one, except in one of those big stores where the toilet bowls had walls between them. And these toilet bowls were short. At home Billy had to climb up to the toilet seat. And those seats were big, so he could fall into the toilet. But in this bathroom his legs would touch the floor!

Miss Bonnie removed Billy's pants and underpants and wiped him off with a damp washcloth. Billy began to sob. And the sobs got bigger and louder. Billy was embarrassed. Here, he'd been so proud of himself for being toilet trained—his mom had told him this showed he was no longer a baby—and now he had made a mess in his pants in front of his teacher.

When they finally came out of the bathroom, Billy gazed around the room, on the lookout for other children making fun of him. But none of the other kids seemed to care one bit that he'd messed his pants. That struck him as just fine!

He wiped his red, puffy eyes with his arm and went to pedal a car.

Soon it was time for mid-morning snacks. Today's snack menu was fruit, and Miss Bonnie announced that each child could pick which fruit to eat: a purple plum, or a yellow banana, or a juicy red and yellow peach. Billy liked "pums," but he had one yesterday. He also liked bananas, and his favorite color was "yeyow," but he remembered he hadn't had a peach in a very long time. Besides, the peach was *two* colors—including yeyow—so he grabbed a big peach. It would be so yummy! He ambled to his seat and chomped a big bite. It tasted just as yummy as he thought it would. Most of what he bit off went into his mouth, but some dribbling juice soaked his chin. And of course, his hand was all covered with peach juice as he continued to scarf that fine fruit.

All of a sudden, Billy's face got all tingly and itchy. It also got warm. Billy couldn't see that his face was flushed a bright pink. He began to scratch it. But scratching didn't do any good. His face became itchier and itchier and began to hurt. While he scratched one side of his face with his free hand, he scratched the other side with the hand holding the peach. Peach juice was now all over his face. His ow-wee was getting worse. Scared, he began to sob. He wondered if he was being punished by the Lord his mom and dad were always talking about for making a mess in his pants.

Miss Bonnie heard whimpering and looked over. She knew an allergic reaction when she saw one. She thought to herself, "Darn that Miss Maplezewski! I bet it's on the missing Child Description Form: allergic to peaches. I just hope his windpipe doesn't close up."

Miss Bonnie strode quickly to Billy, knelt, and took the peach from his hand. Billy objecting, "No, that my peach."

"No, Billy, the peach is what's making you hurt," she said gently but firmly.

Billy couldn't believe a peach could make him sick. His mom had told him poison could make you sick and even die, but a peach wasn't poison, it was yummy food. He knew something that didn't taste so good could make you sick, like probly bussel spouts. But not something yummy like a peach!

Meanwhile, Billy kept scratching his face. Miss Bonnie told him, "Billy, I want you to do me a favor. Don't scratch your face. If you stop scratching, the itch will go away."

Billy wondered why Miss Bonnie wanted him to do her a favor at a time like this, when his ow-wee was really hurting. He also couldn't figure out why she didn't want him to scratch. Whenever he had an itch, he scratched it. Like, after a fly landed on his nose, he scratched it. How were you supposed to get rid of an itch unless you scratched it? And here Miss Bonnie was telling him the itch would go away if he *didn't* scratch it! This school sure was a very strange place! He bawled even harder.

Miss Bonnie finally took Billy to the bathroom, where she dabbed his face and hands with a washcloth. Billy told himself he was certainly spending a lot of time in the bathroom being wiped with a washcloth by Miss Bonnie.

In a few minutes, Billy's face began to itch less and less. And before you knew it, it was back to normal, and they left the bathroom.

But now Billy noticed some of the kids were looking very strangely at him. Billy suddenly felt a little proud. Here he was a new boy, and he was getting so much attention from Miss Bonnie! He was obviously very special! If the other kids were jealous, poo-poo on them!

Billy toddled over to a boy playing with blocks, who took one look at Billy, and said, "No! You cannot play with these blocks."

So, he strode to another boy playing with a ball of wool that had many colors, and who told him, "This mine. Go away."

He went to a girl named Joannie reading a book with pictures, who said, "Go away. My mom said I shouldn't stay near sick childrens." For some reason he didn't call her "Dumbbell-head."

Nobody wanted to play with Billy! So, he sat quietly in a corner of the room, breaking crayons.

Miss Bonnie came over and patted him on the head. He hated being patted on the head. It made him feel like a real baby.

One by one, many kids were picked up by a mom or dad. But not Billy's mom. His mom had told him she'd be back to get him later, but here it was later and she still had not shown up!

At noon it was lunch time. Billy was happy when Miss Bonnie said they'd be eating what the school usually served on Tuesdays—tacos. And the "wed" dink Miss Bonnie said was "cool" something or another.

Billy was very hungry. Why shouldn't he be, since he wasn't allowed to finish his peach? He ate everything on his plate and drank everything in his cup, and his face did not tingle at all!

After lunch came story time and nap mats. Miss Bonnie's stories were boring, with many long words and no funny voices. Miss Bonnie really didn't mind if some kids drifted off into sleep in the middle of her story. Billy himself dropped into a deep sleep shortly after the boy in the story fell down a big dark hole to escape a wicked lumberjack wearing a red shirt.

Later—he didn't know how much later since he couldn't tell time, but it seemed to him a long time, much longer than the five minutes his mom usually sentenced him for time out—Billy suddenly was awakened by a loud buzzer, even louder than on his mom and dad's alarm clock.

He looked around. Lots of kids were in the room. Some were the same as before, but he was sure he hadn't seen many of the others. There was also a grown-up, but it was a man, not a woman. He was wearing gray pants—and a red shirt!

Where were Miss Bonnie and Miss Wendy? Why was there a lumberjack in his class? And why didn't someone shut off that alarm clock?

The man clapped his hands many times and announced loudly, "Fire drill."

He said it again, much louder than sweet Miss Bonnie had ever talked. Billy knew what fire was—something hot that could be your friend but could hurt you too. He knew what a drill was—something his dad used to make holes in things. But he didn't know what a fire drill was. Maybe it was fire that burned holes in things. The man strode toward Billy, still lying on his mat. Closer and closer. Billy's eyes opened wider and wider! He thought the man might drill a hole in him with fire. It would really hurt. Billy began to wail. Would he ever see his family again? He wished he had a dark hole to jump into, just like the boy in the story good old Miss Bonnie told.

Billy didn't move. So, the man picked him up and carried him outside to the yard, where he set him down among other kids. Billy was wailing his head off and thinking, "Okay, maybe *all* the kids are going to have a hole burned in them, not just me. But why weren't they crying? What *is* going on here anyway? And why isn't anyone still not shutting off that stupid-bell alarm clock?"

Then the man strolled to Billy, knelt, and introduced himself, "Hi Billy! I'm Mr. Dave, your afternoon teacher. You're new here, aren't you? I guess you're left over from this morning. Most kids in the morning stay just a half day. Have a good nap?"

Billy was suspicious. Women always took care of kids his age. His mom, or a girl babysitter. Or even Miss Bonnie. Not a man. So, he didn't answer. He thought of calling Mr. Dave "Dumbbell-head" but didn't, afraid what the man might do to him.

But when Mr. Dave announced, "Okay. Everybody back in the room," and all the other kids followed, Billy thought he might be all right after all. Maybe!

An hour later, Billy's mom came to pick him up. He ran over and hugged her leg tightly, hiding his face from Mr. Dave.

She carried him to the car, Billy toting the pizza he'd glued together. As she belted him in, she asked brightly, "Billy, what did you learn today?"

Billy's only answer was sobs.

"Did you have fun?"

He continued to weep.

"You must be tired from your first day at school," she soothed, noticing he wasn't even playing with his miniature cars. Later on the trip home, he ripped apart his pizza.

After dinner—a meal Billy hardly touched, even though he usually loved racaroni—his dad placed his pipe down, took a sulking Billy on his knee and said, "I'm glad you had such a good first day at school, Billy. I remember before I became a college professor, on my first day at the tire plant I caught my finger in some machinery, and it was almost amputated— that's cut off, Billy. And then I puked after lunch, right on the foreman's uniform. And later, someone slashed my tires intentionally—that's ripped it on purpose. We all have bad days, Billy. Even when you think your bad days are over with, another one comes up suddenly out of nowhere. But for you, Billy, Lord willing, I hope all your days at Cedar Glen Nursery are like today."

"Amen," his mom pronounced from the hallway, scaring Billy no end.

The next morning, Billy was screaming his lungs out, begging his mom, "No make me go! Not want to go there."

Mrs. Harrington was mystified. Billy hadn't cried yesterday on the trip to preschool. It seemed like such a wonderful place. And Miss Bonnie appeared to be such a caring, creative teacher. But then, oh dear, she recalled that Billy seemed so glad to see her when she'd come to pick him up. On the trip home he whimpered and wailed, though not as loudly as now. What had happened?

Still, she encouraged, "You'll have so much fun today. You like riding cars, and you can color, and cut things with a scissors, and go on the slide. And besides, your mom—that's me, Billy—has to take care of your little brother. He's a baby, you know, not like you, my big boy."

"Big boy?" He realized that he was that—a big boy. Billy stopped crying.

When Billy and mom entered Room 2, Miss Bonnie immediately asked Billy if he'd like to play with the big car again.

Billy ambled toward the corner with all the cars, tricycles, and scooters. A boy was already there, humming to himself. When Billy looked to Miss Bonnie, the new boy's mom was handing her a Child Description Form. It must be the new boy's first day at Cedar Glen Nursery School.

Billy marched to the new boy and told him, "My name Billy."

The new boy replied, "My name Todd."

Billy took Todd's hand and led him to the back of the room, where he opened a door and showed the new boy four short toilet bowls, all in a row!

Then he looked over to his mom and flashed her thumbs up!

Spill?

I hadn't spoken to anyone yet about the problem, the predicament. What do you call something that blackens and imperils the rest of your life? Of course, I hadn't had the chance. My family was all in deep slumber when I tiptoed home last night. How would they react?

My younger brother, now taller than me, just by an inch or so, would snicker and say, "That sucks," and then bounce on to some other subject. Andrew seemed allergic to staying in one place to hold a conversation.

My older sister Susie, typically overreacting theatrically, would gasp, and say something brilliant, like "Omigod!"

My tenured college professor dad would huffily accuse me of being thoughtless, short-sighted, a poor planner, and damaging my chance to obtain a good higher education and "get ahead in today's cutthroat marketplace, a ruthless socioeconomic matrix."

My disappointed mom would get all prissy and accuse me of acting counter to the Lord's word.

I didn't have to spill right away. Maybe I wouldn't have to tell them at all. Maybe somehow the problem would just go away, leaving a wispy trace of bad memory. Divine intervention, maybe. You reach and wish when you're desperate. But—reality—sooner or later, I'd have to spill to them.

And sooner or later I'd have to face Mrs. Gold! Not to forget—gulp—husky weightlifter Mr. Gold, when he returned from delivering furniture cross-country. What would they say? Or, in the case of the temperamental Mr. Gold, what would he do? A Jewish mover? He just had to be unpredictable.

I thought I'd distract myself by taking refuge in the age-old pastime of watching insects crawling on the wall or floor, but I couldn't find a single one, not even an ant or a spider. And where was a roach when you really needed one? Nor was there even a fly to follow. I regretted foolishly ceasing scarfing down cookies in my room a few weeks ago, which my mom said drew bugs.

"Bugs aren't necessarily bad. Some of them eat other bugs," I half-heartedly told her, though not also mentioning their use as a visual distraction in times of stress.

"That may be true," she conceded, "but I don't want any bugs in your room. They breed all sorts of germs."

I was unable to distract myself from the idea of ... abortion, with its repulsive connotation, more heinous and sinister than other terms we covered in biology, like "mutation" or "deviancy." Abortions had associations with coat hangers, helpless fetuses, and bloody placentas tossed in a dumpster. They were grotesque acts of desperation, performed by the unsanitary money-grubbing hands of ungodly, unshaven degenerates with no concern about snuffing out a life. Who was worse, the twisted unfortunates who went in for them, or the immoralists who performed them?

In addition to meaning a termination of pregnancy, kids in school referred to hideous situations or objects as abortions. Like when most of my friend Alice's hair fell out after her brother prankishly placed a diluted solution of hydrochloric acid in her shampoo bottle.

I'd felt it entirely appropriate when my archrival Scott flubbed most of his lines in the school play and the performance was termed an abortion by the school newspaper drama critic, who happened to be me! Sure, terming the performance an abortion in bold print might not be tasteful, but I didn't think it was right when the school principal accused me of a lack of school spirit.

The advantages of abortions promoted by the pro-choice movement weren't nearly as appealing as the arguments provided by the pro-lifers for their position, which was probably why I'd leaned toward the pro-lifers until now. Life was sacred. And what would you even say to a person if they were aborted before they were born? And a fetus is a human being that isn't fully developed yet. Actual babies aren't fully developed either, and no one's saying get rid of babies.

Yet now that I had to deal with my future at stake, other images emerged—hopelessly living in a dimly lit apartment, sleeping with Joannie in the living room on a used convertible sofa with a thin mattress insufficient to cushion the metal underframe. I saw myself wearing a bow tie clasped over a tight collar, selling women's shoes by day, while struggling to keep awake through night college classes, with much of my little free time usurped by wiping away baby dribble.

The likelihood of a career with an "ist" at the end drifted away. I visualized myself putting on weight and Andrew being able to outrace me.

Instead of impulsively jumping into Jake's Spirit for a jaunty ride to anywhere, I saw myself loading my beloved vehicle with endless objets d'baby, like a folding playpen, a stroller, a bag of disposable diapers, toys, and a stuffed animal, all for a brief visit with my family.

I'd have to get a car seat for the baby. A car seat in Jake's Spirit? No way! It just didn't belong.

Things would never again be as they belonged, or at least as I was used to. I was bewildered, blindly entangled in an unfamiliar network of beleaguered circumstance rather than the comfortable world in which most everyone judged me a success. The structure I knew was being obscured, crumbling, vanishing. I felt helplessly imbalanced, lost.

Lost at the Mall

Knowing he was being brave, Billy sat humming to himself on the wooden bench near the frozen yogurt store, waiting for his lost mom to show up. She was lost somewhere in the mall. All he'd been doing was looking up at store windows, when all of a sudden, he turned around and didn't see her. He gazed around for her, and she didn't show up in his eyesight. He'd waited a few minutes, and still she didn't appear. His silly mom! After telling him the rule was that *he* shouldn't get lost. Well, she'd find herself soon. As he was waiting, he began to think about his life.

Billy knew just about all there was to know about life! He had most things figured out perfectly. He knew his friends were the kids he was playing with that day. And that he'd marry his mom when he grew up. And that, even though they didn't know him well, Santa Claus, the Easter bunny, and the tooth fairy liked him because they brought him presents. And that if he said "Diddle dumpling" when he woke up, he wouldn't see any snakes that day.

He knew just about all the rules a four-year-old boy, or any boy, for that matter, should know. His mom and dad were always telling him rules. Every day, it seemed, he learned another rule. A lot of them started with "Don't." Don't talk to strangers and certainly don't get in a car with them. Don't throw things so they break. Don't touch things that are very, very hot.

Generally, he didn't mind as much the rules starting with some other word than "Don't." Wash your hands before dinner. Say your prayers at night.

Stay out of the street. Be nice to your little brother, even if he was a little jerk most of the time, even though everybody thought he was so cute! Listen to your teacher at school. Obey the Ten Commandments, though he didn't really know what the Ten Commandments were, just that they should be obeyed.

He also knew he should obey the Golden Rule, which sounded like a very valuable rule to learn. But right now, he didn't know exactly what that rule was either. It probably had something to do with the "value of a dollar" his dad was always talking about.

It was fun to dress up like his dad, but it was his dad's rule that he shouldn't dress up like his mom. He couldn't figure out why girls like his older sister Susie could dress up as either a man or a woman. That was unfair, but it was the rule. Girls had all the fun!

Not that they always knew how to have fun. Like when he played house with Susie, sometimes she wanted to be the baby! Why would she want to be the baby? Why would anybody want to be a baby that couldn't do anything but cry? Girls sure were weird!

Another dad rule was that it was okay for him to play with dolls, as long as no one else was around, except the family. Whenever his dad saw him with dolls, he suggested having a catch.

Speaking of catching, Billy knew he didn't understand *all* the rules, like for Huckle Buckle, for instance. Susie tried to teach him once, but it was too complicated. It was a stupid game, he concluded. All games with rules he couldn't understand were stupid.

Sometimes the rules didn't make sense. Like being nice to everybody! Why should you be nice to everybody? Even those people who weren't nice to you. And why did you have to take a bath if you were going to get dirty again anyway? And why should you make your bed in the morning if you were going to sleep in it again that night? And why did you have to eat dessert *after* you ate dinner, when you might not be that hungry anymore? And why should you have to go to bed if you weren't tired? You didn't have to drink water if you weren't thirsty!

Well, maybe some of the rules didn't make sense, but Billy knew he had to obey them, because his mom and dad told him he had to. Sometimes they gave him a choice, and he didn't have to obey a rule. Like, sometimes they told him he had the choice of putting away his toys or having them thrown out. Usually, Billy decided to follow the rule. But he liked having a choice.

Besides some rules not making sense, sometimes there were two rules that told Billy to do two completely different things, and Billy got all mixed up. Like just before! Billy saw a lady with a stupid hat and said loudly, "That lady's hat is stupid!" The lady turned around and gave his mom a mean look and said something about teaching children manners.

His mom leaned down to Billy and told him he'd made the woman feel bad, and he should follow the rule, "Don't hurt other people's feelings." But Billy told her he *was* following a rule, just a different one, a rule his mom and dad had told him over and over again: "Always tell the truth."

His mom said, "Sometimes more than one rule applies to a situation."

So, Billy asked, "How do you tell which rule to listen to?"

"Well, you have to decide which of the rules is bigger, Billy," she explained.

"How can I tell which rule is bigger?"

His mom mulled it over. "Hmmm." Then, once she figured it out, she told him, "You have to consider the whole situation."

Feeling smarter, Billy informed, "I get it. If two rules are mixed up with each other, you pick the one that is bigger, and the rule for one being bigger is you consider the whole situation."

"Exactly," she praised.

"What does 'consider the whole situation' mean, Mom?" he asked.

She mulled that one over too. "Hmm."

Then, she said, "Follow the rule of common sense!"

"What is the rule of common sense?"

"Well, usually it makes sense to do one thing rather than the other. So, you do that thing, and you've followed the rule of common sense."

Billy did his own mulling, then asked, "Mom, if we have the rule of common sense, why do we need all those other rules? Why don't we have just one rule, the rule of common sense?"

"Billy, are you sure you're just four?" she preened, tousling his hair, which annoyed Billy. Someone patting his head was treating him like a baby. There should be a rule against his mom messing up his hair. Why didn't she know common sense, and stop doing that?

Then she added, "Why don't we just forget the rule of common sense, just now. I think you need to become just a little older before using that rule. You'll have plenty of time for that."

That was just fine with Billy. Having to use the rule of common sense was way too confusing. Here he had to decide which of two rules was bigger, and all of a sudden there was another rule to think about!

But now, Billy began to get scared! Just a little bit. He was scared for his mom, of course, not for himself. One second, she was with him, and then as quick as his dad finishing a plate of mashed potatoes, she suddenly disappeared. Who knows what happened? Maybe she was kidnapped. Or she was flattened in between the steps of the eshcalator and was now on the other side of the metal steps. Or she was locked inside a trying-on room. Or maybe a ghost took her. He knew there were ghosts in this mall. There had to be. He couldn't exactly see them, but he could feel the wind whoosh each time the door to the outside opened.

How silly of her! She had warned *him* so many times not to get lost! And now she got lost herself. He wondered if she'd get afraid once she learned she was lost. He wished she would be there right by him so he could tell her not to be afraid! Would she cry? He certainly wasn't going to cry! Crying was for babies!

Then he turned around for a moment, and maybe looked in the toy store, and maybe also turned into the store with all those shoes, and then she was gone, lost. He wasn't silly enough to get lost. He knew exactly where he was. On the bench right in front of the frozen yogurt store. Well, at least *he* was safe!

Once in a while, he heard an announcer's voice coming to his ears. Once the voice told about winning a car. Another time it told about something a store was selling. Sometimes it told about a child that was found. It must be a baby, Billy concluded, to get lost. His mom was acting like a baby, he'd sure tell her when he finally found her. He wondered how he could get his voice to tell everyone his mom was lost. Where was that voice coming from, anyway?

Well, maybe he'd try to find her. She could be in that store across the way selling paintings. So, he strolled there. Some of the paintings on the walls looked just like the pictures on the walls of his nursery school class, except they had frames. He looked around, but his mom wasn't there. Also, he couldn't see a drawing of a car. Not one!

Just then, a skinny lady in a long dress peered through glasses on the tip of her nose, and said, "Yes?" He wasn't sure if it was a question or a sentence. But Billy knew one of the most important rules to follow, one his parents emphasized over and over, was, "Don't talk to strangers." And he didn't know the lady, so she was a stranger. He just walked out of the store, proud of himself for following the rule.

Then he thought his mom might be at the store where they sold clothes with holes. So, he went there and was greeted by a young man with a funny green haircut, who called him, "Yo pal."

He knew his name wasn't Yo, and indeed he wasn't the young man's pal. He didn't even know the young man. So, he turned and walked out of the store, certainly not talking to that stranger!

Next, he went to the store where they sold candy. He walked near the counter and looked around for his mom. She wasn't there. The older gray-haired woman behind the counter blinked at him many times and then sweetly said, "Hello there! Can I help you?"

Of course, Billy knew better than to answer. But he thought it would be okay to shake his head no. He didn't know of any rule that said you shouldn't shake your head to a stranger. But before he could shake it, the woman offered, "How would you like a piece of free candy?"

Billy thought about taking the candy. It was chocolate and might have a cherry inside. And he was a little hungry. And with his mom being lost, she might not even have time to make dinner. A little candy could certainly help out until he was able to eat his next meal.

But the rule was "Don't take anything from someone you don't know." Look what happened to Snow White! And Hansel and Gretel!

So, Billy wagged his head from side to side, meaning a definite "no," and walked out that store. In quick order he walked into and out of stores that sold pets, popcorn, shoes for big boys, shoes for big girls, books, toys, balls, bikes, eyeglasses, and all sorts of other things. Obviously, his mom was not lost in any of those places!

Then he thought, "Maybe she's lost in the parking room." So, Billy waited for somebody to open those big heavy doors with the metal bar going across, that he himself was too small to push open. Then he snuck in behind them and stepped in.

He walked this way and that way, and up this row, and down that one, higher up, and lower down. He was also keeping an eye out for a red car, his mom's car. He figured if she was smart, she'd just go to the red car and wait there for him to show up, and she'd no longer be lost. There were lots of red cars in the parking place, but none of them was his mom's. He knew, because his mom's car had yellow dice on the front mirror. "So, it will be easy to find in a parking lot," he remembered her telling his dad. His mom sure was smart, even though she sometimes did dumb things, like getting lost and going to the gambling casino.

Soon it came to his mind that the parking room didn't have any floors. He'd been in places before where you took stairs to get from one floor to another. When you reached the top of the stairs, you reached another floor. When you reached the bottom of a stairs, you were on a lower floor. But this place was really strange. It didn't have any stairs he could see. It didn't even have eshcalators for the cars. Instead, the floor tilted, and you never reached a new floor. It was always the same floor. It was one big floor that tilted this way and that way. And you certainly couldn't have a ball catch on this floor. If you missed, it would roll down all the way to the end of the floor, and you'd have to chase it forever! No way you could play Huckle Buckle here! Even if you knew the rules. This parking garage sure was strange!

A couple drivers honked at him. Who did they think they were? Just wait until he got bigger. Then he'd stick out his finger at them, just like his mom sometimes did when other drivers made her mad! His mom sometimes seemed like a different mom when she was driving. He didn't remember whether it was Pointer or Tall Man his mom held up, but it was definitely one of those fingers, and not Ringman, Thumbkin, or Pinkie! Thinking of his mom doing that helped him keep from crying, because Billy knew that it was hard to laugh and cry at the same time, though it could be done. Like when his dad tickled him very hard for a long time.

Soon, Billy saw a man in a uniform of a white shirt, black tie, and gray pants with a black stripe down the side. The man held a wooden stick in one hand and a walkie-talkie in the other. On his shirt was a silver badge, and he had a gun in his holster. It must be a policeman, Billy concluded. Billy knew that policemans caught criminals and bad guys. The policeman walked over to him, bent down, and asked, "Hey little boy, I'd say it's a little dangerous here with all the cars driving past. Where's your mom or dad?"

Billy didn't answer, knowing not to talk to strangers, even if they were policemans. Billy thought it would be nice if he could think of another rule which said to talk to the policeman, but he couldn't. And he couldn't even use the rule of common sense, because you only used that rule when you had two rules that mixed up with each other and told you to do different things.

"Are they around here?" the man asked, looking to one side, then another. At first, Billy didn't reply, but then he thought it would be okay if he shrugged, as long as he didn't say any words. He didn't remember any rule against that. So, he moved his shoulders up, and then down.

"Okay. What's your name?" the policeman inquired. Billy didn't answer. Neither did he shrug, because he certainly *did* know the answer to that question, even if he couldn't tell that stranger—Billy Harrington.

"Are you lost?" asked the policeman.

Billy moved his head from side to side. Of course, he wasn't lost! Didn't the policeman know it was his mom who was lost?

"Where is your mom or dad?" the policeman repeated.

Billy shrugged. He didn't know! If he knew, then he could find her himself, and she wouldn't be lost.

"Well, let's the two of us go to the office." And he took Billy's hand and started walking. "Wilson coming in," he said to the walkie-talkie. Billy wished he could have the fun of talking to the walkie-talkie. But he knew he wasn't allowed to speak. They walked through the doors, and down the hallway, and through a door, and then they were in an office with other policemans. Billy looked around, thinking maybe his mom was there, and that was why the policeman took him here. But she wasn't. So why did the policeman bring him here? He could think of only one reason.

Billy wanted to tell the policeman, "You have made a big mistake. I am not a bad guy! My mom is lost, and I'm trying to find her. Why did you take me here if my mom's not here?"

But since the rule was not to talk to strangers, he didn't say anything. They sat him on a bench, and one policeman whispered something to another policeman. Then the second policeman peeked at him and said something he couldn't hear into a microphone. He was probably telling other policemans that Billy was caught.

Except for thinking he was a bad guy, the policemans were pretty friendly. They gave him a cup of ice cream. He knew it was safe to eat, since policemans didn't serve poison to anyone, even the worst bad guys, so he ate it.

While he was eating, a policeman unlocked a door, and behind it Billy could see a man wearing handcuffs. That man was going to jail. Then— whoa!—soon the policemans would put handcuffs on him! And he had left his handcuff key at home, in his Official Detective Kit!

Billy knew just what was happening! They were going to put him in jail! Why? Why weren't they doing more important things, like finding his lost mom? They weren't very smart policemans. Why didn't they ask questions he could answer by nodding or shrugging, instead of ones he'd have to speak to answer, like what was his name?

He figured he'd be put in handcuffs as soon as he finished his ice cream. They knew he couldn't eat ice cream from a cup while wearing handcuffs. Who could? He'd be in handcuffs unless he could do something about it first! Like escape!

So, when none of the policemans were watching, Billy put his ice cream cup on the floor, crouched down low over to the door, opened it very, very quietly, and tiptoed out. Once the door closed, he ran as fast as he could to one side of the hallway, and he finally reached a door. He tried to turn the knob, but it was locked! He saw some other doors nearby, but they were locked too! He noticed two doors together, but they didn't have any knobs on them at all! What kinds of doors didn't have any knobs on them? Probably doors to rooms that people never came out of because they were captured there forever! He ran away in the opposite direction, past the door to the policemans' room, and tried some more doors, but they were locked too!

How was he going to get out of this place and stay out of jail, where he might be locked up forever? Even if his mom found *herself,* she might never find him in there.

Billy at last began to cry! Tears slid down his face. Billy wiped his eyes, but he couldn't stop those stupid-head tears.

Pretty soon Billy found himself sitting in the hallway, sobbing, "Mom! I want my mom!"

Then, out of an eye corner, Billy saw a door open. Two doors, actually. It was those two doors Billy had noticed down the hall earlier, the ones without any knobs on them. They really were funny doors. Instead of opening in or out they opened to the side, just like they went into the wall! Billy raised himself up, ready to run away again, though he really didn't know a safe place to go.

All of a sudden, who should be coming out of the elevator, but his mom! Billy ran toward her, calling, "Mom! Mom! I'm here!"

When they finally reached each other, Billy saw her go down to her knees, felt her arms tight around him, and heard her sweet voice reassure, "Billy! Billy! Land o'holy buffalo me! I'm so glad to see you."

Gasping between each word, he managed to get out, "Me … too … Mom!"

"Billy, you are a brave, stalwit boy," he heard her say as she patted his head, tightly pressed against her toasty shoulder.

Billy knew what brave was, but not stalwit. He hoped it wasn't anything like the 'nitwit' his older sister Susie sometimes called him for no good reason at all! Nah! His mom wouldn't call him a bad name, not at a time like this.

Billy, sniffling between words, told her sternly, "You …were … lost and … I … found you! … I knew … if … I looked … hard … enough … I'd … find you. … You … are … never … to get … lost again. … That's … the rule!"

No Agreeable Option

I pictured a lonely Joannie, flat on her back, sobbing into a pillow, disheartened, frightened. Poor girl! My friend, a better friend than I'd ever thought a girl could be, privy to my nature, like when she said she knew the true Billy was sensitive and introverted inside. No one else had ever acknowledged my delicate internal aspect; it was assumed I was a cheerful boy who fit in and never felt unworthy. Occasionally mischievous or silly, but never sinful.

We confessed the most private emotions to each other. I'd told you how I resented Andrew when he was little, my fear of snakes, and that I felt clumsy and wasn't at all sure what to do when we first mattressed. She'd told me how downcast she felt sometimes because her father didn't pay attention to her, making her feel invisible. To make me feel that the two of us belonged together, she added that she, too, didn't care for snakes. She laughed at my wordplay, even added her own, whereas many kids just groaned and walked away as if I were a drippy noodlehead when I put words together in just such a way.

I liked Joannie a lot. No, scratch that—enormously. And I had the strong suspicion she liked me even more than I liked her, girls generally having greater emotional depth than boys, including boys they were mattressing with. We never argued, and I sensed she watched over me, with always the word to deflect my self-doubts. Being with her was like snuggling under a warm, fuzzy blanket that told me everything was okay. Usually.

Was it love? Was I in love? Was I too young to be in love? Then I decided if I was old enough to produce a baby, I was old enough to be in love. But still, *was* I in love? I'd never been in love before, so I wasn't at all sure what signs to look for, but I concluded that if I was in love, I'd surely know it. I'd feel that DING, hear sweet romantic music. So, absent a ding and such imagined music, I must not be in love. It was an infatuation, I told myself. Then I realized an infatuation was an immature preoccupation teens were susceptible to. Here I was, not mature enough to be in love, and now a baby was on the way. Was I merely like a naïve puppy?

A question drifted into mind of why Joannie hadn't told me she too wasn't sure what to do when we first mattressed. Maybe she *did* know what to do. Maybe she'd read the kind of do-it-yourself manual that would not be present in the Harrington household and that some libraries banned, as they were what they called adult sites, banned from most good-people households in Cedar Glen. Or was there another way she got educated? I considered the inquiry momentarily but then allowed the issue to fade.

I wasn't angry at Joannie. It wasn't her fault she got pregnant. We knew birth control pills didn't work all the time. The odds were minuscule—was it one in a thousand, or one in a hundred thousand? I didn't remember what Joannie said. But it was a statistical certainty that some women on the pill would conceive anyway. Just like it was a statistical certainty that while it was unlikely any given person would win the lottery big prize, someone would win. And now we had won the lottery. But it wasn't winning, was it? It wasn't even bad luck we had, just the misfortunate side of statistical probability. No, Billy Harrington would not allow himself to be considered the object of hard luck. Such an attitude tended to perpetuate and provide the reason for excuse.

Understanding that birth control pills weren't foolproof, we'd agreed it was better to go overboard, double-up in protection, just to be safe. So, in addition to her pills, I wore a condom. Maybe I should have said something that night when the condom broke inside her, but what was the point? She was on the pill anyway! Why ruin her mood? So, maybe I was more to blame for her being pregnant than she was. I couldn't be mad at her!

And what about how Joannie felt? She was as bright in school as me! She wrote dazzling essays, solved complex math problems, and was one of the few in high school who understood that history was interpretation as much as facts. She had plans, too. She wanted to be a doctor. Would they even let her into med school if they knew she'd had an abortion? Okay, Billy. Get real; they don't disqualify people from med school for that, but what about the scandal if she decided to change majors and was up to be a Supreme Court justice?

Would she ever have *any* career if she started having babies now? Would she be any happier than me spending time tending an infant? Spooning mush, speaking babble, and changing diapers?

And if we kept the baby, were we supposed to marry? Have a wedding? At seventeen, we'd need our parents' written permission to get a marriage license, just the same as they had to consent to a school field trip to a local candy factory. Sure, I'd given Joannie my athletic letter, but that was many footfalls from an engagement ring and wedding vows.

How did someone arrange for an abortion anyway? Google it? Would it even be covered under the Golds' health insurance plan? Did we even want to tell Joannie's parents about her getting an abortion? And how much did it cost? Could I pay in installments? Were coupons available for a discount? I had some money saved from my job at the convenience store, but was a few hundred dollars enough? Were the payment terms negotiable, or did they know you'd agree to whatever they demanded?

Adoption? Yes, a possibility. But how could I surrender a child? Early in teenhood, I'd strongly suspected I was adopted. Even if I did have my dad's legs, eye color and large forehead, and my mom's tweaky nose and summertime allergies, there are so many traits, just by chance you're bound to have some of the ones your caretakers have! How else could I account for my being so different from my conservative parents with their traditional attitudes?

I was quite angry at my "real" biological parents for giving me up! Whatever happens, a parent shouldn't give up a child! Didn't they know the Lord will always provide? Now, maybe I realized that no, the Lord wouldn't always provide. At least in a way to keep the parents' lives from being wrecked. Still, how could I give up my own real child, who'd go through life knowing he was adopted and wondering what was wrong about them that a parent would give them up, and speculating what his real dad was like?

NO! Adoption was not an agreeable option.

What was an agreeable option? There didn't seem to be any! I felt like I was taking a test I hadn't studied for, in a language I didn't speak. An incompetent novice at a severe disadvantage, about to be ravaged by a swirl of bizarre circumstances begat by the true world I'd been protected from. Maybe I was a baby, after all. If not a baby, certainly not full-grown. Adults took charge of a situation. They decided what to do and handled it. But I felt incapable of dealing with anything. It was the biggest crisis of my life, and I was frozen. And I knew I was frozen.

If I only could determine what I wanted, maybe I could figure out what to do. In my life I'd learned to get things done. When I craved something badly enough, determination drove me to achieve it, whether it involved hard work or coming to terms with other people.

I WANT A COOKIE!

Billy was very, very sure he was a very, very smart five-year-old boy. Dad was a college professor, and Mom worked at the library, where there were lots and lots of books to make you smart. They read him stories almost every evening—about trains that huffed and puffed climbing hills, and fat tubas that talked, and princesses who wanted a boyfriend, and princes who liked asking girls to try on shoes, and a man with a long beard taking very long naps, and people disguised as frogs. He could tie his own shoelaces. He knew how to spell his name. And he'd memorized a song whose words were his address and telephone number, just in case he got lost.

He remembered once overhearing his dad say something like, "In this crazy world we live in, there are good people and there are bad people. Sometimes it's necessary for strong people to protect the weak people from the bad, and sometimes the weak people don't know what's best for them, and someone good and smart is needed to take over. That's why we need Republicans!"

Billy got a bit confused between good and bad and strong and weak people and didn't quite get why some people argued about which was better—an elephant or a donkey. But one thing he did know was he was a smart person who could take over. He must be a Republican, he figured.

Now a proud member of the kindergarten class at Cedar Glen Elementary, Billy thought, "Now I'm in real school, and a leader of this class. So, in case some stupid dumbbell-head wants to do something I don't want them to do, I can just push them away. Or give them the mean eye."

Billy also couldn't get why, as an almost grown-up person, he couldn't always get what he wanted. Like sometimes, when he asked very nicely for a cookie before dinner, his mom would say, "No, it's almost time for dinner."

Why shouldn't he have that cookie? It wasn't as if he was asking his mom to bake the cookie right then! He was big enough to reach the countertop and open the cookie jar himself. And for a year already he'd been opening the refrigerator, taking out a box of milk, and pouring it into the mug with "Billy" on it.

If he was hungry for a cookie, he should be able to have one! His stomach was getting bigger all the time, with lots of room for cookies *and* dinner.

So, he thought especially hard and finally figured out how to get that cookie. If he squawked loud enough his mom would gladly give him one. So, the next time she told him he couldn't have one, he went, "WAA-WAA-WAA! I WANT A COOKIE! I WANT A COOKIE! I WANT A COOKIE NOW!"

Sure enough, Billy soon had a tasty cookie in his hand. And his mom had quiet in her kitchen. She also had a big puddle of milk on the countertop. When he poured from the milk box, Billy didn't always get every drop in his mug. Sometimes the milk box slid from his hands because, as his mom had told him, they were slippy.

After learning this valuable lesson, not only was Billy able to get a cookie before dinner when he wanted, but he could stay up later than his bedtime, get his mom to hang up her phone and play with him, put on whatever clothes he wanted, and play with *all* the toys in the house, even if they belonged to Andrew or Susie.

Billy thought some of the other kids in his kindergarten class were dumbbell-heads. They probably didn't have moms and dads that read them stories. And they didn't learn yet that grown-ups will usually give you what you want if you yell loud enough.

So what if other kids in class didn't want to play with him! He didn't want to play with them either. The babies! If they didn't want to play the games he wanted, then too bad for them. Just too bad! If they built a castle, he could just tear it down. It wasn't as good as the castle he could make, anyway!

And how dare that new boy play with *his* blocks! The very blocks he played with every once in a while.

At least Miss Garden, his teacher, knew Billy was special. While she let the other kids play in groups, she gave him special jobs that he could do all by himself. Like today, when the other kids had to share finger paints, he got his own and didn't have to share with anybody. Miss Garden knew he was the best finger painter in the whole class!

One day his mom came into Miss Garden's classroom, and the two talked. No doubt they were telling each other what a special boy he was! Miss Garden must have thought his mom was a great mom and gave her a gift of a blue book.

The next day, after his mom took him home, Billy noticed her reading that blue book with white letters on the side. He recognized some of the letters, like B, R, and T. But he couldn't tell what the book was about. He looked over his mom's shoulder and saw there were no pictures in the book, so how interesting could it be? He quickly forgot about it and decided he was hungry. So, he asked his mom for a cookie.

"No, dear. It's almost dinnertime. You may have a cookie *after* dinner."

Billy knew just what to do! "WAA-WAA-WAA! I WANT A COOKIE! I WANT A COOKIE! I WANT A COOKIE NOW!"

His mom continued reading the book, as if he hadn't been screaming his lungs out. Maybe she was so interested in the book she didn't hear him.

"WAA-WAA-WAA! I WANT A COOKIE! I WANT A COOKIE! I WANT A COOKIE NOW!" Still his mom didn't move or say anything. Maybe she was sick. He hoped it wasn't really serious, like poison ivy, or varicose vanes, or chicken pops. Or maybe, just maybe, clogged ears. He'd give it another try.

"WAA-WAA-WAA! I WANT A COOKIE! I WANT A COOKIE! I WANT A COOKIE NOW!"

His mom still didn't move, except to turn the book pages.

"WAA-WAA-WAA!"

What was wrong with his mom? She told him, "Billy, I am reading a book. If you must make loud noise, then you'll have to go to your room for five minutes. That's the rule.

"WAA-WAA-WAA!"

"Okay, Billy. I asked you not to make loud noise. Now, five minutes of time out."

Billy was so mad that he ran to his room. He thought about turning and jinxing her, "I hope you get poison ivy!" But it might make her say, "Now, ten minutes of time out." So, he didn't.

He pouted in his room until his mom arrived to say five minutes was up and he could come out. He decided he wasn't hungry for cookies anymore and stayed in his room until dinnertime, putting out a pretend fire with his pretend fire engine and rescuing babies from the flames.

In class the next day, Miss Garden asked her pupils to draw a picture of where they lived. Billy used his crayons to draw the front of a dark brown house. It had a front door and four windows and a pointy roof. On the green lawn was a tree with a brown trunk and a green ball of leaves.

He wanted to put a yellow circle of sun in the sky but didn't have a yellow crayon. Joannie, the girl sitting across his table, had a yellow crayon. Soon, Billy had that yellow crayon in his hand, and Joannie had tears on her face.

"Why is she crying so much?" Billy wondered. He looked at her picture. Her stupid house also had a door and four windows. But it was leaning so much! She was crying because she was afraid her rickety old house might fall down. Even if he lived in a house like that, he wouldn't cry.

When Miss Garden asked why she was crying, Joannie explained, "Billy stoled my yellow crayon!"

"Well, Billy?"

"She's not a good drawer. Why shouldn't I have the crayon? Look at my beautiful house!"

"Billy, in this classroom we do not take crayons from each other. For the rest of the afternoon, you may sit by yourself next to the goldfish bowl!"

Billy rose with a sneer and ambled to the chair next to the goldfish bowl. He wanted to tell his teacher that she was a dumbbell-head, but then he thought she might make him sit facing the wall with *nothing* at all to look at. Billy got bored looking at goldfish for the next hour, complaining to himself, "They never do anything!"

Later, when his mom picked him up, she again spoke with Miss Garden. They nodded a lot to each other. Miss Garden probably told her about how the baby other kids were so jealous of him that when he came over to play with them, they just walked away. Most of them probably weren't even Republicans! But it didn't make him feel good. He really wanted everybody in the class to like him, even if they were dumbbell-heads.

On the way home his mom stated, "You probably didn't like it too well when Miss Garden made you sit near the goldfish!"

"No!"

"Want to talk about it?"

"She's a stupid dumbbell-head!"

"And you probably don't like it when the other kids won't play with you!" she declared.

"They're dumbbell-heads!"

"But you like it when kids are friends with you."

"Uh-huh."

"It feels good to have friends, and when people are nice to you, right?

"Yeah!"

"You really like it when somebody asks you to play with them," she added.

"A lot."

"You don't like it when somebody messes up *your* toys."

"No no no, I don't."

"Sometimes it's fun to help somebody out."

"Amen," said Billy, repeating a word one of his parents used when they agreed with what the other parent said.

"When we get home, will you help me wash the potatoes for dinner? You're really good at washing potatoes," she told him.

Billy knew he was good at washing potatoes. Just one of the many things he was good at. He did wonder, "Why doesn't mom let me use soap when I wash them? I have to use soap when I wash my hands to get them really clean. How can potatoes get really clean without soap?" He thought he'd ask his mom that question when they got home. But he started thinking about other things, and he forgot to ask.

For now, he asked, "Can I mash them too?"

"Only after they're cooked. Billy. But you'll have to ask your dad. That's his job, you know."

When they arrived home, Billy helped his mom wash potatoes, and after she cut them into pieces, he dropped them in the boil pot. Meanwhile, he forgot all about the cookie he usually wanted this time of day.

What was wrong with his mom? She was being nice, but she sure was acting strange! And look what she was doing now! Instead of reading from a recipe book, like usual, she was reading from that silly blue book without any pictures.

After dinner his mom served her famous deep-dish apple pie. Billy loved apple pie, and when she put a wedge into his plate, he knew he'd want more, and demanded, "I want two apple pies."

His mom replied, "If you're still hungry after you finish this piece, you may have another."

Billy would not back down. "WAA-WAA-WAA! I WANT TWO PIES! I WANT TWO PIES! I WANT TWO PIES NOW!"

His mom stated sternly, "Billy, listen to me. If you finish your pie and are still hungry, you may have another piece."

Billy was getting mad at his mom's poor behavior and shifted to the approach that worked so many times before. So, he said, *"DAD, DAD.* WAA-WAA-WAA! I WANT TWO PIES! I WANT TWO PIES! I WANT TWO PIES NOW!"

His dad began to reach for another slab of pie for Billy, when his mom said, "Gordon dear, remember what's in the book."

She then notified Billy, "If you keep yelling, you cannot have *any* pie."

"WAA-WAA-WAA! Gimme that piece of pie, right now, or I won't love you anymore. I WANT TWO PIES! I WANT TWO PIES NOW!"

His mom then interrupted, "Okay, Billy, I'm going to count to three. If you don't quiet down and start eating by the time I reach three, I'll have to send you to your room for time out. One..."

"WAA-WAA-WAA!"

"Two..."

"WAA-WAA!"

"Two and a baff …"

"WA!"

"Two and free quitters … There! Thank you, Billy. If you want another piece when you're done, remember it's good manners to say please."

This counting by mom was new. At first Billy thought it was a way mom was teaching him numbers. But then he decided it wasn't, because he knew the number after two was definitely three, not a baff and free quitters.

When he was done eating, Billy decided he wasn't hungry for more pie. But crumbs and pieces of apple were scattered around his plate, along with a small pool of milk that fell out of his mug. His mom gave Billy a sponge and asked him, "Will you please clean up your place?"

Billy again wondered what was wrong with his mom. She never before asked him to clean up. Why was she suddenly acting like other mothers he'd heard about? After all, it was an accident.

"Accident or not, please clean up your place."

Billy grumbled to himself. He'd always been able to get two pieces of pie before. And also cleaning up! What was going on? And what was that book his mom had mentioned to his dad, and what did it have to do with pies?

When everyone left the room, Billy noticed the blue book was on the countertop. He stood on his toes, quickly turned some pages, and sure enough, there was not one picture of pie in the whole book. Not one. What kind of book was this, anyway?

He decided to think about how to get his mom back to how she used to be, the good old mom who gave him a cookie or extra pie when he wanted and never made him clean up after accidents!

In bed later, he thought and thought. This was really annoying. So, he thought some more. He kept thinking. Something was different. But what? Maybe he'd find out what it was in a dream. But his dreams that night were about playing Huckle Buckle, which seemed fun.

The next day at school, Billy noticed someone had wrecked the castle made by another boy in the class. Billy went to the boy castle builder, "You must feel really sad your castle was wrecked."

"Yes," sniffled the boy.

"You worked hard to build it!"

The boy nodded.

"Well, why don't we build it again."

"Yeah!" the other boy said, excited. And so, the two of them made another castle and played with each other much of the day. Billy even showed him how to do the frog hop. Later on, Billy even told the other boy, "You have a fine voice for singing," after Miss Garden had them all sing, "Hi-Ho, Hi-Ho."

They called each other friend!

After school Billy popped into the room he shared with three-year-old Andrew, as his brother with a bright red mustache was eating a cherry possicle. Billy marched to his brother, and said, "I bet you really like eating that possicle."

After Andrew nodded, Billy added, "But the rule in our family is that you have to be four years old to eat possicles in your room. So please give me the possicle."

As Billy reached for the possicle, Andrew began sobbing, "MY POSSICLE! MY POSSICLE!" and refused to hand the snack to his brother.

Billy then advised him, "Andrew, I'm going to count, and if you don't give me the possicle I'm going to tell Mom and she'll put you in time out for a whole year. One … two … two and a baff … two and free quitters …" And just then Andrew handed over the possicle.

Billy then told him, "I've got a great idea! You can play with my sandals!"

Billy handed the sandals to his brother, saying, "You really look handsome in sandals. Put them on!" As Andrew was putting on the sandals, which were really much too big for him, Billy left the room stating, "Wow! You are good at putting on sandals! Now you can stay here and pretend you're me."

Then Billy sat on a chair in the kitchen and devoured the rest of the possicle.

His mom returned from the laundry room a few minutes later and began to wash potatoes. He dragged the chair to the sink, stood on it beside her, took a potato, and put it under the running water. Then he stated, "Being a mom can be a hard job."

"It sure can," she agreed.

"You must have lots of things on your mind. I bet sometimes you feel you have no time for yourself," he sympathized.

"That's true, Billy."

"Sometimes you get mad at people and say things you shouldn't and then feel bad about it later."

"I know," she answered.

"Sometimes I bet you just want to tell people you're sorry and do them a favor."

"Uh-huh."

"Sometimes I bet you think there should be less rules for kids. That way you wouldn't have to be mean sometimes."

"Billy, you're such an understanding boy. Have a cookie!"

"Amen," Billy responded before taking a large bite from his chewy oatmeal-raisin treat.

What to Do? What to Do?

Suppose my mom had had an abortion! I might never have been born; I couldn't say I *definitely never* would have been born. I might have popped out of some other mom instead. Who could know with any certainty? Not anyone I knew.

If Mary didn't exist, wouldn't Jesus have been born to some other nice lady? Of course! Just imagine Jesus not being born! Who's to say unborn baby souls don't gather somewhere in the spiritual universe, waiting to be assigned to moms' bellies?

I wondered if, once a baby was assigned a woman who then had an abortion, was the baby's soul destroyed forever, zapped into oblivion—that seemed unfair—or got another chance by being reassigned to a different mom. I'd feel awful if Joannie and I decided on abortion and the baby soul didn't get another opportunity. Or, if it did, whether whenever Joannie and me saw a baby, we'd be thinking that baby's soul might be ours genetically and we'd want to kidnap him home. That assumes, of course, that souls are defined by genes, not only bodies.

Then, I concluded that of course the baby soul got another chance! If it didn't, the Lord would be nasty and heartless, which wasn't possible! When it got another chance, I pondered whether the baby soul got special preference toward the front of the birthing line, or did it have to queue up at the back, awaiting its turn again, like at the deli counter or the bank?

I wondered whether the soul of baby Jesus had had to wait in line, or got special preference, much as the doormen at hot clubs unhitched the velvet rope for movie or rock music stars?

If I'd been born to some other mom, I'd be a very different Billy than I was now—most likely I wouldn't even be a Billy, but an Abdul or Moshe or Leroy or Takahashi or …?

What happened in my life would be way different. I might have the same soul, but the rest of me would be completely unlike the now me. I'd have a different family, wear different clothes, and what I knew and didn't know wouldn't be the same.

I'd probably live in a land where English wasn't spoken, and my talent for wordplay would go unappreciated. Was my talent transferable to other languages? And even if it was, it might not be at all prized, especially if I lived in some Third World aboriginal land, where, even at the age of seventeen, I might struggle to feed a large family through a famine, and neither my family nor my scrawny neighbors would value genius for puns as highly as a slice of bread. Their groans would be reserved for pleas to relieve starvation rather than appreciation of my humor.

On the other hand, I might be a rich, carefree prince of a small European principality, who yachted, poloed, hired world-class hairstylists, and cut ribbons with big scissors in honor of new warships. And if Joannie was pregnant, I'd have the resources to cope, not worry about having to sell shoes for a living. Moreover, perhaps I'd even be secretly admired as a fascinating rogue!

Wait! I might never have met Joannie!

Back to reality.

Dinner at the in-laws—if marriage was in the offing—would forever be strained. And what would I do if Mr. Gold, upon learning his daughter was expecting a baby, lost his temper and decided to beat me up? I could imagine ringing the doorbell at the Gold residence and hearing Mr. Gold holler, "I'll break his neck."

Fighting back would be dumbbellish. The stocky Mr. Gold had me by fifty pounds at least, and, according to Joannie, survived being raised in a neighborhood called Devil's Dungeon. The knowledge that Mr. Gold was later arrested for assault and battery would not compensate for me whistling words between broken front teeth, having at least one broken limb, requiring stitches that messed with my youthful appearance, sipping dinner through a straw, or squinting through at least one blackened eye.

All this damage inflicted should the furious Mr. Gold succeed in apprehending his scoundrelous quarry.

In the unlikely event of me landing a lucky punch stopping Mr. Gold, I'd still ultimately lose. Mrs. Gold might never speak to me again.

Well, actually, she might. Joannie had told me the marriage between Gwen and Shlomo wasn't quite a modern cruise liner but more like a Titanic.

Ask Mr. Gold to have a reasonable discussion? Too feeble to have any chance of success, given Mr. Gold's probable mindset!

Plead for mercy? No! I was not the type of boy—no, man—to supplicate himself before anyone. Except the Lord, of course.

Run away? I remembered what I used to singsong teasingly years ago when Andrew chased after me in anger—"Ya-ya-ya-ya-ya. You ca-an't catch me." I imagined the farcical chase where I'd elude the pursuing, furious, teeth-gnashing Mr. Gold by darting in different directions, wheeling around obstacles. As Joannie raced behind, screaming, "Billy, run! Daddy, stop!" I'd shout, "It wasn't my fault."

"Whose fault was it, then, you little rooster?" Mr. Gold would roar, panting more heavily and dripping perspiration as the chase continued.

What was I to say? "It was my fault, and I sincerely apologize?" Hardly words encouraging Mr. Gold to withhold his heavy-duty fists.

"Joannie's fault?"

Mr. Gold would hardly appreciate that dismissal of personal responsibility!

"Your wife, Mrs. Gold, who blundered by leaving with your daughter the decision of whether to mattress?" Then Mrs. Gold would be furious with me as well, though at least she'd be unlikely to join the chase. And her weapons would be words, not fists.

"It was just fate," I'd resort to.

Mr. Gold would respond, "Fate? I'll show you fate, you little hedonistic beaver thief."

I'd explain, "The Lord's will?" But Mr. Gold would answer, "Not any Lord I know, you substandard weasel!"

"Joannie's dermatologist?" No. No. No.

No answer seemed correct. Later I'd think more on what I'd say, or need to shout, to Mr. Gold as he inevitably became upset. I had time.

I hated my new situation. I knew most people admired me as a likable and smart young man. I was a good athlete, not stuck-up, an attentive listener, and someone with spare change in his pocket. At least enough not to be concerned about finances when I bought a large waffle cone of Neapolitan ice cream at the food court. I suspected most boys at school envied me, and I was careful to say hi to them when they crossed my path, to suppress their venting of resentment, or to avoid enhancing their jealousy through a flaunting of humility.

Now, who'd be jealous of who?

I realize now that others value me as worthier than I am. In point of fact, I am a miserable example.

They incorrectly believe I can easily handle what few problems I have. But I wish I could be someone else, someone who could be effective. Someone who wasn't a loser.

Billy Bad Guy

Billy was annoyed! Those grown-ups on the other side of the doors just weren't taking him seriously. Here he was, his silver six-gun at his side, letting them know, "I'm Billy the Bad-Guy Bandit. Trick or Treat," and they didn't seem scared one bit. They should be. Just because they were bigger didn't mean they were braver. Just because they had skeletons on their doors, or stuffed bodies hanging from trees in their yards, or spider webs on their porch! That didn't mean anything!

They just smiled, as if he was just cute, not realizing he was dangerous and mean. They just didn't believe a six-year-old boy would blast them away. "PSH-PSH-PSH," he could go, if he wanted, plugging them with three bullets before they knew it.

But his dad had told Billy to not actually point the gun at anyone, or they might just shut the door in his face. Or, in some extreme cases, shoot him first.

Of course, he didn't expect many people in houses *on his block* to be scared. They knew in everyday life he was Billy Harrington, first-grade pupil. But the people who didn't live on his block should've been able to tell that he was a dangerous varmint, a buckaroo to be reckoned with. On purpose he didn't cover his mouth with the bandana tied around his neck. Just by looking at him, they should be able to tell that treating him well was good for their health!

Of course, he didn't have to waste anyone yet because, so far, everyone had given him something. He didn't have to give anyone the mean eye and threaten them with blasting holes through them.

Billy's sack was almost half full. He'd been collecting treats—"riding the range," his dad said—for over two hours now, proudly wearing his wide-brim cowboy hat, blue jeans, a cowboy shirt, and brown boots. His holster was strapped around his waist.

But why did his dad need to stand behind him each time he rang a doorbell? He didn't need protection! He could take care of himself. And he didn't need his dad to tell him, as he had, that there was only a half hour left before they'd need to "amble on back to the ranch." What was his dad talking about? A ranch? They didn't own any cattle. They lived in a house in the town of Cedar Glen with a backyard where squirrels scampered. No cattle!

But more important than showing he was a terrible desperado was gathering lots of goodies in his sack. His older sister Susie, who was trick-or-treating with friends and one of their moms, just bragged how much she was going to bring home. She pranced around, boasting how last year she brought home more goodies than any other member of the Harrington family *ever* had.

Big deal! That was when her competition was a five-year-old who got tired so early they didn't even count how much he collected. Now that he was a bigger six, it would be very different. Very, very different. She just thought she was the living princess highness! Or, even higher, The Queen of Halloween. He'd show her he could do better than her any time!

He wasn't exactly sure just how long or short a half hour was. Oh, he knew it was from when the small hand on the clock went halfway around, but did that take a long time or a short time? Sometimes it felt long and sometimes it felt short. From his dad's voice, he thought it must not be very long, though it wasn't very short either. But now that he might have only a little time, he needed to fill his sack quickly. An idea popped up. He'd just ask for more! Just like at home, when he wanted more mashed potatoes, he held out his plate and asked, "May I please have some more mashed potatoes?"

So, after the lady with blood on her face at the next house handed him a candy bar, he asked, "May I please have another candy bar?"

The lady answered. "Whoa, cowboy! One to a customer. Say, aren't you the kid who came around selling magazine subscriptions for your school?"

Billy shook his head no.

"Kids are pushy these days. Sorry, little boy! I must have confused you with someone else. Well, have a happy Halloween."

What did she mean by "little boy"? He should have plugged her. Except she did end up giving him another candy.

At the next house, after the man with fangs gave him a nickel, Billy asked, "May I have another money? It's for my brother, at home."

The man leaned down and dribbled out through his fangs, "Well now pardnah, you ask your brother to mosey around these here parts and I'll toss him a nickel too."

Billy decided, "He should make up his mind if he's a cowboy, talking like that, or a vampire."

At the next house the woman in a dressy gown and carrying a tinsel magic wand gave him a lollipop. He then asked, "May I please have another lollipop? It's for my brother. He's got a sore throat at home and can't come out."

The woman bent over and replied in a voice so unnaturally sweet Billy thought it was disgusting. "Sorry to hear that. Lollipops help people feel better, but I only have a few left. So, tell your sick brother the angel fairy wishes him well, and she hopes he comes around next year."

Billy wondered, if lollipops helped make people better, did that mean they were medicine? He hoped not, since as good Christian Scientists, his family wasn't allowed to take medicine. He wondered, too, whether Christian Scientists believed in fairies. He'd ask his dad on the way home, if he remembered.

He also recognized that all this nice asking wasn't getting him anywhere near enough treats.

At the next house the Frankenstein gave Billy an apple. Billy then threatened, "Give me another apple, or I'll plug ya!" and thrust the silver six-shooter into the man's fleshy belly, at the same time giving him the mean eye.

The man gushed, "Certainly," and hurriedly threw another apple into Billy's sack.

Billy continued to threaten people for a second handout, and before long, his little sack was almost full. By now it was eight o'clock, almost bedtime, and a half hour later than before, so, carrying the heavy bag of goodies, he and his dad moseyed back to the ranch.

On the way, Billy asked his dad why *he* always came along for trick-or-treating, and his mom didn't. "It's a long story, Billy," his dad answered, and then stayed quiet. Billy knew his dad didn't want to tell him, because his dad usually never minded telling long stories. In fact, many times his dad told him a long story when he was in the mood for a short story, or no story at all. And many times, he told a long story that he could just as well have told as a short story. Actually, that was most of the time.

Back at home, after Billy forgot about asking his dad if Christian Scientists believed in fairies, he entered the living room, where his mom asked Billy to empty his sack onto the kitchen table. Billy dumped very carefully, so as not to let anything fall to the floor. As he reached his hand into the cloth bag to make sure nothing was left, he asked his mom, "Why does dad always go with me on Halloween, and not you?"

She explained, "Part of the reason is my work as chairperson of the Parent's Association climate change committee. There are always things for me to do. Call this person or that person, remind folks that old newspapers can be used as wrapping paper, publicize that composting is patriotic, remind folks the city dump is getting full. Gracious sakes alive me, this is quite a responsibility!"

"What's the other part of the reason?" he inquired.

His mom sighed and said, "It's a long story." Then she fell silent.

Billy now really wanted to hear it. It must be a really good story. Or else why would both his mom and dad say it was a long story and act like they didn't want him to know it?

So, he said, "Tell me the long story while I'm counting all my treats."

She conceded, "Oh mercy percy! I suppose you might as well hear it sooner than later. A few years ago, when you were just two and your brother Andrew was only a few months old, your father suggested it would be a good idea for me to take Susie out trick-or-treating. In his words, 'It will get you away from the house, giving you a brief but well-deserved respite from the weary chores of the workaday homemaker.'

"So, he volunteered to watch you and your brother while handing out trick-or-treat goodies at the door. It was early in the evening, and he decided to pretend he was a witch. Well, since witches don't have hair on their faces, he thought he should shave. He was in the middle of changing the blades on his double-edged razor, when you came in screaming about a big bug. So, he hustled with you to the kitchen, carrying his razor. You pointed to the fat spider in the corner and then, while he was admiring the spider's fascinating web, the razor blade accidentally fell out of the razor and into the big bag of apples we were giving out. When your father returned to the bathroom, he forgot about the fallen blade that had been in his razor and put in a new one.

"Well, a little later on, kids started to come, and your father tried to scare them, cackling, all dressed up in a fake long nose and black cape and pointed black cap. Then he told them to reach into the big brown bag to pick themselves an apple. Maybe ten or fifteen kids came by, and they each plucked a big, juicy apple and thanked your father the witch for it. But the next little girl stuck her hand into the bag and came out with both an apple and a razor blade in her hand. She showed her pickings to her mom, who was standing just behind her.

"Your father tried to explain it must've been an accident, but the woman wouldn't hear of it. Minutes later a squad car arrived at the house and carted your father off to the police station. We finally bailed him out, but by then the damage was done. The rumor spread quickly that there was a weirdo maniac in the neighborhood who was handing out apples with razor blades. And over time the rumor spread to other neighborhoods, to the rest of Cedar Glen, to the rest of the state, and then to the rest of the country. And that's why to this day parents around the country throw away apples given to their children on Halloween night!

"So, from that day forward, we thought it would be a good idea for your father to take you trick-or-treating while I stayed home to hand out treats to the kids who came by."

"Wow!" Billy said. He was impressed. His dad was a much bigger menace than he ever was as Billy Buckaroo! Or was he Billy Bad Guy? He couldn't remember.

Billy was listening so hard to his mom's story that he lost count of his pickings and began again. He'd already divided everything into four piles. One pile had the coins. The second pile was candy. The third was little toys and gadgets. The fourth was apples. His mom took the fourth pile and tossed it into the trash, assuring Billy, "When we count, we'll remember those three apples."

"Why did you throw away those apples, Mom? Did they have worms?" he asked.

"No, maniacs may be out there, and I don't want to take a chance and experiment on you. You're my Billy, and you're much too valuable to me."

Billy thought it wonderful that his mom worried about his safety. Though somehow what she said didn't make sense.

As he began counting his coins, Billy put two pieces of bubble gum in his mouth, one after the other. He tried to blow a bubble but couldn't. Maybe when he grew up some more, he'd be able to. It used to be that he couldn't blow up balloons. Bubble gum was harder than balloons.

Soon, his dad returned from the living room, where he'd been reading a book. Spying a fine red apple on top of the trash, he picked it up, took a massive chomp into it, and asked through a full mouth, "Why is this good apple in the trash?"

Then he asked Billy how much money he had. Billy counted his coins. "I've got nineteen moneys."

His dad sat down at the table, and said, "In the traditional Harrington accounting system for Halloween, actually for all holidays, and every day as well, the value of the money counts more than the number of coins. So, a nickel is the same as five pennies, a dime is worth the same as ten pennies. All the way up to a hundred-dollar bill, which is worth a thousand pennies.

"Ten thousand pennies," interrupted his mom, who was better with figures than his dad and thought her numbers talent was a fine reason to attend the gambling casino.

"Ten thousand pennies," repeated his dad, as if this was the amount he stated all along. "Now, what do we have here?" And Billy saw him push some big coins here, and smaller coins there, mumbling as he pushed. Then his dad announced, "Well, Billy, we seem to have one hundred and four cents! Fine job, son."

Then they tallied up the candy and gum. His dad pointed out, "According to family tradition, each small candy and gum counts as one, and big candies and gums count as three. It's important for children to understand the concept of value. Bigger things are often worth more than smaller things, although children should also learn the concept of quality versus quantity. But let's not get into that, or else soon enough we'll be arguing about whether a Snickers is worth more than a Tootsie Roll of equivalent weight."

Billy let his dad compute it all out, and it came to sixty-four candies. Then they counted toys and gadgets, like rubber soldiers, tops, key chains, which added to thirteen.

His dad took a pencil and wrote the counts for Billy's piles. "Let's see. One hundred four cents, plus sixty-four in candy and gum, plus thirteen toys and gadgets."

His mom chimed in, "Don't forget three apples, dear."

His dad, a little annoyed, shook his head, grumbling, "How can I forget apples, dear? Plus, three apples. That's a four, and carry the one, which makes eight, carry the one, one plus one. That's one hundred and eighty-four. A fine haul for you, Billy."

Billy saw his mom go to her cookie jar and remove some change. She placed the money on the table and began to scoop up all of Billy's candy and gum. "Here Billy, sixty-four cents. I'm trading it for your candy and gum."

She tossed all his candy and gum in the trash. "Why did you do that?" he asked, confused, and slightly annoyed. He'd seen his snacks for the next week just thrown away.

"Billy, there are weirdo maniacs out there who will stoop to putting poison in the candy and gum they give kids on Halloween. Even candy that looks like it hasn't been opened. They could inject poison with a needle. We just don't want to take any chances. You're too precious, honey."

His dad, who did not quite approve of his wife tossing away all those perfectly good snacks, interjected, "Billy also could get killed crossing the …" but cut himself short when he remembered that Billy was just learning how to cross the wide street by himself—looking both ways. He reminded himself to teach Billy how to count money as soon as his son mastered crossing the street. One skill at a time!

It crossed Billy's mind that if he went to the store and bought candy with the sixty-four cents, he'd get much less candy than the amount his mom just threw out. Though he really wasn't very sure. He really didn't have a good idea of how much candy sixty-four cents could buy. And he didn't think his mom would intentionally cheat him. She was his mom, after all.

Well, at least he still had his toys and gadgets!

Just then he watched as his mom began to pick up the toys and gadgets—for his own benefit, he knew. But to be sure he asked, "Some weirdo maniac might have poisoned the toys, huh, Mom?"

"No, dear, don't be silly," she replied. "I'm just trying to clear the table. Your sister will be home soon, and we'll need to count her swag."

Billy asked, "Mom, how many weirdo maniacs are there? I mean just in Cedar Glen."

"Including the Democrats, or not including the Democrats?"

"Including."

"It's hard to know, Billy. But goodness, it seems there are more and more every day. Land of my ancestors, you should hear the number of people who think saving a few jobs here and there is more important than saving the habitat of the hairless terrapin," she answered, causing his dad to comment, "Molly, you seem to be becoming less Republican with each passing day."

A few minutes later Susie trudged in. Her sack looked pretty full. Maybe even fuller than his was. "Hi, Mom! Dad!" she greeted, before slinging the sack onto the kitchen table.

"Hello, little Billy," she said ever so sweetly, making him want to stick the gum in his mouth up her snoot!

She then said, "Trick or treat, Mom. Can I have some of those gumdrop packets?" and pointed to the candy in the bowl her mom had set out for kids who rang her doorbell.

"Sure," his mom approved. And Susie placed two of the packets in her sack.

"Let's see what we have here," his dad said as he dumped the contents of her bag onto the kitchen table. Then he began to divide them into piles, just as Billy had done. His mom reached down and took four apples, which she tossed into the trash. Susie didn't complain. She already knew the story.

"That's four apples for Susie," she reminded his dad.

Soon Billy saw him start to count. Shortly he announced that Susie had two quarters, two dimes, five nickels, and thirteen pennies, which amounted to one hundred and eight cents.

There were sixty candy and gums, and thirteen toys and gadgets. Mumbling arithmetic calculations, his dad summed it all up while his mom scooped up all Susie's candy and gum and threw them in the trash, including the two packets of her own gumdrops.

His dad began to mumble again. "That's five, carry the one, plus six and one is eight, one added to one is two."

Then he announced, "Susie has a total of one-hundred and eighty-five. Well, Billy, it looks as though Susie's the family champion again this year. She just beat you by one. It couldn't have been any closer. Congratulations, Susie! But Billy, don't get discouraged. Next year, when you'll be a little older, why, as some wise philosophers have pointed out—several of them in fact—next year will be another year."

"No fair," Billy shouted. "She took two gumdrops from our own bowl. It's no fair when you take candy from your own house! Take those gumdrops away and I win!"

"It's not my fault you didn't ask for the gumdrops. I asked for them fair and square, for Trick or Treat. Experience Halloween Heartbreak!" she taunted, sticking out her pink eight-year-old tongue, thrusting her face forward.

"She has a point there," agreed his mom. "Although it is a trifle on the borderline of fair play," she afterthoughted.

"No fair!" Billy pouted again, and stomped off to his room, where he removed his cowboy outfit. He stewed in his room for a minute or so but then had a thought.

Suddenly, Billy marched to the kitchen, just as his mom finished placing sixty cents on the table to pay Susie for the candy she'd trashed. He crossed his arms, cleared his throat and tapped the floor with the toe of his hard boot. When he had their attention, he untwisted the lips he'd puckered to the side and announced, "Mom, Dad, Susie. Look!"

They all watched as he gaped open his jaws, slowly moved his hand up to his mouth, and used Thumbkin and Pointer to remove a wad of gum. He held it out to them in the palm of his hand, showing each of them the wet pink glob. He then informed them, "This is two gums that a lady gave me. I put them in my mouth here in the kitchen before. You can add these two to my pile. Ha! I beat Susie, by one! I am the champion! I am the champion!"

"He does have a point there, dear," his mom advised her daughter, who angrily strode off to her room with a final gasp of disbelief, as Billy called after her, "Halloween Heart Attack!"

"Nitwit!" he heard her mutter before she disappeared around the corner.

"Billy, you certainly snared victory from your jaws and left your astonished, defeated sibling sister with hers open," stated his dad to his proud, grinning son.

Look to Enlight

The round wood clock over my dresser told me it was already mid-morning. Ugh! Time didn't pause because my life had. Sensing I shouldn't remain in bed daydreaming the day away, I slogged to the bathroom. Normally, I was very conscientious about flossing, probably one of the few teenagers in Cedar Glen who was. But I rationalized it wasn't necessary today, a one-day build-up of plaque and gook between my molars not being fatal. I brushed my teeth, spending only one up and down per tooth, and the cold water I splashed on my face didn't jolt me to a state of alertness as it usually did, nor did it rouse me from a semi-trance of dejection. I still was wearily burdened as I trudged from the bathroom.

I wasn't at all hungry, despite not eating since dinner yesterday, and decided against leaving the sanctuary of my room to munch, gobble, or scarf. The sight of my desk reminded me that final exams were coming up in a few weeks. After I emitted a loud wailing yawn that comatose Andrew gave no sign of hearing, I considered whether I should study Greek classics or trigonometry. Trigonometry didn't seem to offer any potential for enlightenment. I thought half-jokingly, "If my problem involved a love triangle it might help, but my problem is not mathematical at all, except for requiring some clear logical thinking just now. Well, maybe it did involve arithmetic—plussing a new person to the world."

But Greek classics might provide insight into my predicament. Ancient Greek writers depicted the struggles of humanity set with complex personal problems, and their gods, who also might have complex personal problems. Of course, ancient Greeks' theology was obviously erroneous—not even real theology. Time had revealed it to be literature, rather than theology, and mythical at that! Nowadays people knew there was one all-powerful Lord of the Universe rather than a bunch of bickering egotistical gods and goddesses those naïve Greeks worshiped.

Still, the ancient Greeks wrote about the basic human condition, which, as my teachers had taught, perpetuated throughout history. That's why the stories were classics, after all. So, reading the classics might somehow clarify my current problems. The Greeks composed great tragedies, and certainly my situation seemed to be developing into tragedy. Or was there already.

So, I opened to the dog-leafed page of *Oedipus Rex* I'd left off at yesterday afternoon, hoping for some clarity and wisdom. But very shortly I considered its ridiculously far-fetched event—a grown man falling in love and marrying a woman not only old enough to be his mother, but his real, actual mother. Totally ludicrous! Bogus!

Would I ever go out on a first date with my own mom, much less marry her? The same with any of my friends and their moms! Not even Charles, whose mother was known as The Milf Who Would. It was wasteful to continuate with that Oedipus story. I just couldn't buy in.

I went to my bookcase and looked at titles of pieces I'd already read. None seemed relevant. Maybe I was being impatient, but how foolish I was to think Greek classics could enlighten me! The Greeks didn't write about real people in authentic situations. I didn't expect to find a story about an unwed Greek teenager who became pregnant and what she and her boyfriend decided to do. Maybe in those days it was taken for granted they'd get married. There was no college to go to. So, maybe you'd get a job working as an assistant to an important philosopher, much like today's

Supreme Court justices have clerks. Or you'd open up a stall selling olives in the agora marketplace. But I couldn't ascertain a single theme in any of the plays or stories I'd read thus far that might be at all germane.

As far as the ancient Greeks were concerned, women seemed to be impregnated just as often by gods as by men, and they were clueless about abortions. Only later in the advancement of civilization was the practice of abortion developed.

"What has school got to do with real life?" I wondered, not for the first time, the thought usually occurring when I found a problem overly perplexing and it was easier to blame the problem instead of my lack of acumen (which is another word for the more understandable "perspicacity"). Most often I was irritable with a school problem. Now it was a real-life problem.

"Maybe I'll crack open the Bible later, for direction," I considered. I didn't remember any stories about biblical characters who knocked up their single girlfriends. But the readers at the church always found something in the Bible that applied to life.

I hadn't attended church in a long while, and I fleetingly considered a visit for personal counsel. But then I feared word of my news might get loose. Not that Christian Scientist readers were blabbermouth gossips! But I wished systematic confidential confession existed in the Christian Science religion, like for those sinful Roman Catholics.

Fatigued, I closed my book and flopped back into bed. Schoolwork later. But I would get back to it. It was urgent that I do well on finals. More than ever, I might need financial aid. Circumstances now were such that I might not go to college at all, no less my goal of Ivy League acceptance. I had to plan as if I would go. But I couldn't concentrate. I could just not get into a study mood.

Next semester, only a few months away, I'd be a senior. So would Joannie. In just a few months, she'd begin to show. Would it be in September, when classes resumed, or October, or November? I'd never paid much attention to when women began to bump. She'd wear looser clothes, but soon her swollen belly would be obvious. Soon she'd waddle down hallways, her face would bloat, and it would be a production to settle into a chair. She'd be excused from phys ed class, and not speak up in classrooms, so she wouldn't look and feel conspicuous. Stares and whispers would surround her, enveloping her in a morass of embarrassment.

I wondered whether they'd even let a pregnant student attend classes at Cedar Glen High. Last year a girl at school had given birth, right in the midst of English Composition class, right on the floor, with my clueless teacher, the balding bachelor Mr. Cox, completely baffled as to what to do. "Call the school nurse! Someone boil some towels!" he ordered no one in particular.

The girl was plump, so her pregnancy hadn't been noticed by anyone. She herself didn't know, it turned out. After the baby arrived, Belinda confessed, "I had no idea I was pregnant. I thought it was just a stomachache."

Joannie had commented, "Suddenly giving birth like that, Belinda definitely wasn't in touch with her body." I knew Joannie would not be like that.

There would be no mistaking the naturally thin Joannie's condition. Everyone would know she was expecting. Know I was the father. I'd be a role model of what not to be, feeling equally victimized by the classmates who snickered behind my back and by the well-intended expressions of compassion dispensed by my friends.

Joannie giving birth in seven months or less! When I was younger, seven months seemed a gazillion years away. Now, it was a fleeting span that would befall in an instant.

Even more imminent was my meeting with Joannie later in the afternoon. Maybe she had a plan. Or maybe we'd sit there, two scared kids pretending to be grown-ups.

And sooner or later I'd need to face my family, schoolmates, teachers, anyone who knew me and didn't expect anything of this sort in the life of Billy Harrington. I was exhausted, vanquished. I wished I could become invisible to the world for a while.

The Reality of Pumpkin

Billy didn't know what to do. Usually, decisions were easy, but now he was stumped. It was because of Pumpkin, his new imaginary friend. He'd had imaginary friends before, but now was different. Yeah, Billy knew it was cute to have an imaginary friend when you were three, or even five. But it was different when a seven-year-old had one.

And this one was a girl!

Should he tell about his imaginary friend? Or not? And tell who?

Billy's imaginary friend was named Pumpkin. She was his friend for about two weeks now. She was very pretty, about his age. Pumpkin had straw blond hair in a ponytail, which she told him was shorter than a horsetail, which was for people with *really* long hair.

Her very large blue eyes seemed to always be winking. Her white straight teeth almost always showed, since she was almost always smiling or laughing, even when nothing was funny, which Billy wondered about, but soon forgot. She wore jeans, just like Billy.

Billy could see Pumpkin very clearly, even with others around. But he *only* talked to her in private so others wouldn't think he was bonkers, talking to himself. Although other people who seemed to talk to themselves in public were just on their phone, he thought they were bonkers too.

So, he spent lots of after-school time with her in his busy room. He was glad his roommate, five-year-old brother Andrew, stayed away from the room a lot. When not in kindergarten class, Andrew usually was outdoors, romping in the fresh spring air with Bozo, the family schnauzer his dad recently brought home, or climbing the big tree in the back yard, or riding his red three-wheeler around the block, warning pedestrians to "Beep beep, out way of firebike."

There was plenty for them to do in his room—storybooks, toys, games, and playing cards. But even without those things they'd keep busy because he had his imagination. And she had a bigger one.

Oh, he knew Pumpkin wasn't *real* real. Like his shoes, or his mom's convection oven, or anything else that really *was*. But she was real in other ways because she made him laugh, and she usually laughed when he said something funny, but not all the time. She usually felt sorry if he said something sad. But not all the time. Because it wasn't all the time, that made her even realer. He told himself.

Yes, Billy knew Pumpkin only existed in his mind. Yet he couldn't help from calling her up. It was like telling yourself to stop thinking about jellybeans. It just couldn't be done!

He and Pumpkin talked a lot. As just two main examples, they agreed combing hair wasn't important and cartoons were fun. He didn't agree when she said kids should do whatever they wanted, but he got her point. When they played cards, it was Old Maid because she said the game he wanted to play—War—was stupid. But she was just giving her opinion, and it's good for people to give their opinions.

They also talked about whether he should tell his family about her. She said it was up to him; she couldn't help there. It made him feel good when Pumpkin said he was old and smart enough to decide on his own. But on the other hand, was she being bossy by insisting it was up to him to decide? Like he didn't have a choice of whether to make that decision. He *had* to decide.

Billy had thought about telling his parents, but a few months ago, once his last imaginary friend, Marco, got interested in Scientology, Billy just banished him from his mind forever. His mom and dad seemed happy about that. How would they feel if Billy had a *new* imaginary friend? Well, maybe they'd be happy it was a girl this time. But maybe not.

He thought of telling his nine-year-old sister, but Susie was very busy thinking about becoming a preteen and dancing around like a drunken octopus. Now, she thought she was so special because she soon would advance from that nondescript group of kids between toddlerhood and preteen, a group having no specific name. She probably wanted to have nothing to do with a babyish kid like him.

He thought about telling Andrew, but Andrew had never had an imaginary friend, and he would probably think Billy was nuts, or acting like a baby, rather than a highly respective older brother who set a good example. Andrew just wouldn't understand.

Just to get it off his chest, to talk to a living being, he thought of telling Bozo, who at least wouldn't blab about it to anyone else. He suspected Bozo already knew. One afternoon Bozo came into the room while he and Pumpkin were reading a storybook, and he began to bark for no good reason. Billy wasn't sure if Bozo actually saw Pumpkin or just smelled her.

Billy knew for sure he wasn't going to tell about Pumpkin to anyone in his class, even his teacher, Miss Wallaby. He'd always been an A student, but Miss Wallaby might wonder why Billy did even better on tests recently—A+. Billy certainly would not inform her it was because Pumpkin whispered the answers in his ear. Billy wondered why she whispered, since no one could hear her anyway, except him. But when he thought about it more, he knew it would be disrespectful if Pumpkin talked very loud, even if no one else could hear.

Billy didn't so much like getting high grades this tricky way, but Pumpkin told him it wasn't really cheating, just some mischief. Besides, Billy really wasn't all that sure it wasn't him who *was* learning more. For again, he knew Pumpkin didn't really exist.

Anyway, if he tried to explain Pumpkin to Miss Wallaby, she might wonder whether he could be trusted to perform his assigned job of placing markers on the ledge of the whiteboard at the beginning of class.

He certainly wasn't going to tell the other kids in his class, especially his archrival Scott, who was always trying to get the better of him. Before, when he'd told one of his classmates about Marco, word got around fast, and the other kids had kept far away from him for weeks. He smartly decided kids didn't want anything to do with classmates their age who had imaginary friends.

It was even more confusing after his dad used his phone one day to take pictures of the family. Billy knew Pumpkin was standing right in front of him when his dad said "Cheesecake." He knew other family members wouldn't see her, but he wondered if he would. Or not.

Not! Billy could not see Pumpkin in the pictures. More proof that Pumpkin existed only in his brain. But he wondered if he should be happy about not seeing that. Or not.

He figured Pumpkin was much like the Lord. Your brain says a being you can't see really exists. But you can never catch it in photos. As far as both Billy and Pumpkin knew, neither the real Lord nor his real son had ever been seen in photos. Ever! Even once when the Pope was the camera snapper.

Yes, Billy told himself, things certainly were confusing! Pumpkin tried to simplify it all. "Of course I'm not in the photos. If I was, I wouldn't be a real imaginary person, would I?"

Because he had an imaginary friend, Billy felt very different from other kids. He knew sometimes kids pretended to have an imaginary friend, just for the sake of playing. He knew most kids were stupidified by magic, ghost stories, and things that weren't real, or at least couldn't be seen in eyesight or heard in the ear but might really be in another dimension. That, he felt, was why he himself liked all the stories from the Bible his parents had told him. But for sure, now was not all pretend. Pumpkin was much realer than his before imaginary friends.

It wasn't as if Billy had planned to have Pumpkin show up in his life. She just popped up one day. One morning he awoke and there she was, sitting on the bedroom floor with her legs crossed, watching him stretch himself awake. Once he saw her, he stopped in mid-yawn and immediately became totally alert, thinking, "I'm glad I'm wearing pajamas."

He asked who she was, and she brightly identified herself. "I'm Pumpkin, your new imaginary friend."

Pumpkin certainly showed up at the right time, for the previous day had been very not nice. He got into a fight with Scott, after an argument at a game of Huckle Buckle, the two boys going at it in the grass patch outside the school entrance, amidst noisy shouts. Some kids loudly rooted for him, the smaller of the two, and some, much fewer, he was certain, cheered for Scott. Some didn't care and were just rooting for one of them to get at least a bloody nose.

He lost badly, in front of almost his whole class. His eye was shut, and his wrist was very sore from when Scott twisted it behind his back until he was forced to say "Scott rules" five times.

After the fight was over, Scott let him go with a shove, it was very quiet. His classmates just walked away. None came over to ask if he was all right. That skinny Joannie girl gave him a tissue for his bleeding nose but wandered off without saying anything. He was all embarrassed. Losing a fight can be a big, big thing in the second grade. Thank goodness he hadn't cried.

When he got home, his mom gasped, seeing the bruise under his eye. Bending to get a closer look, she determined, "You must have been in a fight. You know I don't like you to fight. Goodness, I would much rather you use your words than your fists. Now let's put ice on this."

Billy explained, "I did use my words. But Scott didn't like them. He said 'liar' and 'cheater' were fighting words. So, he beat me up, in front of almost the whole class."

"You must have felt humiliated," she said.

"Yes," admitted Billy, "I was miliated."

"While the whole class watched? You probably feel they don't think you're truly boyish."

"Uh-huh."

"I bet you feel worse about being ashamed you lost the fight than about your eye hurting," she sympathized.

"Yep!" Billy answered, barely holding in tears. He wasn't sure, though, whether he wanted to cry because he had such an understanding mom, or because he lost the fight.

Gloomy, he wasn't hungry and stayed in his room during family dinner. Later, his dad came to his room with food on a tray, and as he put it down, related, "Your mom informed me what transpired at school today. Something like that happened to me when I was a boy, just about the same age as you. I got into a fight with a bully at school and had the living daylights knocked out of me. I had two black eyes, and the bully gave me a spanking, in front of everyone. You can imagine how I felt. I think that might have been the cause of all the hemorrhoid problems I had later in life. Who can be sure?

"Anyway, I then had a choice. I could train to get stronger and be a better fighter, so I could beat up the bully. But he was pretty big and almost had his orange belt in karate—that's about halfway between a yellow belt and a red belt, Billy—so that wasn't a very promising option. Or I could just let things be and stay away from the bully. But that would mean I'd constantly feel ridiculed by the other kids at school and just know in my heart I was a coward. Or I could turn to the Lord and place my trust in him. And that's what I did. And here I am today. So, let that be a lesson to you, my boy."

With a wink his dad strolled toward the door. As he reached the doorway he turned to Billy and added, "By the way, the boy who beat me up—today he is the governor of this state. So, you never can know. Now eat up." And he winked again as he left the room.

Wow! His dad personally knew the governor, even if it was years ago. If you're going to be a victim, it was partly made up for if the guy who beat you up was now a star person.

But his dad didn't supply any direction as to what Billy should do about Scott. He knew the Lord was his shepherd, but the Lord wasn't always clear about what he wanted from his human flock. The Bible kept changing its mind. Maybe the Lord wanted him to give Scott a bruised eye in return for his bruised eye. Or maybe the Lord wanted him to turn his cheek and live in Christian harmonica with Scott. Or maybe it was the Lord's will that he get beat up again. Billy was very confused and in need of sympathy.

The very next morning, Pumpkin just popped up. She'd been his imaginary friend for two weeks now. But he missed playing more with Bozo and having conversations with his mom and dad, where he learned about life. And he felt a little guilty for not telling them about Pumpkin.

He didn't hang with friends. After school he went straight home. He missed the happiness of the games he played with them. He was one of the best in the class at Huckle Buckle, and he hadn't played a single game, or even had a scrummage, since Pumpkin arrived. She said she didn't know how to play Huckle Buckle and really wasn't interested in learning.

"Let's make fun of Scott, the stupid gorilla geek," she suggested once. They had a good time calling Scott all sorts of names. Billy liked that! He didn't even mind when she said Scott was fine-looking and smart, since she added she didn't care so much that he was a good fighter.

One night, after his mom kissed his cheek, tucked him in to bed, and reminded him to have sweet dreams, Pumpkin rose from the floor where she slept, tiptoed over. Then … BIG SURPRISE. She kissed his cheek and also reminded him to have sweet dreams. He felt warm about that. Sort of.

The next night she did the same thing. He said to himself that he sort of liked being kissed on his cheek before falling asleep, whether it was done by his mom or by Pumpkin. But he wasn't sure.

The next night Billy received an even bigger surprise. Pumpkin kissed him, but this time smack on the lips!

This was a different story altogether! Being kissed on the cheek was nice, but being kissed on the lips was yucky! When he used his wrist to wipe the kiss off his lips, Pumpkin said, "Oh, don't be a baby! It was just a kiss between boy and girl."

Billy said nothing and pretended to fall asleep. After a few minutes his eyes opened wide, and all he could think about was that Pumpkin was changing, and how much he didn't like being kissed on the lips, even by her. And for certain he'd never like it. It was awfuller than being hugged by your mom in front of all the guys.

When he woke up the next day, Pumpkin was wearing a dress! A dress! A light blue dress with lace on the bottom! Why? She never told him she even owned a dress. Something was really wrong, but he wasn't sure if he should ask her about it. So, he didn't.

Billy and Pumpkin didn't talk on the walk to school, except for him warning her not to step in the poop a dog had left in the middle of the sidewalk, and she said, "Thanks." The whole morning, he paid all his mind to hearing what Miss Wallaby taught. At lunchtime Pumpkin was nowhere to be seen. He closed his eyes, trying to concentrate, for he knew she was in his brain. But still, she didn't show. She would not be summoned.

After he opened his eyes and looked at a window reflection, he noticed his bruised eye was all healed.

Finally, he gave up searching for Pumpkin. Obviously, he put down the idea of asking any classmates if they'd seen her. After being with her over two weeks, she went poof.

Strangely, he felt less jittery. Calmer, like after a good night's sleep, or finishing a Neapolitan ice cream waffle cone. Maybe she'd show up later, but he realized he hoped not. She'd probably want to do more yucky kissing!

"Later on," he reflected, "I'll play Huckle Buckle with Andrew, and maybe chat with my mom and dad. I'll take Bozo for a run. I probably won't play with Susie, though. She'll most likely be too busy, doing that silly stuff girls her age do."

Returning to the classroom after lunch, Billy noticed Scott walking up the aisle to his seat. Scott seemed to be talking to himself.

Hmmmm!

Will It Ever Go Away?

I had a hunch that when I finally spilled my predicament to someone besides Joannie, I'd be lectured in a "count your blessings" way. Told I still had health, enough food, a home to live, the whole family not moving away without telling me where they were going. And whatever.

Yet knowing logically that others are worse off doesn't necessarily make you feel any better. Though it can make you less likely to complain out loud.

So, reversing course, I thought that perhaps my whole attitude was wastefully misdirected, that I needed a dramatic change in perspective. Stop the panicky and contrary. Be thoughtful and positive. Open-minded. Find a solution, a way to cope, instead of "woe is me."

Up to now I assumed the baby would be a burden. But surely many men wanted children to play with. They hoped to pass along a heritage, deliver personal nuggets of wisdom, secrets for success, and other important stuff, and not just because their girlfriend accidentally got knocked up.

I hadn't even thought yet about whether what popped out of Joannie would be a boy or a girl. Was it because I suspected the baby would never be born, that I didn't care, procrastination, or because I just didn't want to even consider the reality of the situation, to admit it *was* all going down? I couldn't get clear about all that.

If someone asked did I want a boy or a girl, would I answer, the possibly true, "Neither." Or would I resort to the possibly true but musty old, "It doesn't matter as long as it's healthy."? Or would I deliver the possibly true, that I preferred … What did I prefer? Probably a boy. If I imagined my little playmate, yes, it was a boy.

I could roughhouse with a boy; as a rule, girls are too delicate. I could teach him to play Huckle Buckle, but most girls didn't care for the game, except to watch a boy they had a crush on. I could raise my son to be smart, athletic, likable, and … not someone who didn't go as far as he could've because he had to get married at seventeen!

I tried to steer my thoughts to a happier, hopeful, and optimistic place. Like, I remember the pleasure my folks often experienced with me when I was young. Like when I was three and crept to the foot of their bed early one morning and noticed how together they were under the covers, my dad breathing hard, making different noises than his irritating snore when he'd fallen fast asleep.

My dad must've said something funny because my mom said, "Oh, Gordon," several times in a row. After she stopped "Gordoning," she noticed me as if I surprised her, and motioned me up, though she made sure I was atop the blanket, and not underneath like them. I climbed and snuggled my mom and sighing dad, feeling safe and warm, loved, cuddly, comfier than in my own bed, despite the sheets on my mom and dad's bed lacking cartoons. I was sure my parents enjoyed the cozy intimacy as much as I did.

I flipped over to my mom's side, held onto her back, and said, "I'm the bread, dad's the bread, you're the jelly." Then I made Dad the jelly. We all giggled.

When I was just a little older, Andrew would join me in their bed. We'd each be bread, while my dad would graduate from bread to peanut butter, with my mom still the jelly.

Of course, now I realize what Mom and Dad were actually doing, but as a kid, who knew of such matters?

I remembered the wonder of pretending I was an airplane as my dad centered his straightened legs on my belly, raised me in the air, then I rode forward and backward to the accompaniment of his "Zoom" sounds.

I laughed when he placed fluttering lips on my bare belly and blew hard, giving me his special raspberry spritz tickle. How scary, but how fun it ended when he slung me backwards over his shoulder and let me slide down his long back!

I'd steal my son's nose and mysteriously find it behind his ear. I'd encourage him, applaud his achievements, not seem to notice his mistakes. I'd accept him being scared by monsters in the closet to the age of three, but after that I'd train him not to be afraid. I'd teach him how to read blueprints. Well, first I'd need to learn myself, but I would. I'd take the Mechanical Drawing elective next year. I'd have taken it this semester if I wasn't required to take Women's Studies!

It would thrill me when my boy first bounded up and down stair steps without placing two legs on each riser. I'd explain the perplexing rules of Huckle Buckle and drill him until the nuances of the game became second nature. I'd cheer in ecstasy when he scored his first bangle at Huckle Buckle or preen when he solvated rudimentary algebra problems before reaching kindergarten.

I wouldn't withhold feelings, intimate thoughts. I might have to behave like a woman sometimes, but I'd do it!

I'd talk to my boy, never deceive him, listen, anticipate and treat his problems with equal or greater concern than my own. I'd make him feel he was the only item on my schedule. My son would not be afraid to speak to me, or avoid seeking my guidance, especially if his girlfriend got pregnant. When he was old enough, I'd make sure he knew the value of protection while mattressing.

I won't allow myself to be baggage to an adorable youngster who'd offer hugs to not only get out of punishments, but to express his love for me.

My son would be a whiz bang boy! I wouldn't be one of those fathers who sat under a shade tree at the lake! Unless he was with me, enjoying the day. Or we were both fishing.

Oh, but what if it was a girl? I'd have to think more about that. Probably most of the same stuff I thought about for a son. Maybe Joannie was thinking on that stuff now, for a girl.

But why couldn't I have the same son a few years from now, when I was less clueless, a college graduate, and really knew how to be a grown-up? WHY? Fantasy! All this about the pleasure of fatherhood was fantasy! Possibly true, but all conjured for now. My life could be totally ruined.

This crazy horrible position I'm in now—would it ever just go away?

Boiling Troubles

Billy couldn't sit down. It wasn't because he was nervous, jumpy, jittery. It wasn't because he had no place to sit down. There was the comfy couch, and his house was jam-packed with chairs. All kinds: armchairs, dining room chairs, bridge chairs. Just plain chairs. Not to mention all the stools.

It wasn't because he was playing musical chairs and the other seats were taken.

It wasn't because he could only stand when doing his daily chores of making his bed and feeding Bozo.

Billy couldn't sit down because he had something no one else in his family had. Neither Susie, his stuck-up older sister, nor Andrew, his scampy little brother, were jealous. They knew they were lucky it wasn't them who possessed the two biggest boils in the recorded history of the Harrington family. Two monstrous boils, bright pink and throbbing, right on the fleshy parts of each side of Billy's eight-year-old butt. Nobody could see them under his pants and underpants, of course. He was glad about that.

The boils started out as small lumps he hardly noticed at first. But soon they got larger and larger until they became huge. Billy, whose class was just starting to study fractions, figured, "They take up about an eighth of my butt, or maybe even more, a ninth."

The boils didn't hurt too much, except when he sat down. Or when he tried to run and his boils scraped against his pants. Walking wasn't too bad, unless he tried to take big steps. Once, soon after Billy first developed the boils, his mom playfully slapped his rear end as she asked him to fetch some jalapeño peppers from the refrigerator to embellish the peanut butter sandwiches she was preparing for her kids' lunches. Billy screamed so loud that she'd told him, "My galoshes, I thought you'd swallowed a jalapeño pepper whole."

Another time Bozo, wanting attention, playfully jumped up and slapped paws against Billy's tender butt. A bewildered Bozo spent the next hour sentenced to his doghouse. Billy then realized, "That's no fair to Bozo. How is he supposed to know about my butt boils? All I'm teaching by punishing him is not to play with me." He released Bozo, but he was careful not to let the dog get behind him.

Bozo, in fact, didn't again slap his paws against Billy's butt. But a few times the beloved canine placed his nose close to his owner's backside and sniffed, sensing something abnormal, but then decided whatever it was, it was beyond his comprehension, unimportant anyway, and dropped it from his doggie mind.

Life isn't easy with big butt boils. Ask anyone who has them. Okay, it's hard to find someone with butt boils to ask. You can't see them, and it's weird to go around asking people if they have them. Even then, they might not want to admit it.

At dinner, the family sat in their usual places, his dad at one end, his mom the other, and the kids on the sides. That is, Susie and Andrew sat. For Billy couldn't sit down without feeling misery and pain. So, he ate standing.

Billy might've eaten while lying on his stomach. But he figured his family wouldn't be able to see him on the floor. Besides, everybody knew when you laid on your stomach, it was hard for food to drop down to your belly!

Bozo also ate standing up, but Billy felt this wasn't equal since Bozo didn't have to use forks, knives, or spoons. Food went right from Bozo's bowl to his mouth. But no way was Billy going to lap up his food from a plate. He sternly told himself, "No! I am not a dog."

Billy didn't like sleeping on his stomach at night, his nose squashed into his pillow. If he woke in the middle of the night, he wouldn't be able to see ghosts or burglars. But he had no choice. "Poor Billy!" he felt self-sorry, actually mentioning his own name aloud.

His family was very sympathetic. A few days ago, his dad reminded Billy that many years ago he'd been a veteran of hemorrhoid surgery. He took Billy to the garage, where he resurrected that blow-up tube, the kind small children use at the pool, pointing out, "This is the tube I sat on after my hemorrhoid surgery. Wow, did it hurt when they took out the stitches! When it was all done, I said to myself, 'There must be a better way.' That's when I converted to Christian Science."

Billy wasn't impressed by the green baby dinosaurs on the tube. Wasn't his dad embarrassed by sitting on such a baby tube? Still, Billy tried sitting on the tube. But his boils squeezed against the plastic, and it didn't do a bit of good. Boils are as painful as hemorrhoid surgery, he deduced.

He appreciated that up to now neither Susie nor Andrew laughed at him. In the past few years, the three forever caught diseases from each other— mumps, colds, and the 24-hour, 48-hour, and 72-hour flus—and he knew Susie and Andrew were concerned they might be next in line to catch the boils. But they couldn't help but laugh when his mom, with all good intentions, told them, "Billy should not be the butt of jokes because of his condition."

Susie, who was prone to jokery that he sometimes laughed at, offered what seemed a protest against his mom's order. "But, but ...," she started to say.

Then, his mom, catching on, smiled and said with a wink, "That's enough, Susie. Thank goodness this family has a sense of humor. Humor certainly helps us to get through the day!"

"Amen," seconded his dad.

Just before bedtime, Billy kept his mom company as she washed dishes to completely immaculate and then stacked them in the dishwasher. She assured him, "Don't worry. I'm sure the boils will soon begin to draw."

Draw? He imagined whatever was inside the boils were sketching pictures, the drawings done by tiny yellow monster artists with ugly fingers.

"Poor Billy!" he pitied himself.

A little concerned, the unsure Billy marched to his dad, who was mindlessly picking at his toenails in the living room, and asked, "Are there little creatures in the boils on my butt?"

His dad put down his unlit pipe and replied, "Why, yes, Billy. I sense in you a knowledge of biology far beyond the ken of most eight-year-olds. How did you know about those troublemaker boil creatures?"

His dad then smiled the same sort of proud smile as when he saw all A's on Billy's report card. And he seemed puzzled when Billy took off to his bedroom, crying.

Billy flopped on his bed, then heard clunky footsteps, and soon saw his dad sit on the nearby chair and then lift him to his lap. Billy screamed in pain as his boils landed smack on his dad's legs. His dad apologized, saying something about not realizing, then set Billy back in bed and told his son that in earlier years he'd been a member of several groups with "Anonymous" in their names, and so he wanted to inform Billy that he wasn't alone, that others shared his problem. Then he went on to tell Billy some jokes he heard about the time he had his hemorrhoids removed. Like folks telling him his problems were all behind him. Billy hoped his dad was nifty enough to not find those jokes funny. But just after his dad said, "Let me tell you the one about the rattlesnake and the stubborn ass," Billy leapt back to his bed, and stomach first, sobbed into his pillow, as quietly as he could manage.

As his dad left the room he encouraged, "Don't worry, Billy. Both your mom and I are going to pray that your boils disappear, and soon."

But the boils just would not improve. Over the next few days his mom tried all sorts of home remedies their church permitted. Once, she placed cotton balls dipped in steaming water on them. That didn't work, and little Billy heard her mumble, "Maybe next I'll try an ice pack."

When he let out a deafening wail in protest, he was relieved to hear her say, "Billy, I said 'ice *pack*,' not 'ice *pick*.'"

But cold didn't work either. She even tried rubbing the boils with homemade apricot marmalade, a traditional family ointment that, of course, served a dual purpose. Useless! Nothing seemed to work.

He stayed home from school, but now his mom felt a week had already been much too long. He dreaded going to school, convinced he'd be the victim of cruel taunts, or made the butt (not that again!) of crude jokes.

"Do I have to?" he asked his mom.

"Yes dear, you do. Schoolwork is very important to the Harringtons, what with me a librarian and your dad a college professor. You know he could be called *Doctor* Harrington if he wanted, but, as a good Christian Scientist, he doesn't want to be confused with the medical profession. Your dad went to school forever to get his degree."

Billy wondered: If it took really long to get his degree, did that mean his dad was left back at school?

Anyway, Billy was worried about the reactions of other kids. He knew that kids nowadays didn't make fun of or think bad about other kids with a lisp, stammer or stutter, kids who were very tall or very short, boys dressed in clothes usually worn by boys, girls dressed in clothes usually worn by boys, boys thinking they were really girls, girls thinking they were really boys, or kids driving a wheelchair. Sympathetically correct like that. But butt boils were an entirely different animal.

Animal? Yeah, there were animals hiding in his butt boils. Maybe they were trying to get out, and that's why his butt skin was swoll.

Soon, most people at school knew, since he had to explain why he couldn't sit down. He felt very conspicuous and embarrassed. He thought, "I stand out like a sore thumb!" And that thought made him feel even worse.

As he expected, some smarty-pants classmates were not very kind. A few were kind, like his best pal Todd and that cute Joannie, who sympathized, "You're brave for coming to school."

But others teased him meanly at recess, using words they thought cute or funny, but which hurt his feelings. Like calling him "Nipplebutt." Or declaring he waddled like a penguin, imitating his bow-legged gait.

His long-time nemesis Scott strolled over and, as if they didn't know each other, introduced himself, "Hi! I'm *Lance*. I don't mean to *pin* you down, but if you need any help, I'm here." Billy felt helpless as Scott joined the snickering classmates who were watching.

Billy had given a note from his mom to his teacher, Miss Simple, explaining his situation. Miss Simple took Billy aside and said, "I overheard some of the comments the other kids made. Kids sometimes are cruel, but take it from me, you should just ignore their cheeky humor."

Billy had a vague idea of what she said, and thought she too might be being cruel, poking fun at him. But he changed his mind when she said with a sad smile, as if he were a grown-up, "I hope you understand what I go through when every year my new class calls me Miss *Pimple* behind my back. As a kid I used to say to myself, 'I can't wait until I get married, so I can change my name.' Those kids teasing you, it's their problem, not yours."

Billy couldn't figure out how the boils on his butt were their problem and not his, but he let it pass, concluding it wasn't that important.

He was very sad when he got home, with no change in his boils. His mom noticed his sorrow, and said, "You must be sad because the kids at school made fun of you."

"Yes," he admitted.

"You must have been embarrassed in front of the whole class," she added.

"Yes," responded Billy.

"I bet the other kids made jokes at your expense."

"They did. It's not fair," he complained.

"You must have felt so silly not being able to sit down with two boils on your butt," she added.

"Uh-huh," conceded Billy, as he thought to himself, "I'm so glad I have a great mom who really understands how I feel. Now I'm not so sad anymore."

The next school day was Show and Tell. Billy was glad it wasn't his turn to present. His boils were the only thing interesting in his life since two weeks ago when he gave his last Show and Tell speech about accidentally entering the ladies' room at a McDonald's.

But the teasing from the other kids continued. Billy felt as if almost everyone in the class was laughing at him, no less behind his back. So to speak.

Right before dinner his mom directed him, just as she had each evening for the past week or so, "Wash your hands especially thoroughly, because if the germs inside the boils get into the food, the whole family just might get food poisoning."

Billy thought his mom was being silly. His boils were in his butt, not on his hands. And besides, if some of what was inside his boils somehow escaped and got in the food, someone would taste it and spit it out before it did any damage. But Billy minded her. She really was a fine mom, he knew, even though she was sometimes too strict for no good reason. Besides, he thought, what was the point of arguing? Even if he got her to agree the boils had nothing to do with poisoning the food, she'd find some other reason for him to wash his hands!

Billy knew that his mom, though at times not very lenient, wanted him to be happy. But what she had to say next was a big surprise, much like he would have been surprised if, say, he expected a Swiss Army knife as a birthday present but got a bow tie instead.

"If your boils don't get better by the weekend, we're taking you to the Practitioner after church services on Sunday. The Practitioner will have some ideas on how to cure your boils."

Billy mulled over having to show his butt to a stranger, maybe even a girl stranger, and asked, "Can't we just pray at home and try some more of your remedies? One of them's bound to work. You're really good at home remedies."

"Billy, sometimes we must place ourselves in the hands of the Lord, and that includes our butts!" she informed.

Billy wished that it was clearer which one of the two, God or Jesus, they were referring to when talking about the Lord. He also grumbled to himself, asking why his family couldn't have a family doctor, like other families. When his mom asked him to speak up, he wondered aloud, "Why me? Why did the Lord choose my butt to put those boils?"

His mom seemed to struggle for a good answer before explaining, "Sometimes bad things happen to good people, without any apparent reason. That just goes to strengthen our belief in the Lord, both of them. For if bad things happened only to bad people, and good things happened only to good people, we wouldn't need the Lord as an explanation now, would we?"

Billy didn't quite understand his mom's message, though it struck him as probably important and deep. He was glad he had a mom who knew so much about the Lord, both of them. He still thought it silly not to be able to visit a doctor. But he didn't at all believe some kids at school who said his parents were child abusers because they refused to seek medical help for their children. Kids said all sorts of things just to seem cool.

Douglas, a chiropractor's son, said, "My dad can get rid of your boils by cracking your spine."

When Billy asked what the spine had to do with the boils on his butt, Douglas replied, "My dad said every part of the body is connected to every other part, and if one part was rotten it could affect other parts of the body far, far away. And the spine is the messenger."

Billy then got to wondering whether his rotten boils would affect other parts of his body. His eyes, maybe. Or his ears. Or his brain! These boils were more serious than just a sore butt.

For some unexplained reason, he started wondering if flies would start to hover around his butt, much like they flitted around rotten fruit. He began to get more and more concerned. "Poor Billy!" he self-pitied, knowing full well, but not caring, that his imagination was making him lose control.

Questions ran through his curious mind. How did he get these boils in the first place? And why are they called boils? And what made a boil different than a big pimple? Or a blister?

The next day at school, just before the bell rang to start class, a concerned Miss Simple strode over to where he stood. She bent down to almost his height and asked in just above a whisper how he was feeling. Billy matter-of-factly said the boils still hurt when he sat. "Maybe I'll be better soon," he offered, to seem hopeful.

At lunch recess, Miss Simple took Billy to the school library. There, she pulled out a book called Medical Guide, quickly flipped to the index, and moved her finger until she found "Boils," mumbling all the while, as he'd seen people do when holding a reference book. She leafed quickly to the "Boils" page. Her lips moved back and forth silently as she read rapidly. Every once in a while, she muttered words like "spontaneous recovery," "white blood cells," "pus," and something he thought sounded like "staff low cock kiss."

He asked, "What's staff low cock kiss, Miss Simple?"

"Some form of bug. They're very small, smaller than you can see."

When she asked just how large his boils were, he said, "I'll show you."

But, alertly aware of lawsuits and criminal charges brought against overly curious schoolteachers, Miss Simple said, "That's okay, I just wanted to know if they were big."

"They sure are, Miss Simple."

"Then they might be carbuncles," she stated firmly.

Billy wondered what carbuncles were. He'd heard of barnacles, which sounded like carbuncles, but he knew those stuck to boat bottoms, not to boys' bottoms.

"What are carbuncles?"

"According to this Medical Guide, they are either 'unusually large boils, or groups of boils joined together by small tunnels in the skin.'"

Billy's mind went directly to the ant farm in his classroom, the squiggly ants marching back and forth through their tunnels. And he imagined ants somehow were under his skin, parading inside his butt.

"Poor me! First flies. Now ants!" he thought pathetically.

Now Billy knew he was in real trouble. If he scratched his boils—or were they carbuncles?—hard, it would really, really hurt. But if he didn't scratch, he'd have the horrible feeling that ants were crawling inside his butt. He wondered whether these ants knew how to draw. Or were they ants at all? Maybe they were creatures other than ants. Like miniature spiders maybe, or roaches, or scorpions. Or what kind of bug was that staff low cock kiss, anyway?'

"Poor Billy me!" he sorrowfully self-sympathized with a shudder.

His mom once explained that sometimes scratching an itch was "sacrificing short-term gratification for long-term benefit," so it was wrong to scratch. But she also told him his body was always giving him signals, and he should pay attention to what his body was telling him. So, it would be wrong *not* to scratch.

Having an itch was so complicated.

He decided not to scratch, which seemed more grown up. A few times in his life he made decisions he thought made him more grown up. Once, for his birthday, his dad gave him the choice of either a new Huckle Buckle rod or new shoes with tassels. He really wanted the rod but thought if he picked the shoes, it would show he was more grown up. But once he put on the shoes for the first time, he knew … but it was too late. His dad told him, "You were out of your gourd to pick shoes over a new rod. But I'm a firm believer in letting a little boy make mistakes. Otherwise, how will he ever learn?"

Figuring that just waiting for boils to disappear might not happen soon, Billy changed his mind and began to scratch his boils, though lightly, with the tips of his fingernails. Too hard would make them really hurt.

Miss Simple, forever heedful of her teaching trust, scolded, "It's not good manners to scratch one's behind in public, Billy." So, he stopped scratching, though he did finish with one hard last scratch and apologized, "Sorry, Miss Simple."

And bombshells and eye-openers, the itching stopped!

That evening, Billy's butt seemed a little different to him. It was still sore, but not as much. He shut the bathroom door, took down his pants and underpants, and looked in the mirror, turning his head so he could see his butt. The skin was definitely less red than before, the bumps seemed smaller, and most of all, the yellow circles weren't there! His boils, or carbuncles, were disappearing. Sure enough, his mom was right again.

He called her into the bathroom, then showed his butt. "Look, Mom! See how small my boils are!" he stated proudly.

She looked, and with a gasp exclaimed, "Wonder and wonder! Yes, they are. Thank the Lord!"

Then she looked at Billy's underwear, hooped on the bottom of his legs. "Goodness gracious Billy, you have yellow stuff on your underpants. Honestly, you've got to change your underwear more often, especially when you have boils!"

Happy his boils were smalling, Billy didn't really mind his mom getting on his case. Soon, he knew, he'd be able to sit down, lie on his back, run and play, and do all the things done by a normal boy without butt boils.

Three days later, Billy's butt was all clear. His mom told him, "We can thank the Lord, Billy. Faith will be rewarded sooner or later."

Billy was about to leave the house to join Andrew in the yard for a Huckle Buckle scrummage when he noticed Bozo lying on his side, whining high pitched, like he did when something was bothering him. Bozo was also scratching his hind quarters furiously with his paw.

"Poor Bozo!" Billy thought.

Laking It

As planned, I picked up Joannie late in the afternoon. To avoid the ignominy of encountering Mrs. Gold, I lingered in Jake's Spirit after honking. Joannie ambled down the concrete path, sluggish and unsmiling, the calves below her shorts seeming spindly and fragile. I passed off as wishful thinking a conception that if she was pregnant, her legs should be thicker, not thinner. Was her lethargic gait due to a similar sadness to my own, or to bodily changes owing to the pregnancy, or to her just being more careful now that she was carrying?

Or, my imagination?

Normally she didn't wear sunglasses, but now she had on a pair with a thick white frame, which made them stand out when hanging next to her tawny complexion. It was obvious her intention was to hide redness, rather than make a fashion statement. As she neared, I reached over to open the door latch on her side.

"Hi," we said at the same time, each pretending a cheerful mood. Was this duplication an indication of mutual awkwardness, or that we were kindred spirits?

"How are you feeling?" I asked, immediately realizing my words were immensely more serious, had more importance, than the flippant "How's it going?" I usually used. I wondered if she'd noticed.

Typically, when I asked how it was going, she answered with her patented silly alliteration to a vegetable—"Calm as a contented corn" or "Excited as an electrified eggplant." Now she answered, "I'm fine. And how are you?"

Perhaps she was only mirroring my reserve. Yet, the severe distancing formality of her reply signaled a change in her attitude toward me, a new hesitancy. My eyebrows flinched. Of course it was different; she was pregnant and didn't know if she could rely on me!

"I've been happier," I admitted.

"Well, on the bright side, my face still isn't broken out," she stated. I wasn't certain if she was being facetious or merely trying to lighten us up.

I responded defeatedly, "I feel like everything else is broken."

She nodded. It was unclear whether she was merely acknowledging my admission or informing me she felt the same way. I started up Jake's Spirit and pulled out. As we neared the end of the street I inhaled deeply, then asked, "How about going to the lake?"

"I thought that's where we decided to go," Joannie asserted.

"Oh, yeah. I forgot. I mean I forgot we *agreed* we were going to go there."

We didn't speak much during the remainder of the ten-minute ride to Cedar Glen Park, as I concentrated on the road, and Joannie stared out the front window. Normally, long silences between us weren't unusual, and were even reassuring. Like, we were cocooned together so firmly that we didn't *have* to talk. Now, the quiet was unsettling. Joannie toyed with her ear and asked if I had anything softer than Mass Massacre, which I'd already turned down to a low volume.

"Sorry," I apologized, and ejected the CD altogether.

Shortly, I maneuvered Jake's Spirit into a slot in one of the parking lots scattered through Cedar Glen Park. I took Joannie's hand, which seemed cool and slack, and guided her to the dirt trail leading to the lake. Our feet crunched small twigs and pebbles, as chickadees and stellar jays fluttered away at our approach. Soon the path narrowed and turned uneven, and I had to release her hand as we snaked up and down small hills until we reached the lake bank.

I again clutched her hand as we stood silently observing the shimmering lake, strewn with freshly painted white rowboats, numbers on their bows. Some boats sat perched and bobbing on the surface, fishing poles extending like antennae from the bare arms of motionless anglers in caps and sunglasses. Others glided over the green-brown water, propelled by the rhythmic pulling of oars. "They sure look relaxed," I commented.

"I guess more relaxed than we are," Joannie observed.

"Yeah," I said. "Don't you wish you could be on that lake, carefree?"

"The lake is calm, but the people on it may not be." It sounded sharp.

"You're right!" I admitted. I wondered if someone in a boat who happened to be gazing at the shoreline might at this moment be incorrectly assuming that a certain young couple standing along the lake bank was enjoying a blissful, carefree afternoon jaunt.

We slowly ambled along the footpath hedging the bank. I was grateful no one else was on the trail. The temperature was in the eighties, but the sun blazing down at an angle was shielded from our faces by the bills of baseball caps, and we were cooled by the breeze sifting through branches of the tall firs lining the banks.

"Well?" she sighed as we again stopped briefly to rest and gaze over the water. She removed her sunglasses and placed them in her shirt pocket, the act both removing a barrier and confirming that this was the start of our discussion, the reason we were meeting.

After a few seconds I admitted, "Well, I've been trying to analyze how I feel, what I want, what's best, but I haven't gotten anywhere. I can't think anymore. My brain has either gone limp or stiffened solid. I can't tell. In either case, it doesn't work. Joannie, I'm scared."

I looked at her eyes. They were clear, with no redness. She cast a knowing, far-away smile that I took as both sympathetic and sardonic, squeezed my hand, and said, "I'm scared too."

"I've been scared before, but this is worse than anything in my brief but scintillating life," I confessed with some sarcasm.

"Just from your gut, do you have any feelings about what we should do?" she asked.

"No. My guts don't work either. I go this way and that way, and nothing seems right. You can ask about my heart, and my liver, and my carotid artery, or any other part of my anatomy, and none of them will get you a different response."

She smiled. Then probed, "What have you been thinking about?"

I shrugged.

Then she asserted, "Well, Billy, I've been thinking, and you're right, it hasn't been very easy. We have a few options. First, I could get an abortion. It's only been a little over a month, and it wouldn't be very difficult. I don't know how you feel about that, you being a Christian Scientist, and all."

Her bringing up Christian Science was peculiar, I thought. She knew I was in retreat from my religion, though not completely detached. Did she think in time of crisis I'd backslide? Or, was it "revert," since "backslide" implied unhealthy, injurious, wrong. Did she hope to hasten a full schism by forcing me to use religion in a situation where it wouldn't work for me? I mulled it over and found myself presenting arguments I thought might be representative of the faith I'd been brought up with. "Well, we don't believe in surgery, and I guess abortions can mean surgery, elective surgery at that. But, on the other hand, we believe in freedom of choice. Salvation is individual, you know."

I didn't feel one bit genuine, uncomfortably impersonating a theological spokesman, a task I wasn't up to.

"I see," she said, seeing through my insincerity, my ineffectualness.

"You're lucky, Joannie. You don't have any religion to think about. A religious person ... well, the religion compels you to do or not to do certain things. Someone like you without a religion, you can do whatever you want."

"Not quite," she corrected. "Atheists also believe in individual choice, but that doesn't mean we don't have a moral code. Each of us has principles to guide our lives by, or at least pay attention to once in a while. We can't be human without ethics. Just because we don't believe in an imaginary deity, and just because we don't see fit to waste our time in subservient worship, doesn't mean we lack morality."

"Joannie, you sound like one of those characters in a dialogue from philosophy class."

"Sorry if it sounds familiar. I've had this type of conversation before. Sometimes I get carried away by my beliefs."

"It's okay. So do I. Sometimes." Sometimes I do know what I believe. At least I did.

We continued along the path.

We had this little routine just before we mattressed. I'd say to her, "You're my blanket." She'd respond, "You're my pillow." Neither of us was exactly sure what we were telling each other, but the exchange bonded our intimacy, a part of the confirmation, at least to ourselves, that we were a couple who warmed and bolstered each other.

We didn't say it now.

But as we walked, I told myself I was glad I was with Joannie. I was comforted to have an ally in working things out, someone I felt I belonged with.

Or was it *used* to feel I belonged with? I sensed a chill, no, the intrusion of a frigid sharp plane beginning to cleave us, causing me to shiver briefly. I didn't know where this pregnancy was taking me, and her. The comfortable nest I belonged in was unraveling, disintegrating. I shivered again. It was important to belong.

The Lion Hearts

Billy was either disappointed, or mad, or maybe both. His club, the Lion Hearts, which it was his idea to form, was almost breaking up. The members had told each other when they first started, "One for all and all for one," which Billy was fairly certain was a line he remembered from *The Wizard of Oz*.

But now, supposed best pals Gary and Bruce kept picking on him and leaving him out, and now they were trying to steal Todd to join them. They were all supposed to be great friends, sworn to a vow of being loyal, and, of course, keeping secrets. Besides, Todd had been his great pal ever since they met at nursery school five years ago, when both were just four.

The day the Lion Hearts were formed, the four boys had just finished an exciting game of Huckle Buckle, he and Todd scoring one more bangle than the Gary-Bruce team, in the last quintum no less. They were hanging near the giant old oak tree in his back yard, drinking pop out of cans, seeing—no, hearing—who could burp the loudest.

When Billy brought up starting a club only nine-year-olds could join, Todd burped and asked what the club's purpose was.

"What do you mean by purpose?" Billy asked before letting out a deep, gurgling burp.

"Well, the purpose of the Red Cross is to give blood to bleeding people. The purpose of the Boy Scouts is to help boys learn to tie knots. The purpose of the Elks is to protect antelopes in danger. We need to have a purpose too."

Billy, as if he was a general addressing the troops said, "Our purpose, our mission, the reason we formed our great club, is ... to have fun."

"How about if our purpose is finding lost treasure?" Todd asked hopefully.

"That's one way how we'll have fun. Treasure hunts, scavenger hunts, spying on girls. Lots of ways to have fun," answered Billy.

"Yeah," agreed the excited Bruce and Gary.

They talked about trading blood to seal their vows of loyalty to the club and each other. But knowing that might hurt or they'd get infections, they decided that, instead of sticking a pin to make real blood, they'd draw an "X" on the backs of their hands with a red marker. Then, rub their X's together.

Gary suggested, "It's better if the group is secret." They all agreed, though they didn't know why. But what was the point of thinking of why? It was obvious a secret club was better than a club that wasn't so secret.

Todd had the idea of a secret handshake. So, they made one up where two boys would each clap once, then the two boys would mesh their fingers together, holding it for five seconds, while they said the secret password three times.

Their secret password, made up by Billy, was "Crusaders." Originally it was, "Crusaders, Brothers, Patriots, and Partners." But none of them could remember all of that, even Billy himself, who had a good memory. Someone always left at least one word out. So, they made it just "Crusaders."

Todd had originally asked, "Isn't our password 'All for one and one for all?'"

But Bruce reminded him, "That's our motto. A motto is different from a password."

Then Gary said, "What kind of club could it be if it didn't have a name?"

I have a good one!" That was Bruce, who was really good at history. "The Lion Hearts. If our secret password is Crusader, then Lion Hearts is a great name."

Billy, with his odd but creative mind suggested, "How about we think of other names that are sort of close, but will throw people off the track about our group being secret. Like, instead of Lion Hearts we call the group – Tiger Spades, or Panther Clubs, or Leopard Diamonds."

"That's stupid," said Gary. The others agreed.

So, Lion Hearts became the secret group's name.

They said no to having uniforms. It would be obvious they all were in the same group. And how could they do a good job of spying if the enemy could tell who they were and clam up or bamboozle them?

Their secret hideout was the wood treehouse between two fat limbs of the large oak in Billy's yard. It only had room for four members to sit—one reason their club wasn't bigger.

Each week members paid dues to the treasury, the money kept by Gary, the Pursekeeper. Todd was made Keeper of the Key—in other groups called President. Billy had asked why, if it was his treehouse, and his idea to start the club, Todd was to be Keeper of the Key.

Gary told him, "The clubhouse doesn't have any keys. It doesn't even have any doors. It's just a name. How about, since it's your treehouse, you be the Lord of the Manor?"

That title at first sounded just fine to Billy. But he wasn't that happy when told his job was just to serve snacks and make sure his little brother Andrew was nowhere around when they met. But he felt his job wasn't as important as Pursekeeper, Keeper of the Key, or Scribe.

When he complained, Bruce told him, "Not everyone can have a high title. You need people to do the work. Besides, we'll change, and soon someone else will be Lord of the Manor."

It didn't quite seem fair to Billy. But he went along.

Todd always started the meeting by banging his hammer. Then Bruce, the Scribe, read the minutes of the before meeting. "Here are the minutes of the official meeting of the Lion Hearts last week. We talked about some stuff and then we ate some snacks. The meeting then was agermed."

Actually, his minutes told the truth about what went down at the meeting. "They talked, ate snacks, and then agermed." Nothing more need be said. Or, in this case, written.

Bruce's minutes were pretty much the same from week to week, making Billy suspicious of just how much effort Bruce was putting into his scribe job.

Once, Billy asked to see the page Bruce was supposedly reading minutes from and noticed it was blank. So, Billy asked, "How can you read the minutes from a blank page?"

Bruce answered, "It's written in invisible ink."

Puzzled, Billy asked, "Well if it's invisible, how can you see it?"

"Special contact lenses."

"I didn't know you wore contact lenses."

"That's because they're invisible. "

"Prove it!"

"If I take them out to prove it, you won't be able to see them. They're invisible."

That answer didn't seem quite right to Billy, but he couldn't exactly catch why.

But now, despite the purpose of the Lion Hearts, Billy wasn't having much fun and thought he deserved a promotion. After six weeks he still was lord of the manor. He'd proven himself by serving tasty snacks and doing a great job looking out for Andrew, certain his immature little pest brother would try to spy on them. He constantly looked down from the treehouse for any sign of a snooping Andrew. He never caught his brother, but he had to keep a wary eye out, so it was hard to relax and have fun.

Andrew asked once if he could join the club. Billy couldn't hurt his brother's feelings by saying the others didn't want him, so he told him he was still too little, and anyway there was only room for four in the treehouse.

"So, I'll stand up," Andrew volunteered. But Billy made it clear that Andrew would not be a true Lion Heart if he had to stand.

Andrew felt left out! Part of Billy also felt left out. The "all for one, one for all" spirit wasn't all there anymore.

In fact, earlier today the three others came to the meeting wearing camouflage shirts that matched each other. Gary said they bought them at a sale at the Army-Navy surplus store, using money they'd collected so far from club dues. "But we only had enough money in the treasury to buy three. We'll buy yours when we have more money. If the sale's still on."

Billy, who now was not sure of himself with his fellow club members, didn't ask why didn't they tell him they were going shopping. And why did they not buy one for Gary, or Bruce, or Todd? Just him. What if they said they didn't like him? At least as well as they liked each other.

But he did ask, "We said no uniforms, but aren't these shirts a uniform?"

"You don't know anything," Bruce accused. "If they were uniforms, we wouldn't have bought them. They're just three exact shirts. You're a doofus!"

"Yeah!" voiced Gary in agreement. So did Todd, but not so easily, Billy could tell. Todd volunteered to give Billy his shirt, but the other boys pointed out the shirt wasn't the right size.

Billy knew very well he wasn't a doofus, though he didn't exactly know what a doofus was. And if he didn't know what a doofus was, how could he even admit being one? Or knowing he wasn't one. It sounded like it meant something like "goofy"! No way was he a doofus or goofy! His friends kept coming up with new names to call people. He wondered how different insult names got people to use them.

What did he do to make them not like him? What makes a person like someone one day and not the next? He hadn't paid much attention before to how they treated him, but now he recalled other times he was left out.

A week ago, he overheard Gary and Bruce talk about the movie *Werewolf From Outer Space,* and they hushed up when seeing him, then wouldn't tell the plot, saying he could see it himself. So, he asked Todd if he'd like to go on Saturday. Todd apologized like he was bashful and told Billy he'd already seen it with Gary and Bruce.

And in the school cafeteria two days ago, he was last in line, and when he came out, they were sitting at a table with no room for him. He had to sit by himself. Well, not exactly by himself. He had to sit next to Thomas, who always had yellow gook coming out of his nose. Who wanted to eat with Thomas?

Was he bossy with them? He did tell them to clean up the crumbs in the treehouse after their meetings, because his mom said so. Although he wondered, why it was okay to throw food to squirrels and put seeds in the bird feeder, but not okay to leave food for them in the treehouse?

Did he do anything to embarrass them? No! Did he do something gross, like kiss a girl? No! Barf on purpose, on demand? … Some people thought that was a real talent. But he hadn't done it yet.

Maybe Bruce and Gary were embarrassed by always losing to Billy and Todd at Huckle Buckle.

Did he make them jealous in any way? Not that he knew! And certainly not on purpose! Was he mean to any of them? No! Did he keep them from doing something they wanted to do? No. Did he use nasty words to them, or insult them? No … No no no no no no!

Late in the afternoon, his mom noticed Billy moping at the kitchen table, nibbling a cookie. Suspecting why he was in this sorrowful glum mood, she asked, "How's your secret club doing these days?"

She knew! The club was supposed to be secret. But now his mom knew! Would he get in worse trouble with the other Lion Hearts because his mom knew, since how else would his mom know unless he blabbed it? Would they think he wasn't trustable?

"Fine," saying no more.

"Something's on your mind. You look like you haven't got a friend in the world."

"How did she know?" Billy wondered.

"Being a good friend is sometimes a hard job."

"I know," agreed Billy.

"But you always have your family. We are your best friends," she counseled.

He thought about saying, but didn't, "Mom, Andrew is not a friend. He's my pesky little brother. And Susie's not a friend either. She thinks she's so special! Just because she's eleven."

After a pause, he asked, "Mom, how do you know if someone's your true friend?"

"A friend is a pal you do stuff with, someone you can talk to, especially when you're not so happy or if you're in trouble. A friend is still your friend even if you've done something bad. A friend doesn't do things behind your back or try to steal your other friends. But you're lucky. You have some nice friends, Billy."

"And some who aren't so nice! No, I take that back, because if they aren't so nice to me, they can't be my friends."

"You're good at figuring things out, Billy. You know how to pick friends!"

"Yeah."

Later on, his dad came into his room for their evening chat. "Billy, Mom told me you and she had a little discussion about friends. When I was a kid, I had so many friends! Scores of really, really, dear, close friends. Scores! And most of them knew I had scores of really, really dear friends. The downside, though, was often my friends wouldn't call on me to play, thinking I'd be busy playing with someone else. So, most of the time I had to play by myself. Did a lot of reading. But don't let anyone tell you, son, that a book is as good as a friend. Just not so. By the way, how's your secret club going?"

"So, everyone knew!" Billy concluded to himself, but said, "Just fine, Dad."

"When I was about your age, I belonged to a secret club, the Desperadoes. Had secret passwords, handshakes. There were four of us. Our motto was, 'Die together.' Not that we expected to die soon. Just that we made a pact that if a hand grenade fell on the floor, we'd all jump to smother it, to save the others. Didn't quite make sense to me, all four. Just one was necessary. But I agreed in the name of brotherhood. Anyway, after a while, some other boys in the club seemed to leave me out of things and tried to make my best friend in the group their best friend. Well, I'm sure you're tired and not interested in one of your dad's boring stories. So, pleasant dreams, Billy."

Then, as his dad marched away and was about to leave the room, Billy called out, "Dad?"

"Yes, son?"

"Um. You have some mashed potato on the corner of your lips … No, the other side."

The next evening Billy was helping his mom wash and peel potatoes, when she asked brightly, "How was your day?"

"Great, Mom. We had the best club meeting. We really got some stuff decided."

"Did you boys remember to clean out the crumbs from the clubhouse?"

"We broke up that club at lunch. Gary and Bruce joined a soccer team and can't meet anymore. We'll still scrummage Huckle Buckle and other stuff together. But I formed a special new club. It's called the Desp… I'm sorry I can't tell you what it's called, because it's a secret."

"Oh! I'm glad you have a club to belong to. Clubs can be fun!"

"Yeah. And mom, I let Andrew in."

"You did?"

"Yeah!"

"Who else is in the club? Todd? Any of your other friends I know?"

"So far only me and Andrew. I'm the Captain-Major, and the Chancellor of the Guard. Plus, I'm in charge of the Intelligent Spying Unit. He's the Writist, and Man-of-Arms. But the neat thing is that me and him will be the only ones to decide who else to let in our club. If we want, we don't have to let anybody else in. Andrew says he's willing to let Todd in. But I have to think about it. I'm not too happy with Todd just now."

"I see."

"Mom, can you increase our allowance? We need money for our treasury."

"I'll think about it."

"Mom, how did you find out about our club? It was supposed to be secret."

"Andrew told me. How else would I know? It seems you were looking for him under the tree. But before your club meetings, he climbed to one of the high branches, where he was hidden by leaves and tree limbs, and listened in. The little guy overheard everything you guys said."

"Hmm," thought Billy. "Maybe I should be the Writist and let Andrew be in charge of the Intelligent Spying Unit."

The Meaning of Tree

We meandered the path circling the lake, passing by a gauntlet of impenetrable boxwood bushes on either side. I hoped Joannie wouldn't bring up religion again. I stopped practicing years ago, not visiting church, or praying, or even singing hymns to myself.

Occasionally my mom and dad went to Sunday services, but when they asked us kids if we'd like to come along, only Andrew volunteered. The family still didn't do doctors. Last year both Andrew and I had bad cases of the flu, coming down with it within an hour of each other. It lasted five days. He prayed. I didn't. We recovered at almost the exact same time. When I brought this up to Andrew, he informed me that our recoveries coincided because he prayed for me too.

The older and more sophisticated I'd become, the less observant, though by no means was I ready to throw in with Joannie's atheism. I still believed there was a Lord, and a Lord's son, and I called on them every once in a while. Sometimes, for no good reason other than something stirring inside me, I'd look up at heaven. I didn't expect to see anything, but maybe the Lord would catch me trying to communicate, worth some heavenly entrance points should the situation arise. I wasn't ready to totally reject Christian Science but also not ready to accept any other approach.

Yet this was not the time to work through personal religious philosophy, and I wished Joannie hadn't raised the subject.

At a clearing, I picked up a roundish stone half the size of my fist and hurled it as high as I could toward the lake. We followed its trajectory until it broke the water, a plop and circular rippling marking entry. As the disturbance faded, Joannie spoke softly, "We don't have to get an abortion. I could give it up for adoption. Or we could keep it."

She peeked at me, checking out my reaction. When I held silent and expressionless, she continued. "If we kept the baby, you don't have to marry me. I wouldn't want to get married just because I'm having a baby. Marriage is a commitment, and I wouldn't want you to make any commitment to me, or the baby, you didn't really feel. I could raise it at home. Maybe my mom would help. And you could visit whenever you wanted."

I nodded, but said nothing, keeping my options, withholding commitment.

Finally, we reached our destination, a clearing at a rise sloping sharply down to the water. Reaching down the slope, extending perhaps a hundred feet to the bank, amidst dried pale amber grass, lay the thick, gnarled trunk of a long-dead tree, cut down at its charred splintered base by the attack of lightning. It had long ago lost its foliage, and its stiffened limbs had silvered. Yet, lying in rigid tautness on the ground, it still retained a majestic power.

I sometimes visited the site of this fallen tree alone, my thinking tree, to meditate. Once, a few years ago, I thought about bringing a date there, but reconsidered. It was my private, almost sacred place, an arena to work out my troubles, not a site to impress girls with a notion of my profundity.

I stepped over the roots to the stump, and then over to the trunk, where I hunkered down facing the water, as Joannie sat holding her knees in the wild grass beside me. The gentle whooshing breeze rustling through branches played over a peaceful, restful silence. For minutes we absorbed the quiet, our eyes drifting over the lake.

Once, I began to say something, but held back. Joannie asked, "What?"

"Nothing," I said, running my fingers over some old bark.

A few minutes later I finally spoke. "I sometimes come here when I need to think something over, when I have a problem I can't solve. Each time, I seem to work out whatever's bothering me. I don't know why exactly, whether it's the quiet, or being lost in nature, or just getting away, but once I've left here, every time I've been with this tree, matters are about to be settled, and I've solved my problem. It's a magic unraveler. My own enchanted magical tree."

"I think I know why," Joannie replied, holding a sharp sliver of dried grass, her expansive eyes expressing wonderment at her discovery.

"You do?" I asked.

"And it has nothing to do with magic!"

"It doesn't?"

"It has to do with a hidden message this tree is sending you."

I stared at her. "What?"

"This tree is so old. Look how tall it grew, dwarfing all the trees around it. It must've survived hundreds of years to stretch this tall and grow so strong, surviving windstorms, attacks by insects, drought, diseases, and competition from other trees and plants. Think about this tree, what its strength was based on."

I looked and saw the tree was even more magnificent than I'd thought. I was about to say something about the Lord creating it when Joannie went on.

"Aside from its size, what's most noticeable about this tree? Its roots! Still extending from the ground. Look how thick they are, the space they occupy, even above the ground. I bet they extend a hundred feet down, anchored to the soil in all directions. When you, Billy Harrington, come to this tree, it sends you a hidden message. You're reminded, though you don't consciously know it, to commune with your own strong roots, the roots that define you. And so, when you have a problem, you refer to your roots to decide what to do. You remind yourself who Billy Harrington is! Then, whatever you need to do to solve your problem just naturally follows."

At first, her explanation seemed a sage psychological conception, a most powerful insight reverberating with accuracy, filling me with admiration. Yet, in what must have been a deep-seated emotional reaction, for it certainly had no logic, I immediately flip-flopped and rejected her reasoning as inventive poetic thought, but incorrect. I could not allow myself to accept her perception as truth.

Was it because by acknowledging her premise, by admitting the legitimacy of her thoughts, I'd be ceding her the leadership role, a role that should be mine?

Was it anger at myself for being so ineffectually muddled while she performed so intelligently? Or irritation for allowing her to get pregnant, for not being more wary?

My magical tree—the one to which I ascribed mystical powers, even quasi-religious significance to—reduced to a poetic analogy with roots!

Or was I upset because her spirituality was stronger than mine?

"You reading Thoreau in English class?" I asked smartly.

Joannie smiled, no doubt believing my query was jokish repartee.

Then foolishly—"How could a girl as smart as you be so dumb as to get herself pregnant? How could a guy as smart as me let it happen?"

"Let's go, Billy," she declared, pushing herself up, braced by a sudden anger. I stared out at the water for a few seconds, then boosted myself down from the fallen trunk.

"Billy, I want to tell you one thing. This baby is growing in my belly. And I will be the one to decide what to do. I will take your wishes into consideration, whatever they might be. But in the end, I will decide how this situation will be resolved."

She snatched the sunglasses from her pocket, put them on. As we silently marched to the car, Joannie resolutely taking the lead, I was snarled in conflict, unsure of how or even whether to respond to her declaration. I was angry she'd taken charge, leaving me a bystander, with her proclamation that *she'd* be the one to decide what to do. Wasn't that the man's job, to take command in a crisis? What right did she have to be the decision-maker? Joannie would never have thought to take control before the class in women's studies. I was to be the father! I was the man!

But what man? I was ashamed because I'd been unable to take charge. So far, I'd been little more than a blocked, paralyzed figure, no man.

Yet despite my annoyance with myself and Joannie's assumption of supremacy, I was relieved because the burden of decision was not finally mine. Even without my participation, a decision would be made.

And I wouldn't have to explain to my parents that I agreed Joannie should have an abortion—if that's what she decided; I could deflect all the blame to her. We wouldn't have to get married, and I'd be able to go to college. Nor would I need to live poor, with no free time.

And if she did want to get married, how could I live with a woman who took it upon herself to make the major decisions? Could I spend the rest of my life with a woman who turned unilateral in times of stress? I'd just seen a surprising Joannie I didn't know about.

As we neared the car, I attempted to diminish the overwhelming tension by remarking, "When I was a kid, I played water Huckle Buckle at the lake. I didn't like it that much, though. The boundaries were too unclear, and being in the water, I really couldn't take advantage of my agility."

Joannie, still furious, didn't respond. I wasn't surprised. She had been definite, defiant, firmly addressing a problem. And now an insipid me babbled about lack of agility in a game of Huckle Buckle.

We rode wordlessly back to her house, where I dropped her off.

I knew for certain I'd never be the same young Billy Harrington. I'd lost too much innocence and realized I could panic. But I was desperate to maintain as much connection as I could to a life that had kept me contented. To hold onto whatever valuable was left of the boy so I could become a man.

The $5 Lunchbox

The alarm clock startled Billy awake, and he quickly shut it quiet. Normally he didn't set the alarm for a Saturday morning. But the Harrington family decided a few weeks ago to hold a yard sale today. Actually, his mom had done the deciding, telling his dad in no uncertain terms, "Either we buy a bigger house, or we get rid of the junk cluttering up the garage, attic, rooms, and closets in this house."

His dad finally agreed, suggesting it would be a good educational experience for the children. "It will approximate having a little business of our own. It'll help teach them the value of a dollar."

Each of them was assigned a task or two. His thrifty mom, who knew the most about shopping, would price the items. She and Susie, Billy's almost teenage sister, would set out attractive displays. Billy and Andrew, his eight-year-old little brother, were to help their dad carry stuff from the house and garage to the front yard. Billy also volunteered to watch for pickpockets and shoplifters. His dad also had the job of placing signs on posts and trees in the neighborhood.

But first, they each had to decide what they wanted to sell, wanted to keep, and wanted to keep but didn't have room for.

Like everyone in the family, except his mom, Billy wanted to keep lots of things he hadn't used or even seen for years. Oh, he was willing to part with an arithmetic book from third grade, thinking the book was probably obsolete by now, what with all the probable new developments in arithmetic in today's fast-paced world. And he didn't object at all to selling some old clothes.

But he especially wanted to keep the Lone Ranger lunchbox he'd taken to school in the first and second grades, before he grew up and began to take lunchboxes with singing groups' pictures. He fondly remembered those olden days of yesteryear. Memories! Those fond memories of a time long ago. Four years ago, almost half a lifetime. Life was so carefree. Girls didn't bug him. Teachers gave homework just twice a week. Those olden days, those cowboy days, when he carried a six-shooter after school and Halloween, and wore a mask, just like the real Lone Ranger.

He was about to hide the lunchbox in the back of his closet, when his mom noticed and told him if she could sell her tutu, from when she took ballet lessons to regain her shape after giving birth to him, if Susie could sell her old Barbie dolls, if Andrew could sell his worn-out Huckle Buckle rod, then he could very well part with an old lunchbox.

Aside from his mom, the family members wanted to put high prices on their items. Either they thought the items were much more valuable than they were, or they didn't want them sold. He heard his dad, for example, tell his mom that $25 was a reasonable price for a certain old lamp. "It's $100 new, and quite a steal for the astute buyer."

"Dear, it's fifteen years old, the lampshade is ripped, the wiring needs fixing, and the switch is broken. Fifty cents is just fine!" his perceptive mom decided as she applied the price tag.

His mom's attitude was, "Get rid of everything," though she called it, "Pricing items to sell." To her, fifty cents was the correct price for most items. There had to be a good reason to have a different price.

Billy, however, was successful in keeping the price of his Lone Ranger lunchbox at a higher amount. He did this, without his mom noticing, by adding a zero to the fifty-cent price his mom had placed on the tag, so it looked like five dollars.

That morning, Billy wasn't sure if he was in for a day of work or a day of fun. Yard sales weren't exactly what most ten-year-old boys did with their time, but Billy guessed it was okay as long as it didn't happen more often than once every ten years.

Everyone ate a quick breakfast of cold cereal with jalapeños and began their chores. Billy, together with his dad and Andrew, began carting items to the driveway and front lawn. It took well over an hour.

"I can't believe we have all these antiques!" his dad exclaimed.

"I can't believe we have all this junk!" exclaimed his mom.

Not everyone did their share of the hauling. Billy was quite miffed at his younger brother for carrying only one small item at a time, walking soooo slowly. Andrew said he was working as fast as he could. Billy threatened, "If you don't work any faster, I'll take your share of the profits."

"You can't do that!" shouted his brother, "All the money's going into the college fund."

Adding to the college fund was how the family had decided to use the money they'd earn, although each of the children had argued in favor of at least giving them five dollars for their work effort. "There are child labor laws in this country," Susie had pointed out.

"Yeah! And I might not even go to college," Andrew had added.

"College is a long way off," Billy had submitted.

His mom chastised, "Now, now, children. A college education is the most valuable gift we can give you. Which would you rather have, an education you can use your whole life, or five dollars that you'll soon spend and have nothing to show for?"

"The five dollars," the children chimed in unison.

"Humph," muttered his mom.

"Amen," his dad, the college professor, said, it being unclear to everyone else whether he agreed with his wife or the kids.

Finally, the merchandise was all set out. Toys and games, some with parts and pieces missing. Stuffed animals—bears, lions, rabbits, cats and dogs, and snakes—some tattered or stained, some looking brand new. Lots of old furniture, books, lamps, framed pictures, old appliances, most of which didn't work—his mom submitting, "I hope some of today's shoppers are handy."

Bozo's old feeding bowl, which he didn't object to us selling, maybe because he was now lying listlessly indoors with a case of what must have been the dog flu. The bird cage of their escaped parakeet. Old cat litter they'd bought for their cat who ran off years ago with the tom two blocks down and never returned. Billy reflected that the Harringtons hadn't always been lucky with pets.

Also laid out was Billy's lunchbox, the one he so badly didn't want to sell. He loved the colorful drawing of the brave masked man sitting atop the spirited white stallion with raised legs, powerfully regal. He still wondered why the horse was named Silver, even though he wasn't the color silver at all. Well, maybe names like Whitey and Snowy were already taken.

In the background were cactus, craggy mountains, and blind canyons, where stampeding cattle or bad guys could be cornered. Billy imagined camping at night in the Old West, hearing tales of outlaws, marshals, gunslingers, and saloons, told by the mysterious masked man with the silver bullets. He fantasized eating his meal off tin plates, rustled up by a crackling campfire under a star-filled sky, and soothed by a harmonica. Since neither the Lone Ranger nor Tonto had much of a musical ear, the harmonica was played by a sidekick named Fuzzy, picked up along the trail.

"Mom, do we really have to sell my old lunchbox?"

"I'm afraid so, Billy. If we all kept what we wanted, we wouldn't have enough for a yard sale."

Buyers began to arrive just as his dad got on his bicycle to check that the signs he'd posted on nearby streets the previous night hadn't come down. Shoppers parked their cars and SUVs at the curb, nodded good morning, and examined and picked.

"How much is this teddy bear?" inquired an older man with a mop of gray hair.

"Fifty cents," answered his mom.

"Sold," said the man, handing over two quarters. "It's for my grandchild," he felt the need to explain. The man looked lonely, and Billy just had a feeling that the friendly soft bear wasn't quite for a grandchild.

"How much is this pipe?" asked a middle-aged man in a turtleneck sweater.

"Fifty cents," responded his mom automatically.

"Quite reasonable, actually," he commented, dispensing two quarters.

"How much for this lunchbox?" asked a woman with a young boy Billy recognized was in the first grade at his school.

His mom was about to answer when Billy interrupted …

"Let me help you. I know lunchboxes." His mom stepped away, and Billy spoke in a hushed voice, as if telling a secret, "That rusty old falling-apart lunchbox with the broken latch is five dollars."

"How about four-fifty?" offered the woman.

"I'm afraid not. Besides, it hasn't got a picture of Tonto. Why don't we look at this blue lunchbox, with Jack—from Jack and the Beanstalk. It's only fifty cents, and a real bargain."

"Why, thank you," she acknowledged. And after examining the blue lunchbox briefly she handed it to her happy little boy, and fifty cents to Billy.

After returning, his dad looked around for his prized briar pipe he'd laid on one of the tables but couldn't find it. "Has anyone seen my pipe? I put it down somewhere."

"Uh-oh!" his mom murmured to herself, then told him, "Oh, dear, I'm afraid I must have sold it. I'm sorry. Here Gordon, the money I sold your pipe for. It's yours. You don't have to put it into the college fund. You can use it toward a new pipe."

"Molly, what kind of pipe will fifty cents get me? That pipe cost fifty dollars!"

"I'm sorry, dear. Maybe next week we can get lucky at someone else's yard sale and find a pipe someone's selling for fifty cents." Then she added, "You never smoke it, though. All you do is keep it in your mouth."

"Good Christian Scientists don't smoke," he reminded before a huffy leave-taking.

Lots of people trooped through. Some looked only for certain types of items. An elderly, white-bearded man limping with a cane asked hopefully if they had any photographs of President Millard Fillmore.

A middle-aged woman with frizzy hair who Billy felt certain also had a frizzy brain and was quite bonkers, asked if they had any portraits of her Aunt Mildred.

A heavily tattooed motorcyclist asked if they had a volume of poems written by his famous great-uncle, Milton Milo Miles. Billy told him he'd never heard of that great-uncle, which is when tattoo-man mentioned he wasn't surprised because his great-uncle was famous for no one having heard of him, considering all the poems he wrote.

That didn't quite make sense to Billy, but he merely apologized for not having such a volume of poems.

A man examined a toaster through thick spectacles and, maybe angling for a lower price, commented to his mom that it was really old. His mom then informed the gentleman, "That old toaster is really exceptional for toasting *stale* bread." The man had no sense of humor and didn't laugh at that old chestnut joke.

Although Billy was not 100 percent sure his mom was joking.

Shoppers busily examined the jumble of merchandise, looking for bargains. Some sniffed around briefly. Others spent lots of time sniffing.

Billy kept a close watch on his lunchbox the whole day and forgot watching for shoplifters and pickpockets.

Most shoppers didn't seem interested at all in his lunchbox, but Billy had to be alert, for occasionally someone picked it up. When a man smiled after examining it, Billy stepped over and said, "The thermos inside is stuck shut, and besides, most people prefer the picture of the Lone Ranger to be when he was young. He looks kind of old and pudgy here. Why not take a look at these other lunch boxes? They're cheaper anyway, and a much better value."

Sure enough, the man chose a box with a python cartoon character swallowing a bank robber.

Not that Billy spent all his time watching the lunchbox. Sometimes he sold something else. Toward day's end, a woman in a beret seemed interested in a lot of items. Billy, having listened in on what his mom was doing, said, "It's late. Tell you what! Everything that says fifty cents, I'll give you for a quarter."

"Great!" said the woman, and within a few minutes she picked out twelve items, including three stuffed animals, four T-shirts, a pair of pants, a strainer, a sweatshirt, and a partly cracked flowerpot.

"Twelve items at a quarter each. That'll be three dollars," said Billy, proud of himself for multiplying in his head so quickly.

"Will you take two bucks for the pile?" she asked.

Billy rechecked his mental arithmetic. It still came to three dollars. Something about the woman being unfair struck him.

"I just love to haggle at yard sales. And this is such a wonderful yard sale," the woman announced cheerily.

Billy frowned, unsure of how to handle the situation. Somehow, he thought, the woman might be trying to take advantage of him, sweet-talking him in the hopes of getting some terrific end-of-the-day bargains. But then again, haggling was a part of the yard sale process. "Two fifty," he countered.

"Sold!" she announced, and gave Billy ten quarters.

But when Billy glanced over, his Lone Ranger lunchbox was no longer there! With wide-open eyes, he marched to where it was. He examined the ground nearby, and it wasn't there either. He peered carefully to see if anyone was carrying it, but no one was. Neither did any of the shoppers look like they were hiding the lunchbox under their clothing. He strode to his mom and asked, "Did anyone buy the Lone Ranger lunchbox?"

"Why, I believe so!" she stated. "A few minutes ago."

A disappointed Billy trudged with sagged shoulders to the lunchboxes area, managing to stifle a tear from dripping down his face. Ten-year-old boys do not cry. But he sure felt like crying!

With about an hour left until dusk, and few shoppers about, his mom decided to close the yard sale. She and Susie packed old clothing in old suitcases, and Billy, Andrew, and his dad carted other stuff to the garage. Billy moved much slower than in the morning. Not only was he tired from working on his feet all day, but he was so, so sad over the loss of his lunchbox. The world didn't seem quite as rich anymore!

After dinner, his dad licked mashed potatoes off his finger, picked up his mug of hot chocolate, and announced, "It was all worthwhile. We made one hundred and fifty-nine dollars for the college fund. And fifty cents," he said, eyeing his mom in particular. "Did we all have a good time?"

"I did," said a drowsy Susie in a sorrowful tone belying her words. "Me too," reported Andrew, not too happily.

"It was a good experience for us all. On Monday, I'll call the Salvation Army to cart away the stuff we couldn't sell. I'm sure someone can use it," his mom stated.

A melancholy Billy didn't say anything, just trudged to his room. When he looked at his bed he noticed a square-shaped object. It looked familiar, but since the light wasn't on, he wasn't sure. He switched on the light and went to the bed. Sure enough, there it was—his Lone Ranger lunchbox!!!

He ran out of his bedroom, down the stairs, and entered the kitchen with a broad smile, clutching the lunchbox. "This was on my bed! I thought you said the lunchbox was sold," he told his mom.

"It was. *I* bought it. Look inside."

He unhooked the rusty latch and opened the lid. Inside the box was a crisp new five-dollar bill! "Mom, you're the best!" he contended with a contented grin, hugging his precious lunchbox.

Susie's eyebrows raised. Then she hustled to her room and soon returned with an old Barbie doll her mom had told her someone had bought. A five-dollar bill was tucked inside the doll's waistband. "It was on my bed!" she exclaimed.

Andrew pushed away his chair and hustled upstairs, returning in less than a minute with his old Huckle Buckle rod that his mom had told him someone had bought. A five-dollar bill was taped to the rod. "Look what was on my bed!"

"My precious children!" his mom exclaimed proudly. They all hugged. Billy even found himself hugging Susie and Andrew. He couldn't remember ever doing that. It wasn't as bad as he expected.

Billy watched as his bemused dad rose and swaggered purposefully into the master bedroom.

His dad returned shortly with a frown, complaining, "Hey, there's no pipe on my bed!"

The Dog Decides

When I returned home, fourteen-year-old Bozo was half-snoozing at the foot of my bed, something he often did in the early evening. I bent to rub his gray coat and greeted, "Hi, boy! I'm glad you're a boy. I'm not doing too well with girls right now."

Bozo remained in place, raised an eye, and sighed. Then he closed his eye and nodded, as if he knew what I was referring to.

When I was little, I thought dogs and cats were the same animals, except dogs were the boys and cats were the girls. Remnants of that early notion stayed with me, so now, if I heard someone call a particular dog "she," or a cat called "he," I had to remind myself nothing wrong had been spoken.

Bozo was my dog, more than my brother Andrew's. Though Andrew probably played with Bozo more often, and everyone in the family contributed at times to Bozo's care, I was ultimately responsible for feeding and walking him. If no one else had done it that day, the duty was mine.

I'd been pretty responsible, caring for Bozo all these years. Bozo seemed happy, though it was hard to tell for sure since dogs didn't laugh or even smile and can't say, "I'm having a great time," even if they were. Unlike my dad, I didn't think a dog wagging its tail was a definite sign of enjoying itself. There were lots of reasons a dog would wag its tail. He could be bored, and tail-wagging passed the time. A tail wag could be equivalation to human doodling, or something to do while mulling another thought. Or air currents that wags made might slake an itch. Or just be fanning a warmish butt! Who knew why dogs wagged a tail at any given moment? Why did some dogs bay at the moon? Paw holes in the garden? Some things just can't be explained!

I wondered if, at this very moment, Joannie was reaching the same conclusion about boys.

Well, if I could care for a dog, I could care for a baby. A lot of the care seemed to correspond. You brought a dog to the vet and a sick child to the Christian Science practitioner. You played with both. Once in a while you checked out the insides of their ears and bathed them. If they made certain sounds, you had to figure out the reason.

I conceded dogs were a little easier to care for than babies. You had to feed them only once or twice a day, and you didn't have to cook. Instead of heating up bottles, you just put fresh water in the bowl in the morning. You didn't have to worry about a dog taking an afternoon nap. It wasn't expected that you teach a dog to learn to read—they probably weren't smart enough to learn anyway, though in certain ways they were smarter than humans. Like, it took my mom and dad only a week to toilet-train Bozo, but three years to toilet-train me.

I plopped onto my bed, then mindlessly reached down to stroke Bozo's back, as I tried to take stock of what happened earlier with Joannie. I concluded I was probably worse off than I'd been before meeting with her. I hadn't told her what I wanted—how could I? I myself didn't know—and she hadn't voiced what she wanted either, except to mention that she'd do as she pleased, regardless of what I had to say. She might have told me more if I hadn't had such a smart lip. Why *did* I react that way?

She was angry at me!

Could I blame her? A girl wants a take-charge man in times of crisis. I'd always thought I'd be the commander on the battlefield. Born with leadership qualities. Able to think clearly under pressure. Courage. Innovative strategy and tactics. Outthink the enemy. Now I wasn't sure if I'd just rather take orders and do whatever I was told. Who was the enemy, anyway? The baby? Joannie? The me who seemed to be hiding?

My respect for Joannie had grown since she told me off. I'd heard of captives who identified with their captors, victims who'd come to revere their tyrannical oppressors. It had never made sense to me. Why would victims identify with their oppressors? Now I understood. If you thought of yourself as helpless, and the other party was a commander, you might want to be like them.

Not that I felt captive or a victim. But my status was lower than hers, at least until the time I straightened out my own mind and could then go after what I wanted, whatever that might be. Maybe I shouldn't even communicate with Joannie until then.

Pet dogs had it easy. Very few major decisions were left to them. Maybe they'd welcome the opportunity, though. I leaned down over my bedside and said, "Okay, Bozo, it's up to you. Yip once and it's an abortion. Yip twice and it's an adoption. Yip three times and I'm a daddy. Got it?"

Bozo, perhaps deeply engrossed in dog fantasy about a bitch down the block, didn't even twitch his head to shoo away the fly on his snout, no less wake from his hedonistic slumber to yip.

"No yips and this whole affair never went down!" I announced, faking a toothy smile.

"Oh, what's the use!"

One thing in my favor was that it seemed Joannie hadn't come to any resolution yet either. She alluded to the same alternatives I listed but didn't yet seem to prefer any one over the others.

I'd have to make major decisions, finalize my priorities, very soon! First, me alone. Then I'd be prepared to discuss them with Joannie, and we'd make a consensus decision—if she was still talking to me and hadn't made up her own incontrovertible mind.

Sometimes you have the ordeal of deciding for yourself.

Sometimes you have the comfort of having other people you trust decide for you.

Sometimes you have the contentment of having other people you care for and trust decide *with* you.

Sometimes the world, which you have limited control of, and which may hardly recognize the genuine you, decides for you, and you have little say.

Why Can't Kids Vote?

Billy wanted to vote. Election Day was a week away, and he aspired to visit the polling place and cast his ballot, just like his mom and dad. It would make him feel like a true American citizen, although he'd heard it was more typical of Americans not to vote.

"Kids are people too, and what's voted on also affects us. So, why can't kids vote?" That's what he told his mom and dad.

"Billy, that's a very good question. But there are some very good reasons why not. Gordon, tell him," his mom directed his dad, whose fingers were scooping mashed potato crumbs from his plate and feeding them to Bozo, the beloved family schnauzer, who had made the decision to scamper over to get his treat.

"Wanting to vote is very admirable, Billy. But I'm not so sure kids understand the issues," his dad explained.

"How is that different from grown-ups? Just tell me. Besides, I do too know the issues. I'm in favor of the environment being cleaned up—getting rid of pollution, and smog, and plastic bottles—and I'm for recycling. And teachers should be paid a lot of money. And the government should do what's good for the majority of the people, not just rich people.

"Doesn't Billy know we're Republicans, Molly?" his dad asked his mom.

"I thought so, Gordon."

"Billy, you can't just clean the environment, enhance education, and feed homeless people willy-nilly. It's more complicated than that."

Billy wondered who this Willie person was, but before he could ask, his dad told him, "Besides, I'm not so sure you know about *all* the issues. Like what should we do about what's going on in Europe?"

Billy replied immediately, "I think we should sit down and carefully weigh all the choices, then make an informed decision."

"Just what I would do," agreed his surprised dad, who didn't know his son was capable of such an incisive, unarguable remark. But he added, "I don't think it's imperative to do it sitting down. Some people think better standing, you know."

Billy argued, "Besides, most *adults* don't know much about the issues, and they're allowed to vote. Like all those people who march and shout slogans about pro-choice or pro-life. Do you think they can possibly know about *all* the issues? Do you think they study all the issues? Do you think they even much care about any other issue?"

"He's got a point there, dear," recognized his mom.

"And another thing, Billy," his dad broke in, "If kids your age had the vote, they'd be swayed by catchy slogans and the promises of crooked politicians who'd say anything to get elected."

"How is that any different from grown-ups?" Billy inquired.

"Hmmm," his mom mumbled.

"Dad, it wasn't me who bought all those things advertised on TV. There's the knife set, the CDs playing the greatest hits of Bach, Beethoven and Elvis Presley, not to mention the memory course."

"I don't remember buying the memory course," his dad muttered.

"And you believed what the governor said before he got elected!"

"He's got another point there, Gordon," conceded his mom.

"And besides," Billy added, "they say the average adult has the intelligence of a twelve-year old. Well, I'm eleven, but I'm at least two years ahead of my grade level. Therefore, if I'm not mistaken, I'm brighter than more than half the grown-up population. Why don't they let me vote, even if they have to take away the vote from some of the stupid people?"

"You'd have quite a tussle trying to take the vote away from stupid people. Most of them are Democrats! Some of them carry knives and guns," he pointed out. "Another thing, you don't own property, and you don't pay taxes."

"I do too own property. My toys and clothes are my property. Not yours! But even if you're talking about land, the grown-ups living in the projects don't own any, and they can vote. And the rich people who own the big houses on the hill don't pay *any* taxes, and they can vote."

"Again, he's got a point there, dear," acknowledged his mom.

His dad tried again. "Well Billy, if kids could vote, they'd be swayed by their parents and would vote like their parents told them."

"Dad, you always say kids should listen to their parents, so what's wrong with that?"

"I just mean they would vote without understanding the issues," he explained, puffing from his new unlit pipe.

"I might not listen to you if you told me how to vote. Like, we disagree on whether or not kids should vote. So, if we voted on that issue, I'd vote different from you. Besides, look how grown-ups have already messed things up! Why don't we give kids a chance? Yes!" Billy said with conviction.

His dad defended the adult generation, asserting, "Why, just because a few things have gone haywire doesn't necessarily mean everything is wrong. Things could be a lot worse! And I don't feel your mother and I should be held responsible for some of the bonehead things the president and Congress have been responsible for over the past few years. This is supposed to be a democracy, and ..."

His mom interrupted, "Billy, if you're so interested in voting, why don't you run for office, say in your class government? Isn't there a class election coming up right after Election Day?"

"We're voting for class president, but I'm not running. Missy's running, and no one else has a chance. All the other girls will vote for her because she's a girl. And even the boys will vote for her, because she's nice to them, and really pretty. We're eleven years old, mom. And besides, I just said I wanted to vote, not get elected to something."

"You'll get your chance to vote in the school election, son," she assured.

"It's not the same thing, Mom," Billy complained crabbily.

That night, as Billy lay in his bed, waiting to fall asleep, he recalled the words of his dad. "Besides, this is supposed to be a democracy, and ..." his dad had said earlier, before being cut off by his mom.

In a democracy, more than one person ran for office. But it looked like no one would run against Missy. This was not right. She should have opposition. Look what happened in countries where only one person was allowed to run for an office.

Of course, it was unlikely Missy would be able to establish a totalitarian government as president of her class, especially since class presidents were changed every few months and stern Miss Grunch was around to make sure Missy wouldn't have more power than she herself, a teacher, did. But a principle was involved.

Billy decided to declare the very next day as a candidate for class president.

In the morning, just after the Pledge of Allegiance, Billy marched to Miss Grunch and informed her he wanted to run for class president too.

"That's fine, Billy. But you can't run just like that. Someone has got to nominate you. Then someone has to second the nomination," she instructed. Billy noted that Miss Grunch seemed to take her Roberta's Rules of Order very seriously. *(Roberta's Rules is the feminist manual, just to make sure that women's rights weren't denied or abused by male-decided parliamentary procedures.)*

He thought, "No wonder the world's a mess. If I have to go through all this rigmarole just to run for class president …"

But he thought better of it, determining he'd not let such silly obstacles hold him back. So, to Miss Grunch he allowed, "Fine," before returning to his seat. He had to find only two people in his class, one to nominate him, and one to second the nomination. He approached Tina, the quiet girl who sat in front of him, and asked her to nominate him.

"Sorry, I'm voting for Missy," she said in just above a whisper.

He approached Sarah, the sprightly red-haired girl who sat behind him.

"Sorry, I'm voting for Missy," she told him, tapping her foot to some song in her mind.

He approached Gillian, the blonde girl who giggled a lot, to his right, and Nancy, the girl with new braces on her teeth, to his left. Both said the same thing, "Sorry, I'm voting for Missy," Gillian with a giggle, Nancy in a mumble.

"Just my luck to be surrounded by girls!" he reflected.

So, during recess he asked some of the boys. Robbie, not one of the brighter students, said, "I'll think on it. Missy sometimes helps me with my homework." Billy knew he was a lost cause.

He solicited shy Phil, who said, "It's kinda like this, well, when it comes down to it, well, the truth is, well, Billy, let me just say it. Missy kissed me yesterday, and … you know!" Phil was a lost cause too.

Scott, his longtime rival and the class bully, definitely was a lost cause. If he ever asked Scott, he'd get a big laugh, followed by something like, "I might nominate you for classroom whiteboard eraser!"

Soon Billy classified as lost causes Rachel, Gilbert, Frank, Taylor, Ann, Larry, Charlie, Marie, Dave, Jessica, Chin, Alyssa, Leroy, Francesca, Lou, and everyone else in his class, except for Romero and maybe Joannie and Lana.

Billy had never talked to Romero, who sat on the other side of the room and was new to the school this year. He came from El Salvador and admitted, "I no speak English good."

Most of the time Romero stayed by himself. He seemed shy and happy to read a book while other kids played. He also had a dignity that made Billy suspect Romero would go far, once he spoke English better. Romero didn't yet have much influence with the other kids, but he didn't need any to nominate Billy. All he had to say was, "I nominate Billy Harrington for class president."

So, Billy approached Romero and said, "I know we haven't talked much, but I'd like to ask you the favor of nominating me for class president. Later on, Miss Grunch is going to ask if there are any more nominations for class president, and all you have to do is say, 'I nominate Billy Harrington.' That's all there is to it!"

"That all?" Romero asked.

"That's it!" responded Billy.

"Okay, I do it," said Romero. Billy shook Romero's hand with both of his, as two hands made it seem twice as thankful. Billy hadn't yet realized that two hands was a sign of wanting power.

Later, when Miss Grunch asked if there were any further nominations, Romero stood and said, "I nominate Billy Harrington for class presidente!"

Some kids sniggered. Billy looked over at Missy who, offended, shot her stuck-up nose at him before turning away.

"Any second for the nomination?" asked Miss Grunch.

"Oops! Forgot about that!" Billy said to himself. But he thought quickly. After waiting a few seconds, on the off chance someone would second him, he rose to his feet and announced, "I second the nomination."

His classmates looked at him. What?!!! Then Missy rose and said, "You can't second your own nomination! Can he, Miss Grunch?"

"No, he can't!" shouted out Scott in agreement.

The teacher was momentarily flustered. "Let me think! Let me think! … This is highly unusual, and it hasn't happened before. Hmmm … But I don't think there's anything against it in Roberta's Rules. So, we'll have to accept the seconding."

Then she loudly announced, as if she was presiding over a national political convention, "The name of Billy Harrington has been placed in nomination and is seconded. So, I hereby declare Billy Harrington officially on the ballot for class presidente—er, class president."

Billy was happy. But just for a moment. He quickly realized that if the election were held today, he'd probably lose twenty-eight to two, or twenty-nine to one, if Missy somehow got around to helping Romero with his homework, or giving him a kiss, or otherwise helping him learn certain curious practices of American culture.

That evening, at the dinner table, Billy announced he'd become a candidate for class president. His mom commented, "Why Billy, I thought you said you weren't interested in running. What changed your mind?"

"It was something Dad said, about living in a democracy. He made me feel patriotic."

His sister Susie, now a high school freshman and feeling superior, broke in, "What has patriotism got to do with running for president of a stupid sixth-grade class? Sounds like a power trip to me!"

"Susie, I am not after power, and if I was, I'd be unlikely to get it. Just about everybody in the class is going to vote for Missy. Unless I think of a clever way to win."

"How about a smear campaign?" interjected younger brother Andrew. "What scandals can you uncover about her? Sex, evilness, dishonesty, addiction, family ugliness, or any other good stuff!"

"She does go around kissing boys. If the voters were parents, that might be a minus, but not if the voters are the boys she's kissing. And she has a nasty streak, but the voting public loves that, at least the grown-up voting public does, thinking it shows leadership and the strength not to be pushed around. She did pee in her pants a lot when she was in second grade."

"Yes, but in third grade, you had butt boils everybody knew about," Susie countered.

His mom interjected, "Children, I'm disappointed in that sort of talk. Elections shouldn't be won on the basis of what trash you turn up about a person. Whiskers and razors, if I listened to everything said about your father, I'd never have married him! You shouldn't be talking about the bad you can find about the other person. You should be speaking about your platform, what you believe in, what you'll do if elected."

Billy thought that was good advice. "That's right. I want people to vote for me because they like what I stand for, not because the other candidate is a cheap kid-kisser. So, tonight I'm going to decide what I stand for."

That evening his dad strolled to Billy, now in bed and said," I'm really proud you're running for class office. You probably have the political itch in your blood. Your great-uncle Cyrus was a politician, you know. Ran for U.S. senator, and he lost. Ran for the state legislature. Didn't win. He set his sights on the city council, and when he lost his first bid, he doggedly continued and lost four more times. Later he was just nosed out in his bid to become town dogcatcher—that was an office they voted on in those days, before they made it civil service. Then, he made up his mind to think big and run for the greatest office of all, president of these United States. He knew it was a long shot, but he was a Harrington, after all! It was just his luck, and perhaps the country's misfortune, that he just slightly miscalculated while racing his bicycle against a train to see who'd be first to the railway crossing. He was flattened before he could ever get on the ballot. But you are on the ballot, Billy, and we're really proud of you. Keep up the family standard, my boy!"

Before he fell asleep, Billy thought about what he really stood for. Then, he thought about what he would *say* he stood for, for even as new an observer of the American politics as he was, he knew these could be two quite different things.

First, he thought about what a president did. He knew the president of the United States was the commander-in-chief of the Armed Forces, but Cedar Glen Elementary didn't even have student school-crossing guards. Nor a junior ROTC chapter. Of course, there was little need for paramilitary activity at the school. There was no reason to expect an invasion in the near future from any source, except perhaps from killer bees rumored to be heading north.

Of course, the class president did get to be Miss Grunch's number one assistant in evacuating during fire drills, but that didn't seem very promising as a campaign theme.

The president of the United States was in charge of the nation's budget, but his sixth-grade class had no budget he knew of. And he couldn't talk about raising or lowering taxes, since his classmates paid no taxes or even dues. Most of the kids would probably be gleeful if he suggested saving money by lowering Miss Grunch's salary, but she might seek revenge by increasing the amount of daily homework.

The class president, like the president of the USA, ran ceremonies, like accepting the gift of a new computer from the head of the Parents Association or donating that new computer to a retiring teacher. But that seemed like an ego thing, and hardly something to address in his campaign.

Then Billy had an idea. It just came to him, like in a vision! His theme would be that, if elected, he would be the "Three E's President—Education, Environment, and Eating," three subjects he felt his classmates were very interested in.

The first thing Billy did the next day was ask Romero to be his campaign manager. He did this, not because he expected Romero to be an effective spokesman, but to make sure Romero would vote for him.

Starting that day, Billy told everyone who would listen about his platform. He'd pitch them by saying something like, "As president, I'll have a Three E's Program. It may not always be popular, but you'll know that I'm an honest person who doesn't say things just to get elected."

To some he said, "I'll be the education president. For us in Cedar Glen Elementary to be the best we can be, we should have *more* homework. I want our school to be tops in the state when they give us all those tests."

He said, "I'll be the environment president. I'll organize a drive where one Saturday a bunch of us students go through the garbage of as many homes as we can and take all the recyclable bottles and cans. Then we'll cash them in and give the money to Save The Rainforest."

He said, "I'll be the eating president. The vending machines should have healthier food. So, replace candy with fruit. Replace soda pop with juices. Serve nutritious vegetables in the cafeteria instead of red meat, like hamburgers!"

He knew his campaign messages would not be popular. But the only way he thought he could win was by seeming to make hard choices.

Missy took a different tack. She courted individual voters, and when asked about Billy's platform, said she'd have a talk with Miss Grunch about having less homework, she was in favor of adding to the selection of candy bars and soda pop in vending machines, and she'd much rather have a class picnic than go through someone else's filthy garbage.

The day after the nation's Election Day, Billy's sixth-grade class had their election. It was a secret ballot, so nobody would know for sure how anybody else voted, although everybody felt pretty certain Missy would vote for herself and Billy would vote for himself. Each child checked one candidate's name on a slip of paper and then put it into a box on Miss Grunch's desk.

Miss Grunch tallied it up, making tick marks with a pencil. She then stood up and announced, "Here, class, is the final tabulation of our class presidential election. Billy Harrington has four votes, and the winner, Missy Barnes, has twenty-six votes. I declare the winner, and next class president, to be Missy Barnes. Congratulations, Missy!"

Missy delivered a brief acceptance speech, which she began by saying, "I want to thank everyone in the class except four people, and my parents who made me what I am today. And my friends, who made me what I am today. And my teachers who ..." and so on, including her orthodontist, who gave her such fine braces.

As she thanked everyone, Billy glanced at Romero, who shrugged a tiny smile along with an eye roll. Billy decided to ask his mom if he could invite the loyal Romero to dinner sometime. Then Billy tallied in his mind who voted for him. It didn't take very long. Himself, of course. And Romero. And, most likely, Joannie and Lana.

He was right. Later on, during recess, skinny Joannie took Billy aside to collect on his promise that if she voted for him, he'd kiss her. On the lips! It wasn't as icky as he thought it would be.

A short while later, messily dressed, smelly Lana came by to collect the smooch she'd been promised. It was *ickier* than he thought it would be!

Billy decided he was handsome enough to run again for class president. Now he knew how to win an election!

At dinner his mom asked Billy how he'd done in the voting. He dejectedly said he hadn't won and added, "Mom and Dad, you were right about not letting kids my age vote. Most of them are kinda dumb and cast votes for the wrong person and the wrong reasons."

His dad, who'd just finished reading an analysis of Election Day results in the Cedar Glen Tribune, asked grumpily, "Hummph! How is that any different from grown-ups?"

Boys and Girls

Yesterday I was lost in an unknown massive cosmos, totally unable to get my bearings, unable even to decipher which ways were north, south, east, and west. I was tumbling, twisting, being tossed, maybe jumping from an air vehicle without a parachute, intercepted mid-flight by an angry space tornado, finding it difficult to breathe, since there was little to inhale up in blank airspace. Not even air, because air is what you found on Earth. And then, later, it was as if I were swimming to reach the side of a pool filled with molasses, flailing aimlessly, slowly, not knowing if I'd ever reach something solid.

In other words, I was a real metaphorical mess, not comprehending if I would ever survive. And if I did, in what type of world.

But today was easier. After yesterday's meeting with Joannie—now disappointed and angry with me—my situation was more defined, had more structure. Like, instead of a vast unfamiliar universe, I was part of the local solar system, with its eight planets. Or was it nine planets? I mulled that one over. The culprit was Pluto. Astronomers kept changing their minds about whether it was a planet. The confusion was understandable, not surprising, and had existed almost since they named it Pluto, after Mickey Mouse's dog pal. Or was it his pet? Who knew? Anyway, why name a hard planet after an imaginary cartoon dog? The world of astronomers waffled about Pluto being a planet. So, I wasn't the only one who found it hard to decide. That was how I thought of it.

Then, I caught myself. Why was I spending so much time reflecting on the cosmos and planets and the Disney universe, or quagmires, and other pretentious, poetic-like metaphors when I had problems in Cedar Glen to solve? Was the type of contemplating I'd been doing a way to avoid the uneasiness of my predicament?

Stop! I needed to work my immediate problem.

On the other hand, sometimes temporarily setting aside an immediate problem allows the brain to percolate without you knowing it and solve that problem.

Maybe later I'll fantasize about not being able to escape from a corn maze. Although that *is* less dramatic. I mean, really, if you can't figure how to get out, you know they'll come get you.

Anyway, my messed-up world was more structured now. There were three alternatives—have the baby, end the pregnancy, or put the baby up for adoption. Each of these had consequences. Like, keeping a baby might result in me having no successful career and working menial jobs, and not going to college, and being otherwise miserable. Or, on the other hand, I might really enjoy raising another human being.

Joannie would be the one to make the final decision, though I would give my opinion. She was the one taking leadership.

No, let me correct that. Me, as the man, would make the final decision. I'd do this by *allowing* Joannie to make the final decision about the pregnancy. Keen delegation is a hallmark of strong leadership. So, as the man, I was in charge. I would not lose that—my masculinity. Not Billy Harrington!

So, I spent most of Sunday morning in bed, weighing the alternatives, the fatiguing dread of yesterday morning thankfully absent.

Yes, Joannie was angry at me, but at least I better understood my position, my alternatives. And at least for the immediate future, she wouldn't break up with me. Our bond was too strong to sever, to untangle, to poofize it.

I was less inclined than I was yesterday to abort. An abortion *might* resolve our immediate problem. But even though the clinics these days had a very high success rate, what if it was botched—complications like hemorrhages, or operating instruments left inside her—or, Lord forbid, unable to conceive later, abandoning both of us to eternal regret?

Suppose the stress, or psychosomatic complications from the operation, resulted in her turning away from me, from men, from marriage, from mattressing.

Suppose the vengeful will of the Lord for undergoing such a blasphemous procedure meant Joannie would never have children. My future wife, even if it wasn't Joannie, might be unable to have children, or not want them.

This might be Joannie's only chance. And mine.

I could end up a lonely bachelor. I'd never have children! Yes, an abortion might get fatherhood out of the way for now and clear me to pursue other ventures. But I had said getting my virginity out of the way would clear me for other ventures, and look where that got me!

Here was a chance to satisfy what my biology teacher proclaimed was my "evolutionary imperative" as a human being to reproduce. But fatherhood also might mean being ensnared by a web of responsibility, denying me the adventures I'd planned.

I wondered whether my biology teacher really was more keyed into the meaning of life than my church. He taught I was put on earth to reproduce, while the church readers were pretty firm that it was to honor the Lord.

I suspected that if you tried to pin the readers down, unwilling to tackle science, they'd waffle by saying you could honor the Lord by reproducing. If that were true, I wondered whether the more children you had the more you'd honor the Lord, or whether the Lord felt that after a certain point—say more than three children—you'd just be cluttering up the earth He created. So, he'd be more annoyed than honored, considering all that added pollution and the effect on climate change.

But now, I was thinking only about a first child, and both biology and church seemed to be saying we should have the baby. Plus, I'd be a young daddy, able to understand and identify with my child's problems; I'd just been a child. Was still?

If I was going to have a child, I still definitely wanted a boy, though I supposed it wouldn't make much of a difference the first year or so. Newborn boys and girls differed trivially at birth, their anatomical variations concealed by diapers anyway. At birth, gender was incidental to the amount of hair on their heads, their helplessness, and the loudness and frequency of their shrieks. For some time afterward, boy-girl differences lay dormant. Color preference, for example.

During their first few months, boys and girls were equally oblivious to pink. And blue, for that matter. But sooner or later in life, girls were drawn to pink, instinctively homing in on it like a gamer to the latest game version— though for some reason, boys weren't correspondingly drawn to blue in the same dependent way. Even militant feminists were tempted by pink; just look at their diligent efforts to avoid wearing the color. From what I could see, the only girls in Western society undrawn to pink were the daughters of militant feminists, who were taught severely from birth to overcome their genes and despise the color.

I recalled the chapter on color in the women's studies textbook. It began, "No other color is as tied to gender as pink," and ended, "So throughout the history of peoplekind, the color most affiliated with slavery is not black, as everyone thinks, but pink."

Of course, the textbook was written by a woman. In fact, all the books used in my women's studies class were written by women. Were they discriminating against men? Just wondering.

I suspected Joannie, the budding feminist—at least she volunteered opinions more often than anyone in women's studies class—would revert and choose pink outfits for a baby girl. Well, she might not actually go out and buy them, but she certainly wouldn't backlash into returning all pink outfits sent as gifts to a girl baby. But she better not buy pink for a son! And return all gifts that were!

The affinity for pink was so strong and widespread, it had to be genetic. I suspected many non-anatomical differences between the sexes were genetically based, even though it was politically correct to state otherwise. For instance, I couldn't quite buy the argument that girls were inherently equal to boys in math and science. According to the women's studies textbook, in elementary school boys and girls were equivalent in these subjects, but girls fell back because of social expectations, both their own and their teachers'.

Well, girls as a group were taller than boys up to about the same age as when boys shot ahead in math and science. If this difference in height was explained away genetically, why shouldn't the differences in math and science achievement? Even Ms. Hutchinson couldn't answer that one!

Of course, there were other differences between the genders. Women's high body fat slowed their running speed but made them more likely to survive a famine. They read weepy novels and reacted to cuteness but secretly admired brute strength. Compared with men, they were more likely to frequently fall in love, have long telephone conversations, confess feelings, and express tenderness. They were also more prone to hysteria and breaking down in tears, more likely to trip and fall when chased by bad guys or monsters, and have no idea what was under the hood of a car.

Yes, I had women pegged. Who was it who mentioned I'd make a good psychiatrist? Or anthropological observer. Or online influencer.

I suspected I might feel different about girls' proclivities if I had a daughter, but I genuinely expected it was a boy in Joannie's belly.

Yes, I definitely wanted a boy!

If I wanted a child at all!

What a way to spend a Sunday morning! Figuring out about a family!

MOO! MEH!

illy was bored and more than a little perturbed, slumped there in the back bench of the family SUV, his arms crossed and his mouth twisted into a serious frown.

"There are lots better things I can do on a Sunday afternoon than this," he thought. "Huckle Buckle. Computer games. Even watch cartoons. Anything would be better than seeing some stupid farms in the stupid country. I'm twelve years old, too old to be doing this."

Once a year his mom and dad took their three children on a day trip to the country. Each year his dad reminded them why. "Our country's pioneer roots are grounded in the soil and livestock, and it's very important that you children be reminded of that every once in a while."

In the medium-sized city of Cedar Glen, children were far from farms and any livestock. The only animals he and his family saw regularly were those cute squirrels meandering the neighborhood, and the everyday dogs and cats, although their own dog, Bozo, was special *every* day. Occasionally they saw other animals friends kept as pets, like hamsters and pythons. Fish, birds, and insects didn't count as animals, since they obviously had no real brains of any consequence. At the Cedar Glen Zoo, he could see wild animals like monkeys, lions, and seals. But only in the country could the Harringtons see useful large farm animals like cows, horses, and sheep.

Billy was quite glad it wasn't more than one day each year the family took this sort of trip, following ever smaller roads winding ultimately to the country. Billy knew his college professor dad wanted to make sure his family was educated, and not just with schoolbooks. But he didn't have to like it.

"Do I have to go?" Billy had pleaded with his mom.

"Yes dear, you do. We're a family, and we do things together!"

Normally, Billy knew, the family would have waited a few months until autumn to trek to the countryside. But this time his dad had told them since he wasn't teaching summer session this year, he was eager to get out of the house. "Even a professor can get tired of reading books."

His dad even complained to his mom, "I wish something fortuitous would occur, like the plumbing system backing up, so I could do something useful."

"You can mow the lawn," his mom said.

"I hate mowing the lawn," his dad replied. "And as a college professor, I'm not good at it."

Billy could hardly believe that older sister Susie and younger brother Andrew, sitting next to each other, weren't complaining about having to go on this trip. Instead, troublemaker Andrew protested that Susie was hogging too much room. His snooty sister retorted she couldn't help it if she was bigger than him, and Andrew was doing disgusting things with his nose. Andrew explained he was merely trying to fish out the fly he thought buzzed into his nostril. Then he complained about her cheap perfume stinking up the whole SUV. In response, Susie called Andrew an infant. To which Andrew singsonged, "Ya-ya-ya-ya-ya."

Sort of typical behavior in the family.

Forty-five minutes out, his mom asked, "Did everyone remember to go to the bathroom?" Billy thought this was a silly question to ask just then, since it was unlikely his dad would turn the SUV around and travel home if one of them forgot.

"Why didn't she ask that question *before* we left home? Am I descended from nitwits?" he wondered crabbily, not for the first time in his life. But then he corrected his thought. His mom wasn't a nitwit. She just did nitwittish things sometimes.

"Gosh darn! I didn't go," reported his dad, "but never you mind. I can go behind a haystack."

Billy wasn't completely sure his dad was joking. Nor was his mom, who best knew his dad.

"This trip is fun," Billy disbelievingly heard his brother say.

"I can't wait to see the animals," Susie added.

Billy didn't know what his siblings' intentions were. They couldn't possibly mean what they'd said.

Soon, they drove through Bracerville, a small town with a few stores, mostly for farmers and ranchers. Near the end of town was a sign reading, "Slow Children at Play." Andrew told his dad, "Watch out not to hit any kids out here, Dad. They walk slow and may not be able to get out of your way."

His mom responded, "Andrew, the sign simply means the children playing here are just a little … special."

Billy's curious brother asked, "Mom, why do you think kids who can't walk fast are special?"

Before she could answer, Susie broke in, "Mom, Andrew was asking that stupid question as a silly joke. Unfunny."

Andrew, who thought his was a serious question, nevertheless thought—Hmm, maybe Susie's right. So, he admitted, "Just a silly joke, Mom. Where's your sense of humor?"

At the outskirts of Bracerville, his mom warned, "Be alert, kids. We may see animals at any time soon."

"Big deal!" Billy grumbled cynically.

Soon the SUV approached horses and colts grazing in a field. His dad pulled to the shoulder, tires crunching the ground and blowing up a small dust cloud. Just beyond the barbed wire fence enclosing the field stood animals leisurely munching grass.

"Everybody out," ordered his dad, and the family stood in a line next to the fence. Then his dad said, "Okay, gang, we all know what to do. Ready? At the count of three. One … Two … Three."
"Neigh, neigh, neigh," brayed Andrew boisterously.
"Neigh, neigh, neigh," brayed Susie loudly.
"Neigh, neigh, neigh," brayed his mom vociferously.
"Neigh, neigh, neigh," brayed his dad stridently.

Billy could tell everyone really meant what they were braying. But when Billy said "Neigh" just once in a quiet, flat voice, it was as if he was saying "No" in an old-fashioned way.

"Let's do it again," suggested his dad. And so, they all did, including Billy saying only, "Neigh."

This may have been fun when he was little, but not now! This is so ridiculous! "I can't believe I'm a member of this family," Billy thought.

One horse seemed to briefly look up but then turned his mouth back to the ground to nibble grass. The other horses didn't even look up.

"Big deal. These horses don't even know or care we're here," Billy judged.

"Wasn't that great! Now, what'll we find next?" asked his dad. So, they rode the road, on the lookout.

Too soon for Billy, but soon enough for the others, they saw a flock of grazing sheep and lambs. Again, his dad pulled over, crunching pebbles and raising a dust cloud. The family got out and lined up next to the fence. "Okay. We all know what to do. Ready gang. One … Two … Three."
   "Baa, baa, baa," bleated Andrew boisterously.
   "Baa, baa, baa," bleated Susie loudly.
   "Baa, baa, baa," bleated his mom vociferously.
   "Baa, baa, baa," bleated his dad stridently.

"Baa," said Billy quietly, not even bleating, again not meaning it.

"Let's do it again," suggested his dad. So, they repeated, including Billy.

One sheep seemed to look up briefly but then turned to nibble grass. The other sheep didn't even look up.

Billy reflected, "Big deal. These sheep don't even know or care we're here. They're just as brilliant as horses. This family should be on a cartoon show, the way they behave!"

His mom asserted, "Okay! Wasn't that great? Now let's see what we can find next." They all got in the SUV, except his dad, who pointed and said, "There's a haystack. Be right back."

He soon returned looking happier and relieved, the family again on the lookout for more animals. Too soon again for Billy, they came to a small herd of grazing cows and calves. His dad pulled over, next to the barbed wire fence, and again they all exited the SUV.

"Great! Now we're all going to moo!" Billy thought, glad none of his friends were around to see this.

"Ready, gang. One … Two … Three," announced his dad.
  "Moo, moo, moo," mooed Andrew boisterously.
  "Moo, moo, moo," mooed Susie loudly.
  "Moo, moo, moo," mooed his mom vociferously.
  "Moo, moo, moo," mooed his dad stridently.

Billy felt this was so stupid! The next thing you knew they'd oink like pigs! He thought he'd no longer go along with his one-word mocking. Let them know he wasn't happy about being here. They stupidly hadn't recognized it yet! So, when they were done, with a cackle in his voice he blasted out a very loud, rebellious, "MEH! MEH! MEH!" Three sounds! And a little different from the sounds of the others.

"This is fun! Let's do it again," suggested his dad. And so, they all repeated their mooing. "Moo! Moo! Moo!" broadcast, according to Billy, that ludicrous Harrington family cacophony.

All except Billy, who again used a loud voice to sound, "MEH MEH! MEH!" Then again Billy's rebellious cackle-like, "MEH! MEH! MEH!" Then again, "MEH! MEH! MEH!"

A couple of cows looked up briefly and groaned, and some other noises came out of their mouths. But the sounds weren't very loud, and you couldn't tell exactly what they were saying, even if you were a cow-speak expert. Those cows soon returned to munching grass.

But a cow who'd been lying on the ground—a black and white—raised her head and gazed about. Rising up on stubby legs, she turned toward the Harringtons and slowly lumbered across the field toward them, wagging her curlicue tail. As she got closer, it became clear she was heading directly toward Billy, who stood slightly apart at the end from the others.

When she reached the fence, there she was, right in front of him, not even a foot away, the moisture on her black nostrils and the rapid blinking of her eyes clearly visible. In a very deep cow voice, she uttered distinctly, "MEH! MEH! MEH!" Then she repeated it. This time just once. "MEH!"

Andrew said, "Moo, moo, moo." But the black and white shook her head and responded only with a very long, cackle-like, "MEHHHHHHHHH."

Billy realized something was very different here. This cow was friendly and seemed to want a connection, maybe even a friend.

Then, Billy again roared, "MEHHHHHH." And the cow stuck out her tongue and licked his bare arm, the raspy wetness pleasantly surprising him, making him feel special. He'd never heard of a cow licking a boy's arm, no less a boy she hadn't met before.

Why would he have heard? Not even in the little children's books his mom read to him when he was little. Those cows did all sorts of things—jumping over a moon, providing milk calcium to a town ravaged by osteoporosis. But never lick a boy's arm.

His arm tingled as air currents wafted over the area he was licked.

Billy repeated, "MEHHHHHH," and this time the cow again bellowed "MEHHHHH," then reached over and licked Billy's nose. Billy did not move away.

Susie reacted, "Ugh! Disgusting."

The cow brought up her cud and spit at Susie.

"That's what I call disgusting," jumped in Andrew. "Why is she talking like she understands Billy and not us?"

Billy told him, "Probably because you don't understand cow speak. 'Meh' is very different from 'moo.' It's like you talking to someone in English who only speaks Kapashi."

"There's no such thing as Kapashi," asserted Susie. "I'm going to check." And she started typing on her cell.

"I'm talking in Kapashi?" Andrew asked.

"No, you're talking in English, obviously," Billy explained. "That's why Betsy didn't understand you. She doesn't speak English. Betsy speaks cow speak."

His dad asked, "You mean all these years I've been telling cows 'Moo,' and they didn't understand what I was saying?"

"Afraid so, Dad."

"Betsy? How do you know her name's Betsy? How do you even know it's a girl?" asked Andrew of Billy.

"Andrew, all cows are girls," chimed in Susie, raising her eyebrows and shaking her head at her brother's ignorance. "A boy cow is a bull."

"I know. I'm ten, not two," Andrew reminded Susie, who was sure her brother didn't know.

Billy pondered once more how he could possibly have come from the same gene pool as this group.

"How do you know her name's Betsy?" Andrew repeated.

"It's obvious," Billy told him, finalizing that discussion, although it wasn't really obvious to him. It just seemed like a suitable name for a cow.

None of the others challenged Billy's "obvious," not wanting to chance being thought of as ignorant and stupid by not recognizing something obvious. Billy registered that this reticent approach to conversation and interpersonal relationships sometimes happened, and maybe that was why the world was screwed up. Well, at least sometimes.

Billy didn't care at all that his arm got all wet from cow slobber. He patted the cow's nose and looked into the heavily lidded eyes on her boxy face. The eyes stared back at him. The other Harringtons looked on while the boy and cow stared at each other.

"Betsy's so cute!" he exclaimed. "I wish we could take her home. But I guess Betsy's too big."

Playing along, Susie added, "Obviously! There's no room. Unless you tie her to the rear bumper and we drag her home!"

"Very insightful, both of you," his dad praised. "First, the SUV payload is under 2,000 pounds, and I'm concerned the cow may damage the axles. Second, you do have a point about the cow not fitting inside our vehicle.

"Third, that cow belongs to somebody. If we took her, we'd be cattle rustlers, and there hasn't been a cattle rustler in the family ever since your great-grandfather Monroe was locked up in Leavenworth penitentiary many years ago, soon after he decided to leave the monastery. He and his gang of …"

"Gordon," his mom scolded her husband, just by saying his name with attitude.

But then his dad added, "I could come back with a trailer tomorrow. Betsy can help me out with the mowing back at our ranch. No doubt about it. She could trim the grass while I enjoy a cold Cheersarsaparilla."

"Gordon! We have no place for a cow anywhere on our property! And we don't have a ranch! We're suburban, not rural." That was his mom, always the one to think things through.

And that was that! … Well, almost.

"Where's your sense of humor, Molly?"

After thinking it over—"Sorry," she said.

Susie finished checking her phone. "Ha! There is no such thing called Kapashi. When I searched, it didn't show up at all. That proves it! If it's not in my phone, it doesn't exist."

Billy's mom interrupted. "Meanwhile, I've got a great idea. Let's all go into that little place in Bracerville and have ice cream sodas!"

"Yeah," agreed Susie and Andrew enthusiastically.

His dad offered, "Well, we haven't seen the pigs yet, but my throat is dry from mooing, and I'm a little hungry too."

"Do we have to leave here *now*?" a sorrowful Billy asked.

"Yes, Billy, we do," said his mom kindly.

After giving Betsy's face a final pat, and bellowing a loud "MEHHHHHH," Billy followed the others back to the SUV. He looked out the window and noticed Betsy, with drooped head, slowly waddling back to the herd. He waved to her, though he knew she couldn't see him.

On the ride to Bracerville, his mom, noticing Billy was moping and reflective, marveled, "I've never before seen a cow attach herself to a boy like that."

Billy nodded in agreement.

"And I've never before seen you attracted to an animal like that. Even when we brought Bozo home."

This observation resulted in Susie chanting, "Billy's in love with a cow! Billy's in love with a cow!"

Billy flushed in embarrassment. Or was it anger?

His mom said, "Susie! Saying a boy is in love with a cow is a very serious accusation. In love?"

Susie answered with "duh" rolling eyes. "Mom, I was once twelve years old. I know love when I see it."

"Oh," said his mom in a "that makes sense" way. But knowing how Billy felt at the moment, she continued. "I'm sure Billy isn't really in love with that cow. He just met her. Oh ... it's just ridiculous he'd fall in love with a cow! Though I suppose at his age it is better than being in love with a girl and getting in all sorts of trouble."

Billy was mystified. What did his mom mean by being in love with a girl? He'd never do that!

His dad commented, "It's apparent Billy's not in love with a cow. You don't see a cow and just fall in love with it. It takes time, just like it took me time to fall in love with you, dear."

"Oh! A cow, am I now?" asked his mom.

"That's not what I meant, dear," trying a conciliatory tone.

"Where's your sense of humor, Gordon?" his mom asked.

"Ho, ho," his dad stated, as if he wanted to communicate that his mom had told a corny joke.

"Say, Billy," his dad said, changing the subject, "Do you think Betsy is a black cow with white patches, or a white cow with black patches?"

"I have no idea. I'll ask her the next time I see her." Then he added, "You asked me that same question when I was four, Dad. Except then it was about zebras."

They reached Bracerville and, in Chuck's Restaurant & Emporium, sat around a large circular table covered by a gorgeous embroidered white Irish linen tablecloth with fringed lace. And paper napkins. By then Billy noticed his mom and dad had made up and held hands. Even when his parents had a little row, they soon made up. How simple life sometimes was, especially if you were simple, like his mom and dad. Obviously!

The proprietor, who was also the waiter, was tall and thin, with a long craggy nose and a bald head. Wearing a white apron with only a few stains, he came from behind the fountain and handed out menus, informing them,

"I'm Chuck, the owner of this here *chuck*wagon." Then he clicked his tongue, smiled, and winked.

"Ha! Ha! You'd think the man would've tired of his silly joke by now," considered Billy, though he kept the judgment to himself. "*Chuck*wagon indeed!"

"No need for those menus, Chuck. We'll all have chocolate ice cream sodas," his mom informed. "It's a family tradition to have chocolate ice cream sodas when we're out together."

"No, make mine a *black-and-white* ice cream soda!" asserted Billy.

The rest of the family just stared at him. No one had ever ordered anything but a chocolate ice cream soda before. There was an awkward moment of silence. Billy saw Chuck's eyeballs move from one family member to another.

His mom, understanding, then declared, "That's a wonderful idea, Billy. You just want your ice cream soda to be in honor of your black-and-white Betsy. Chuck, change my order to a black-and-white ice cream soda."

"Mine too," chimed in his dad. Susie and Andrew joined the cavalcade and changed their orders too.

So, Chuck crossed out the old order on his pad and wrote in "Black and white" five times on his pad, stating what he wrote each time.
"Black and white."
"Black and white."
"Black and white."
"Black and white."
"Black and white."

Then he asked, "Sure you don't want burgers? This is a *cow* town, you know."

Susie commented, "We know it's a cow town!".

"No thanks. I speak for all of us," stated his dad, perhaps trying to reinforce the perception that he was the head of this family.

"I'll tell the cook about the black-and-whites," informed Chuck, who was, of course, also the cook.

Although Billy couldn't quite understand how you "cook" ice cream sodas.

Shortly, Chuck delivered five tall, frosty glasses, each filled with stirred chocolate syrup, a big ball of vanilla ice cream, and topped by a thick whipped cream swirl and a red cherry. And five tall spoons, of course.

Billy announced, "I would like to propose a toast."

He noted that everyone in the family was surprised, for he'd never before proposed a toast in his whole life. When all were silent, he cleared his throat, raised his glass and announced, "To the best cow in the whole world—Betsy!"

They clinked glasses all around. Then his dad said, "Ready gang. One … Two … Three."

And the whole family loudly roared, "MEH! MEH! MEH!"

When Billy looked up, he saw Chuck shaking his head at the preposterous behavior of these big city tourists, probably thinking, "Urban folks certainly are mindless sometimes. Total rubes!"

Then Billy asked, "Dad, can we come back to the country next week?"

Asking Myself

I was reserved and distant at school the next day. Not once did I raise my hand in class. At lunch, instead of joining Joannie in the cafeteria, I isolated myself under an oak tree in the quadrangle and barely took three bites from my peanut butter and jalapeño sandwich as I stared emptily ahead. I answered classmates' questions in monosyllable monotones. I avoided eye contact with Joannie and noticed she was ducking me as well. I attended my Huckle Buckle team practice, diligently going through the drills but hardly saying a word to teammates.

Perhaps prompted by the academic backdrop, I daydreamed about living away at college and experiencing the camaraderie of dorm life, cheering at football rallies, carousing at parties, pulling all-night study sessions with fraternity brothers, and simultaneously chewing on both a crisp apple and philosophical enigmas while sitting cross-legged on a shaded lawn beside a venerable stone building clung with ivy. And being hugged by my gushing mom and dad after commencement ceremonies for not only graduating but making magna cum laude in journalism.

Who were the boys who got girls pregnant and became teenage fathers? Weren't they usually the dull boys whose wit was mainly based in profanity, who dropped out of school, and whose grades were so low, except maybe not in wood shop, they weren't going to graduate anyway? Who took substances to get high and who never read books for pleasure? The irresponsible boys who'd never amount to anything truly admirable?

Did I want to go through the ignominy of Scott calling me Papa for years?

Did I want to be responsible for supporting a family, be forced into tiresome caretaker activities and the repetitive, mindless chores of caring for a baby?

Could I ever again play freely with my friends? Wouldn't they look at me as someone separate, no longer one of them? A person suddenly of a different generation?

Would marriage revert me to being a stay-at-home gamer, entertained by cartoon images on screens?

Would I *have* to recycle, setting aside used cans and bottles, to provide a good example for my child, even when the baby hadn't yet sounded "mama" or "dada" and was years away from learning about ecology, pollution, and conservation?

Would I recycle simply for the extra nickels?

Would I really enjoy showing off baby photographs I knew very well were not much different from the mass of baby photos? Or would I pocket the photographs and have the world wonder why I didn't show them?

What would my relationship with Joannie be like? Would we ever be close again? How do a mother and a father survive when they resent each other?

I concluded I had not advanced very far in my thinking, in arriving at even a solution to my current dilemma of a strained relationship with Joannie.

Serious Silence

Billy wasn't happy! Neither was anyone in the Harrington household. Things had been gloomy for months, ever since his mom and dad—Molly and Gordon—virtually ceased talking to each other. Sunday morning visits to Christian Science church services ended—although Billy was not all displeased about that. There was no more planning for the weekends, no more inside jokes between the two of them. No more saying "Amen" when one of them agreed with what the other said.

Even aside from the two of them, hardly anyone played with Bozo, or even patted his back. His dad even stopped telling Billy stories about the Harrington ancestors.

Billy didn't know why they were angry with each other. It wasn't as if she bopped him over the head, or he called her nasty names. At least that he knew about.

He could tell things really were serious when his dad stopped mashing the potatoes for dinner, and his mom then ceased making mashed potatoes altogether and began to prepare all sorts of other potatoes—baked, scalloped, Lyonnaise, hash browns, French fries. Some of them were very tasty, he had to admit, but they just weren't as luscious as mashed potatoes. And besides, mashed potatoes were the family tradition. Any other potato type just seemed wrong.

Billy, his older sister Susie, and his younger brother Andrew often moped and kept to themselves. In moody despair, Billy listened to pensive, sluggish classical music, read poetry, and sometimes spoke using poetic imagery.

He suspected his parents were thinking about divorce, but as far as he knew neither had done anything about it yet, like lawyer-up, or squirrel away money the other didn't know about, though if they were good squirrels— well, of course he wouldn't know about it. Each night his dad slept on the couch, and the heads of the Harrington household only communicated about ordinary housekeeping matters. His dad would let his mom know they were nearly out of toilet tissue, and his mom would inform his dad the lightbulb in the basement needed changing.

Billy, in a moment of metaphorical hopefulness, thought the small amount of verbal contact at least provided a beacon of opportunity. He told himself, "The secluding wall of silence had doors that were ajar perhaps, but not shut, and so a silken beam of light gleamed through." His dad could've set out on a brave and audacious journey to buy toilet paper himself. His mom could well have changed the lightbulb herself, handyman-like. At least Billy thought she knew how to change a lightbulb. Well, even if she didn't, she could have asked him, rather than his dad.

Anyway, the schism was not totally finalized. But still ...

Andrew, especially, seemed cheerless. Just before bedtime one chilly evening when Andrew was particularly melancholy, Billy asked his normally impish brother why he seemed so unhappy. His despondent brother told Billy, "It's my fault they aren't happy and aren't talking to each other. If it wasn't for me, they'd have more money and could buy more things, and if I were a better boy they wouldn't be so angry, and it's all my fault."

Billy, who at thirteen was more mature and more insightful than his eleven-year-old brother, thought of telling Andrew, "Stop being so dramatic!"

But instead, he counseled him, "Andrew, blaming yourself for mom and dad not talking to each other is completely ridiculous. The currents in the ocean run deep, and riptides oft pull weary stragglers out to sea. In other words, you have zip to do with it! And neither does Susie! It's just the typical cliché tendency of children to think they're the cause of the parents' breakup. So, just stop! It has nothing to do with you being to blame. The truth is, all these problems they're having are my fault."

Billy thought he was being mature by accepting blame. Gone were the days he excused himself by saying, "It's not *my* fault." Nowadays, he accepted blame for lots of things. Even stuff he had nothing to do with. Once, someone in his English class stole the teacher's beloved fountain pen. Mr. Dinkle warned if the thief didn't come forth, the whole class would have extra homework. Billy then confessed, telling Mr. Dinkle he'd since lost the pen. In reality, Billy had nothing to do with the theft. He wasn't even the lookout.

A few in the class knew Billy hadn't stolen the pen—the real thief and one or two others were aware—and Billy was beginning to get the reputation of being disruptive.

Another time, Billy's team lost at Huckle Buckle, and he told his teammates the loss was his fault, even though the person he guarded hadn't scored a single bangle all day.

Still another time, his good friend and the eighth-grade class president, Romero, came to school limping badly with a sprained ankle. After Romero explained to Billy at recess that he'd gotten the sprained ankle stepping in a ditch while mowing the lawn—Billy, in his habit of absorbing blame, said seriously, "It's my fault."

Romero looked at him, puzzled, and said, "Billy, I won't even ask you how my ankle sprain was your fault. But it bothers me you're always willing to take the blame. You confessed about the pen, when I saw with my own eyes Scott taking it. You say "My fault" automatically, whenever anything goes wrong. Your grades are just passing, when you used to be at the top of the class. You've been moody and unhappy, and sometimes you speak very strangely, as if you're in a dreamworld of poetry. You even listen to music without a beat. What is wrong, my friend?"

Billy contemplated. Why indeed was he always taking the blame? Was he in fact acting the dreamy poet? And what was wrong with listening to slow, soothing music without a beat?

"I don't know," he told Romero, his eyes tearing up, staring into a distant void.

"Do you have bodily changes you can't understand?" asked Romero, aware that boys' bodies changed considerably at their age, becoming more manlike. Or at least hairier under the armpits.

"I don't think so," replied Billy.

"Are you in good health? Are you sick?" inquired a concerned Romero.

"No, I'm feeling as idyllic as a blissful robin in harmonious flight."

"There, you're doing it again," Romero pointed out.

"Doing what again?"

"Talking poetry … Is everything all right at home?"

Billy hesitated. Romero waited. Billy hesitated. Romero waited. Romero's waiting outlasted Billy's hesitations, and finally Billy admitted, "No, it's not. I think my mom and dad are going to get a divorce!"

"What's up, my friend? Spill!"

"For the past few months, they haven't talked to each other except when they have to. We don't eat mashed potatoes anymore. And things may be coming to a head. Last week my mom forgot twice to put mayo in our sandwiches. And my dad didn't put transmission fluid in the SUV and now the engine's all wonky. These things never went down before. The house is so quiet, and there's always tension. We kids are all afraid to make a peep and upset one of them."

Romero offered, "You might find value in joining the 'Children of Divorced and Separated Parents Club.' It meets after school on Thursdays. It has twelve steps …"

"Stop right there, Romero," Billy interrupted.

"Billy, you are not the first kid at this school whose parents are no longer together. It's time you took a trip to the school psychologist."

But Billy didn't want an outsider involved in his family's affairs. Romero meant well, but Billy didn't even know the school psychologist, and the psychologist sure didn't know what his parents were like. Anyway, it was his parents who needed a psychologist, not him. So he told Romero, "Instead, my mom has books on psychology. Maybe I'll get some ideas."

After school that afternoon, Billy perused titles in the living room bookcase. He was a little skittish about picking up *Psychopathology, Deviancy, and Abnormality.* If that applied to even one of his parents, maybe they *should* get a divorce. So, he put it back on the shelf. (Although he did wonder why it was there in the first place.)

There were books on *child* development. One seemed familiar—the thin blue book with the white lettering, the very one he remembered his mom reading when he was about five. It was called *Converting the Brat*, with the subtitle *How to Manipulate Your Child and Save Your Sanity*. He pulled it off the shelf and sat down with it.

The table of contents showed different chapter names, like "Guilt Doesn't Work," "Spanking Doesn't Work," "Accusing Doesn't Work," "Understanding Works," "Ignoring Isn't Ignorance," "Giving Choices," "Making Lists," and "Criticizing the Behavior and Not the Person."

He was particularly drawn to the last chapter, "Why to Never Ever Let Your Child Get His Hands on This Book." It was short, merely advising that a child reading the book might one day exploit some of the same methods to use on the parent!

So, Billy realized this book really might be useful.

He opened randomly to "Guilt Doesn't Work." There he read that parents trying to change behavior by making their child feel guilty are actually teaching the skill of how to make someone else feel guilty, and the child will soon know how to make the parent feel guilty. Besides, even if the parent succeeds in making the child feel guilty, it may backfire. A child made to feel guilty about being messy may go his whole life considering himself a slob.

So, Billy decided not to make his parents feel guilty.

He skipped over "Spanking Doesn't Work." Even if the chapter was called "Spanking *Does* Work," he would've skipped it. He intuitively knew there was something wrong about spanking one's own parents, even if they deserved it and didn't smack you back.

He turned to "Understanding Works," and learned if you "get" your child's situation, rather than yell or scream, he'll develop his own insights, and you'll save your voice. His supportive mom had always seemed to "get" him, ever since she brought home that book. A few times in his life he'd wondered, "Why is my mom like that? I can do anything, and she'll understand. If I burned down the house, she'd point out I must have been in a bad mood and then ask kindly if I'd like to talk about it. What was wrong with her? Why don't I have a normal mom who yells at me sometimes?"

So, he decided not to use that approach.

Billy then read through another chapter, "Making Lists." But this time he thought, "This may very well work. If I take the viewpoint that mom and dad are acting like children, and I apply some of the hints in this chapter ..."

That evening, after his dad went to the movies by himself (at least he said he was going to the movies), Billy approached his mom. "Mom, got a minute?" he asked.

"I suppose so," she responded grudgingly.

"I have a problem that I wonder if you can help me out with. I see a mom who doesn't talk to a dad. And then I see a dad who doesn't talk to a mom. And I see a houseful of unhappy people. This makes me sad and mad and not glad. And I want to do something about it. So, I've brought this paper and pencil, and let's write down everything we can think of that might solve this problem."

"Goodness, Billy! This does sound a little familiar. But I guess it can't do much harm. I guess you've noticed your dad and I have grown apart. It's not easy to live your life with someone moody and stubborn and yes, arrogant like him."

"Mm-hmm. Well, what should I write down first?"

"Dad will move out!" she blurted.

Billy wrote that down, knowing it was important to record everything during the brainstorming and not make any judgments until later. Then he said, "Okay, now here's another suggestion—Mom will move out."

His mom frowned but then offered another solution. Then Billy made a suggestion. They each contributed to the list of suggestions until they ended up with:

Dad will move out.
Mom will move out.
Mom will stop going to the gambling casino, where she drinks tequila.
Dad will stop saying he's going to the movies when he's really going to a bar.
Dad will go to therapy.
Mom will go to therapy.
Mom and Dad will go to therapy together.
Mom and Dad will go to therapy along with the kids.
Dad will change his behavior and be nicer to Mom.
Mom will change her behavior and be nicer to Dad.
Mom and Dad will take a square-dance class together.
Mom and Dad will just kiss and make up.
Dad will stop being so gosh-darned stubborn.
Dad will get rid of the hair sticking out of his ears and nostrils.
Dad will begin to be considerate of Mom's feelings.

Billy was especially curious about the items about alcohol consumption, which violated Christian Science dictum. But he didn't want to press his mom too hard. Still, when they were done, Billy told her, "Okay, Mom, now it's time to review what we've written down. I'm especially interested in what you said about ..."

Which his mom then offered, "Why don't you just give me the list, and I'll think about it!"

The book said people are more likely to commit to something if you simply gave them a choice. So, he told her, "You have two choices. You can tell me *now* which suggestions you like the most and which you don't like, or you can wait until tomorrow night. Which is your choice?"

"Tomorrow night," she stated with conviction. So, he handed her the list.

When his dad returned home later, Billy couldn't help but wonder if the movie theater had started serving beer along with their popcorn. Billy approached as his dad removed his shoes and stated, "I have a problem that I wonder if you can help me out with. I see a dad who doesn't talk to a mom. And then I see a mom that doesn't talk to a dad. And I see a houseful of unhappy people. This makes me mad. And I would like to do something about it. So, I've brought this paper and pencil, and let's write down everything we can think that might solve this problem."

"Hmmm. Sounds like something your mother would have done when you were a little kid. But I guess it can't do much harm. Your mom and I have just grown apart, our lives have gone in different directions. And, well, your mom's not what I'd call a constant nagger, but she does have her annoying ways of getting what she wants. And darn it, sometimes it's downright irritating!"

"Well, what should I write down first?"

"I remember when your grandparents once had a spat. It was in the summertime, and we were in the middle of a drought ..."

"Dad, what should I write down first?" Billy repeated.

"Mom will move out!" he blurted.

Billy wrote that down, then announced, "Okay, now here's another suggestion—dad will move out."

They made suggestions until they ended up with:
Mom will move out.
Dad will move out.
Dad will stop visiting bars after dinner.
Mom will stop going to the gambling casino, where she drinks tequila.
Mom will go to therapy.
Dad will go to therapy.
Dad and Mom will go to therapy together.
Dad and Mom will go to therapy along with the kids.
Mom will change her behavior and be nicer to Dad.
Dad will change his behavior and be nicer to Mom.
Dad and Mom will take a square-dance class together.
Dad and Mom will just kiss and make up.
Mom will stop being so gosh-darned stubborn.
Mom will get rid of the hair under her armpits.
Mom will begin to be considerate of Dad's feelings.

Billy was again especially curious about the items about alcohol consumption. But didn't want to press his dad too hard either. Still, when they were done, Billy told him, "Okay, Dad, now it's time to review what we've written down. I'm especially interested in what you said about …"

But his dad announced, "I'm a little sleepy just now, Billy. Why don't you just give me the list, and I'll think about it!"

So, Billy told him, "You have two choices. You can discuss this with me now, and tell me which suggestions you like the most and which ones you don't like, or you can wait until tomorrow night. Which is your choice?"

"Tomorrow night!" his dad asserted. So, Billy handed him the list.

He hoped his mom and dad wouldn't see each other's list. The chances of the two discussing their lists was minuscule, given the extent of their communication these days. But one of them could leave it where the other would see it. The lists were so much alike, his mom or dad might think he violated a confidence by showing one of them the other's list.

The next day Billy couldn't concentrate at school. He wondered whether his parents would really talk to him about their lists, and what they'd say, so he barely heard what his teachers taught. He'd surprised his folks the first time. Now they might just treat him like a kid. Or they just might come out and say it was none of his business.

Later, Billy returned home after halfheartedly playing a losing game of Huckle Buckle, causing his good friend Todd to accuse him of not hustling. It was close to dinner time, and as Billy entered the house, he sensed a familiar scent. It couldn't be anything but the fragrant aroma of mashed potatoes! He entered the kitchen, and sure enough there was his dad happily adding a little warmed milk to the bowl and blending, his wooden spoon confidently whooshing. And Susie was teasing Andrew again! And his mom was whistling.

"You sound like a tea kettle, Mom," Billy said. She smiled but kept whistling.

Dinner was the best meal Billy had had in months, and not just because mashed potatoes were on the menu. Billy didn't have to hear his dad ask one of the kids to pass a dish sitting right in front of his mom. He didn't have to watch his mom poke at her food.

After dinner, when Susie and Andrew had gone to their rooms, and his dad retreated to the living room to read the newspaper, his mom told him, "Your dad decided things were pretty rotten, and it just might be a good idea if we discussed the suggestions on the list you drew up with him. I had sort of been thinking the same thing.

"Anyway, he called me at the library and asked if I was free for lunch. I was momentarily flustered, but I realized I wanted to discuss the suggestions on my list with him. So, I agreed.

"At the restaurant, where he bluntly ordered mashed potatoes as his meal, your dad told me what he'd gone through with you last night and pulled out his list. Then I exclaimed, 'Gracious goodness,' and pulled out my list. We compared lists; almost exactly the same. Almost.

"Then your dad said, "You know, Molly, we are so much alike. I don't know whether we're alike because of all those years we've been together or whether we've been together all these years because we're so much alike. But I guess it doesn't matter."

"He asked me, 'Do you remember how our troubles began?'

"I answered, 'Not at all.'

"'Neither do I,' he said.

"'I've been very foolish,' I confessed.

"'So have I,' he admitted.

"'Amen,' we said together, and we gave each other a little kiss. Then, to seal the reconciliation, I reached over to his plate, and Billy, I don't know if you'll believe this, but I grabbed a fistful of mashed potatoes and placed it in his mouth! I paid no mind whatsoever to what the other diners might think!"

After she disclosed the day's events, his dad returned and told him, "Billy, tonight your mom and I will do something we've always wanted to do, but somehow never got around to."

"Go to a motel on a second honeymoon?" he guessed.

"No," his dad disclosed. "We spent our first honeymoon on a cruise, not in a motel. It was a ship from a port far, far away. The captain of the ship was your great-uncle Stanley, who …"

"Drive out to Moonlight Bluffs and park?" Billy interrupted with a sly grin.

"No. Why don't you tell him, Molly?"

"We're going …"

"To square-dancing lessons," they said in unison.

Just before they were ready to leave, his mom told Billy, "I see a boy who did something very wise, a boy who cares very much about his mom and dad. I see a boy I love very much."

Billy, at first not knowing what to say, stated, "I see a mom and dad who seem very happy."

"One more thing," his mom added. "It *was* all your doing."

Billy flinched, awaiting an accusation that he'd done something to cause the schism. She paused before going on. "It was your doing that your dad and I got to be friends again."

As tears were about to depart his eyeballs, his mom raised her arm. "Look, Billy! No hair," nodding toward her armpit. Billy then raised his arm, pulled up the edge of his T-shirt sleeve, nodded toward his armpit, and said, "But Mom, look! Hair! I must be becoming a man."

"I think you're just about there!" she concluded.

As he moseyed off to listen to some good old Mass Massacre, he heard his mom continue, "I wonder if we could convince your dad to do something about that hair in his ears and nostrils …"

Billy was now convinced things were back to normal.

The Confession

Late in the afternoon I was mopily drifting into a nap when my mom rapped softly on the door and called my name. I heard, but preferring solitude, I didn't respond. She tapped and called again. Again, I didn't acknowledge. The door to my room slowly nudged open, my mom peeked her head in, then walked to the chair near my bed.

I hadn't known it was my mom because she normally didn't gently rap on the door, softly call my name, slowly nudge the door open, and sit in the chair near my bed. Normally she thumped hard, broadcast loudly she was coming in, and barged in as if she had every right to.

I wasn't happy about her intrusion but also relieved that someone might care, even if they weren't yet aware of exactly what they cared about. She folded her hands on her lap, saying, "I've noticed you've been listless and withdrawn, not like my normal Billy. You stay in your room all the time. Goodness, is there anything you'd like to talk about?"

I froze. I wasn't yet ready to confess my impending fatherhood. Not yet. Nevertheless, I longed to speak with someone about my predicament. "No, nothing's wrong."

She persisted, "Sometimes when we talk things out, we realize they aren't so bad after all."

She was right. Holding in feelings usually was no solution. Not that procrastination never works. Sometimes problems fade away when you do absolutely nothing. Pregnancies could reverse by themselves, with the fetus shrinking into the remnants of dried out sperm and shriveled ovum, I thought wishfully. Sure, and Scott, my rival, could spontaneously combust.

More realistically, miscarriages occur. But what kind of person roots for a miscarriage?

Strong unexpressed emotion can agitate your body, or mix your mind so you act strangely, even crazily. Still, I wasn't prepared to tell my mom. How could I admit to becoming so sordid? I'd feel disgraced, even if it was to her. Because it was sordid. I'd have to hear her gasp and then get that pontifical lecture about the Lord's expectations. Or would it be a colossal sigh of disappointment?

"So …?"

"It's nothing I can't work out myself," I tried to assert firmly, aware I probably didn't sound very confident.

"Well, I'm just in the kitchen if you need me," she informed.

Blurt time!

"Mom. Joannie's pregnant!"

"Oh! I see."

"I'm the father."

"So that's it! Whoopsie-Doopsie!"

I looked down and nodded, a muted vertical nod. A "Yes" dip. I shut my eyes so tears wouldn't emerge.

"Well, how do you feel about it?" she asked.

"Awful. Just awful."

Her kind face waited for me to continue. I asserted, "Mom, it's wrong to get a girl pregnant who you're not married to. It's unfair to the baby, and unfair to the mother."

"And to the father too."

"And to the father too," I echoed.

"Well, what are we going to do about it?" she probed helpfully. That soothing "we" made me feel I had company, that my problem had a resolution, yet undetermined, but one we'd find. Tension in my jaw and shoulders dissipated. My family, at least my mom, was on my side.

"I don't know, Mom," I stated glumly.

"Have you prayed on it?"

My mom surely knew I was no longer observant, so I suspected she mentioned prayer out of duty. Or maybe she thought a reminder could prompt me back to the fold. But I hadn't yet reached the bottom people usually require to revert to religion. Although in the past day or so I'd had more thoughts about the Lord than I'd had in the past six months. Out of respect I answered, "Not yet. Besides, I'm not sure I want the Lord to know what a mess I've caused."

"He already knows. How does Joannie feel about it?"

"I don't exactly know. We're both so unsure."

"Well, there's just one solution," she affirmed.

Did her solution involve getting married and having the baby, giving the baby up for adoption, or an abortion? The solution wasn't so easy for me. How did it come so easily to her? Or did her solution involve a lengthy prayer session?

"What's the solution?" I asked.

"Both you and Joannie need to think about the type of people you are. What are you rooted in that makes you *you*? People grow from their roots. Take stock, and I'm quite sure the solution will be right there."

"You're right, Mom. Thanks!" I said gratefully, amazed. There it was, so clear! So often she managed to put things in perspective. She kissed my forehead, stroked my cheek, and left. Happily, she didn't pat my head like a baby.

I closed my eyes and thought. It didn't take long before a conception dawned! I emitted an open-mouthed, wide-eyed "Hah!" Or maybe it was "Aha." I don't remember.

Now I knew I'd be prepared when I met with Joannie again, which would be once I'd done some hard reflecting that shouldn't take too long. I texted her and without moving our thumbs much at all, we arranged that I'd pick her up the next morning, an hour and a half before classes started at Cedar Glen High.

Teen Types

Billy lazed in bed, gazing at the patternless spackle on the ceiling and mulling over the direction of the rest of his life. Now fourteen, he realized he was no longer the carefree kid who shimmied up trees, vaulted over fences, and intentionally splashed in puddles. He was now a teenager, it being widely recognized that boys usually skidded into teenagerhood at the age of fourteen, while girls generally tumbled into teenagerhood at age twelve.

Teenagerhood was serious business. His voice no longer cracked, but stayed a decent deep, and downy filaments of hair appeared over his top lip, so he'd soon incur shaving expenses, or else share a razor and cream with his dad. Now that he was capable, maybe he'd cultivate a beard, at least a mustache. He'd have a few weeks to decide, the growth over his lip now only a faint fuzz.

He didn't think teenagerhood was a mere bridge from child to adult. Being a teenager wasn't just age driven. It was a matter of attitude. When he reached eighteen, he'd officially be an adult. But he'd always keep the unspoiled, fair-minded outlook of a teenager. He wouldn't make compromises with justice, with truth, ways in which teens excelled. Of that, he was sure.

But right now, he was both excited and nervous. Tomorrow was to be his first day at Cedar Glen High School.

As he prepared for bed, his dad came into his room. Andrew was fast asleep. "Sit down, Billy," he told his son, who was already lying in his bed. His dad sat in the nearby chair and continued, "I remember my first year in high school. Believe it or not, I was a member of the Cheerleader Squad. Carried a megaphone and cheered for the good old Cedar Glen High Ostriches. That was the team nickname then, before they changed it to Pit Bulls. Ostriches are fast and powerful! Vicious only when provoked! One year, at the state cheerleader championship competition, we took first prize in the Most Original Cheer Lyrics event. We'd scream:

Wallaga wisp gayoo gayam,
Touchdown, field goal, here I am.
Caloo, calla, caya, cayam,
Hullabaloo and a body slam.

"Those were the days! I was the first boy member of the Cheerleaders, the only one that first year, my senior year. I guess I'm a trend setter. Your mom was a cheerleader too. Spunky lass back then. Wore that short skirt! Hadn't of been for cheerleading, and that short skirt, I don't know if we'd be married now. Don't know if you'd've been born. You may owe your existence to the good old Cheerleader Squad. And that short skirt, Billy. Well, I suppose you're trying out for the football team and have the squad cheer for you! Nice chatting with you, big guy. Have sweet dreams!"

So, as Billy closed his eyes he determined he *would* have sweet dreams.

In the morning, now in his first year at Cedar Glen High, he had to decide just what type of teenager he'd be. His sister Susie, who was now a senior and mature enough to be helpful to others in the family, gave Billy a heads-up on the possibilities. Each option suited him in some ways and not others.

He could be a Cheerleader. He'd meet popular pretty girls, not that he really knew how to talk to girls. But then again, by being on the same squad, he might learn. Billy had just begun to recognize that girls were sometimes pleasing to be around. Not all of them made him feel awkward. Many were not goofy at all.

What most appealed to Billy about becoming a cheerleader, though, was building the famous Cedar Glen High Human Pyramid. Eight cheerleaders linked arms side by side, and four more cheerleaders rose to stand on their shoulders. Then two new cheerleaders scaled the shoulders of those four. Finally, a lone cheerleader climbed up past the base of eight, past the next tier of four, atop the next two, at last proudly standing at the apex of the pyramid, waving to the astounded, applauding crowd! The Cedar Glen High Human Pyramid was well known, and even fans of opposing schools cheered their mind-boggling, gravity-defying feat.

But, on the downside, to be a cheerleader he'd have to trim his hair short. His clothes had to be neat. Yes, his dad had been a Cheerleader, but Billy wanted to be his own person, not a follower of footsteps. And when it came down to it, the things Cheerleaders cared most about weren't very meaningful. Cheerleaders joined country clubs later in life, and played golf or tennis or pickleball. In the end, most Cheerleaders were rather shallow. Though not his dad or mom, of course.

Some Cheerleaders were also Suntanners, school socialites with the latest hairstyle and clothes. Who wouldn't want to be popular with girls, attend a party every Friday night, go on dates, and hang out at the right places? He was certainly good-looking enough, and his face was clear, so far, knock on wood. No! Thank the Lord, instead of knocking on wood. Always better to pursue the spiritual instead of the superstitious.

But he wasn't completely confident yet about talking to girls. Suntanners were pretty self-assured. He wasn't. For now, of course. Even if they seemed to have the most fun, gathering rays, basking at the pool, not needing Vitamin D supplements, and all that, Suntanners were rather trivial. Imagine holding a serious discussion with a Suntanner on the significance of the

Eskimo Revolution, no less the meaning of existence! Besides, weren't they the most apt of all to develop skin cancer in later life?

He thought about being a Jock, on a sports team. He was coordinated, quick. But the only sport he truly excelled at was Huckle Buckle, and the school had no Huckle Buckle team yet. He was sure on his feet and had good balance. Too bad the school didn't have a gymnastics team either. Although even then, he wasn't sure he'd be thought of as a Jock. Gymnasts were more like dancers than Jocks.

The most popular sports were football and basketball. But he was too light for football and just wasn't very skilled in basketball.

Jocks were admired by other students, but they generally weren't known for being smart or perceptive. And their athletic achievements weren't all that significant in the grand scheme. Athletic prowess did not necessarily translate to winning in life.

He could become a Brain. He was smart enough and liked when people pointed out he was bright. He was the only kid he knew who did cryptic crossword puzzles regularly. Often, he solved brain teasers on the computer, and he imagined taking a Mensa test, correctly answering every question and receiving a standing ovation from other Mensa members, whose huge heads were dominated by protruding foreheads.

But most Brains were nerdy, messy-haired dweebs who later became bald! At least the boys. And yes, Brains could code and knew the meanings of words most others didn't know. But how much of it was just showing off? Brains didn't seem too aware of goings-on in their very own school. And plenty of what they knew wasn't very useful. When Brains used obscure esoteric words, no one but other Brains understood what they wanted to get across! No, Brains were so inconsequential. At least in high school.

It was a little surprising that his professor dad, as a teenager, wasn't a Brain rather than a Cheerleader.

He could become a Hoodlum. Not that he'd do any real damage. He wouldn't violate any of the Ten Commandments, for instance. Maybe some graffiti or vandalism. The Ten Commandments didn't say anything about property damage. But he wouldn't harm any churches. And certainly not hurt people or steal.

There just was something glamorous about Hoodlums. Girls seemed drawn to them. And life was filled with exciting action. Hoodlums did stuff. He wouldn't be sitting around reading or small-talking all day. Hoodlums were highly respected at school.

But while Hoodlums in big cities often were training to become real adult hoodlums, most Hoodlums in Cedar Glen seemed to become auto mechanics or truck drivers when they grew up. Billy had more professional aspirations in mind. And to become a Hoodlum, he'd have to plummet in his studies. No self-respecting Hoodlum went to all his classes and did well on tests.

When you really came down to it, Hoodlums were trivial, at least at the high-school level in Cedar Glen.

He could become a Slapper! He liked loud music, and it might be nice to see what it was like to have hair over just part of his head—the right side, for instance. Slappers were rebels, and they were on it about rebelling, there being lots of things that just stunk in this doggone world we live in today. He'd think about wearing an earring in his nose. He knew one thing. His dad was never man enough to wear an earring when he was a teenager.

But Slappers didn't seem to believe in anything. Except loud music. If you asked one of them, "What do you believe in?" most likely you'd hear the name of a singing group. They didn't even believe in anarchy. Most of them probably would have never heard of "anarchy" if it wasn't for the name of a band of the same name. It was hard to believe you'd end up eminent in any field by being a Slapper. Besides, it must hurt, continually being cuffed in the face like that when buddies greeted you.

Or he could become a Dreamer. There was just something about him meshing with Dreamers. He sometimes liked to be alone, thinking deeply, like that Thoreau guy he'd studied in eighth-grade English class, the one who spent so much time at a lake. Or was it just a pond?

Occasionally, he felt he was almost entering a trance. He liked the idea of others believing he had complex, profound thoughts. Some girls were attracted by the reflections of a moody loner. And he wouldn't have to talk much with them. His normal reticence might even make them think he was more profound than he really was, enhancing his allure. There was something romantic about imaginative Dreamers.

On the other hand, Dreamers seemed the most likely of all the groups to step on their own toes since they didn't watch where they were going. Or become Democrats. Most of the time they weren't *that* creative. And their moodiness could be depressing. Unless they wised up to reality, what kind of lucrative work could Dreamers expect later on in life? All in all, there didn't seem to be much future in being a Dreamer.

Maybe he could be a Goodie, a student who obeyed all the rules and got A's in just about everything and ran for student government. He had always thought of himself as a well-rounded person who would make something of himself one day.

But Goodies were sort of boring. Of course, teachers liked them! But a lot of the kids made snide remarks about them being slick and fake. And besides, they weren't advocates for honest-to-goodness change to improve the world, or even the school. If they had genuine substance, they'd do something radical to shake things up. But they had a stake in keeping the status quo they flourished in, the status quo including becoming crooked politicians. Deep-down, the Goodies were shallow as well, if not immoral and decadent.

Of course, he could become none of these. If he did, he'd be a Nobody, no different from anybody else, one of the crowd that was just there. He'd have no worthwhile identity, not be exceptional in any way, go through life without anyone pointing him out, part of a bland, faceless audience attending the true luminaries. One thing for sure is that *he* wouldn't become a Nobody.

There it was, week two of school, and Billy still hadn't decided on the type of teenager. He knew he had to pick one. He probably couldn't do a combination. Whoever heard of a Goodie-Hoodlum, for instance? They didn't exist in high school. Maybe in the adult world, where organized crime required attorneys, and embezzlers thrived. But not at Cedar Glen High!

Thinking about what his friends were doing wasn't very helpful. Gary was clearly a Jock, Bruce was a Dreamer, Todd was a Slapper. It was sort of sad to realize the four of them might never have much in common ever again.

Romero, of course, was a Goodie. Billy realized he himself used to be a Goodie, but this time around he wanted to be something different. He reveled in teachers liking him. But that was last year, before he was in high school and a real teenager.

As Billy lay back on his pillow, reflecting, his mom entered his room, politely knocking on his door beforehand, and said, "Hi, Billy. You seem to be thinking about something."

"Yeah!"

"It sounds pretty serious."

"Yeah," he agreed.

"Sometimes it's hard to think and get the answer," she asserted.

"I know."

"Sometimes you think and think, and it doesn't do any good," she pointed out.

"Uh-huh."

"Well, I'm going now," she declared, and left the room, gently shutting the door behind her.

"Thanks, Mom," Billy shouted as the door closed, appreciative that she'd led him to the insight of who he wanted to be. He could always count on his mom!

For some reason he couldn't figure, it had come to him, just like that, when she was speaking. He needed to identify what he really wanted. And ever so clearly, he visualized himself climbing atop the Human Pyramid. Yes, maybe cheerleading was once associated more with girls than guys. But nowadays cheerleaders had to be athletic. He was nimble, loved to climb, and he was light enough that his weight wouldn't topple the rest of the pyramid. He saw himself atop the pyramid, waving to the crowd magnanimously, wallowing in his accomplishment!

Tomorrow he'd go to Cheerleader Squad tryouts!

Billy wondered whether he should tell his family about his decision. But, no! He was a teenager, and parents didn't have to know everything going on in a teenager's life! It was anti-teenage morality and scruples to spill important decisions to parents.

Besides, his sister Susie might proclaim that cheerleading was solely a girl's job. What did she know? She was one of those Suntanners who dumbly refused to use sunblock.

He knew better. Maybe girl cheerleaders do sissy stuff, like punch pom-poms into the air and yell nonsense like "Boom-bah-sis-boom-bah." But boy cheerleaders nowadays were athletic—climbing, tumbling, balancing kids standing on you while keeping your balance. When he was a kid, had he ever fallen off a log, or the top of a wall, or his bike? Never!

In addition to going to Cheer tryouts, Billy thought he could also become a Slapper. So, before school the next morning, with some, but not enough, misgivings, he went to his friend Todd's house. They found scissors, and before you knew it, Billy had fuzz on the left side of his head, with the long hair on the right side tied into a ponytail by a string of rawhide.

Todd said "Congratulations" just before he slapped Billy hard, but not too hard, on the cheek.

At school his new hairstyle got mixed reactions. Some kids just laughed when they saw him. Others, like Romero, merely shook their heads. But a few came over and slapped his face, then gave him a hug, greeting him in Slapper comradeship. "Way to blankety-blank go!" said the encouraging Pignose before delivering a huge open slap to Billy's cheek.

Cruel Martin, known for mistreating cats, asked if he planned to go to the Mass Massacre concert that weekend. Trashhead Annie offered to take him to a jeweler to get his nose pierced but continued, "Or, I can do it for you. It doesn't really hurt. Much. But we'll have to buy a training ring so you don't get infected."

Billy was partially pleased. He had an identity now as a nonconformist, a mutineer against the bland status quo. He'd taken a stand, telling the screwed-up world he wasn't going to go along blindly with society's absurdity.

But on the other hand, he really did want to be a part of the traditional famed Cedar Glen High Human Pyramid! Well, yes! He could do both! No harm in trying!

So, after last period he went to the athletic field, where more than fifty kids were trying out for the Cheerleader Squad. Mrs. Dunkirk and Mr. Carlyle, co-leaders, put the candidates through drills. Billy enthusiastically jumped, followed dance steps, somersaulted, cartwheeled, and stood on his head. He thought his facial expression masked his feeling of looking stupid when shaking pom-poms. Then, they were led inside the gym by Mr. Carlyle, who timed them climbing a twenty-foot rope.

Billy's shinny to the top was the fastest of all. He slid down smoothly, feeling masterful as he dismounted. He thought to himself, "I'm a cinch. I'm the best climber here. Top of the pyramid, here I come!"

When the session was over, Mrs. Dunkirk read the names of those making the cut. Billy waited for his name to be called. He tried to find a pattern as to why some kids were chosen, but couldn't. Obviously, it wasn't in order of rope climb time, nor was it alphabetical. Boy after boy had his name called. He kept waiting. Until she announced, "To all those whose names have not been called, thanks for trying out."

He couldn't believe it! How could they not choose the best climber in school?

As the teachers walked off, after announcing practice would begin the next afternoon, Billy caught up with Mr. Carlyle. "Excuse me, Mr. Carlyle. I'm Billy Harrington. A mistake may have been made. I didn't hear my name read. I was the fastest rope climber, and I can tumble."

The teacher said, "No mistake was made, Billy. Athletic ability is just one component of what we're looking for. We're also looking for character, someone who moms with small kids could point to and say, 'I want my kid to be like that.' Your hair, Billy, indicates that you are not the type of person those moms are looking for. Of course, you may try again next year!"

A shaken Billy thought, "It's unconstitutional to reject kids as cheerleaders because of hairstyle! It tramples on First Amendment free speech! My new hairstyle puts me in a protected class, protected by the Constitution." But then he figured he wouldn't get much support, even from his own family, for a lawsuit. So, he benched that idea.

He kept his baseball cap pulled down over his head the rest of the afternoon and evening, so no one in his family was aware of his new hairstyle. He also planted on the cap when he woke in the morning and wore it through breakfast.

When Billy arrived at the schoolyard before classes began, he took off his cap, exposing his new hairstyle. But no one came by to slap him. Not Todd, not Pignose, not Trashhead Annie, not Cruel Martin. And Raw Meat Gus, the leader of the Slappers, turned his back in avoidance when Billy came over. So, Billy didn't get the chance to slap a face or get his own face slapped. The ignored Billy *did* feel his face was slapped, but only in a manner of speaking.

On the way to first period Billy jogged to Todd and asked, "What gives? How come nobody's coming over to slap me? Everyone's avoiding me?"

Todd peered around to make sure no one else heard, then informed him, "We heard you tried out for the Cheerleaders yesterday. Slappers don't do that! The guys figure you obviously weren't cut out to be a Slapper! So, decide what you want to be, and when you've got your mind made up to be a real Slapper, see me. Maybe you can do penance, or something!"

Through the rest of the school day Billy spoke with few fellow students. The Slappers had nothing to do with him, and Billy was sure some friends were avoiding him because he looked like a Slapper. Well, maybe they weren't true friends, after all.

He was a boy of no world.

The only person greeting him was Joannie, that Nobody girl he sometimes caught unexpectedly walking behind him, who said, "Hi, Billy."

It wasn't much comfort, a Nobody like that saying hello to you, he thought, while minding manners, he grunted acknowledgment to her. She was real pretty, though.

Once home, later, he had an idea. He set his books down, pulled out scissors from a drawer, and hustled to his parents' bathroom. Neither of them was home. He stood over the sink, raised the scissors, looked in the mirror, and lopped off all the hair he could hold in his hand. After further pruning himself, leaving uneven stubble, he wrapped a towel around his neck, washed the top of his head with soap and warm water, and lathered up his skull with his dad's kiwi-scented shaving cream. He took a razor from a drawer. If he had no hair at all, he couldn't be confused with a Slapper. He certainly wouldn't be seen as a Dreamer, a Brain, a Suntanner, or any other group known to Cedar Glen High students. He'd at last be different! A true teenager!

Of course, he'd never shaved before. But how hard could it be?

He set the blade against his flesh and pulled forward. He examined the blade. It contained flecks amid a clod of white cream. He did it again. This time amongst flecks and shaving cream there was some red. But it didn't hurt. So, he continued shaving. And soon he was the owner of one completely bald skull, which contained eight small gouges that didn't hurt.

He washed his head and went to study in his room, where he stayed until dinner. The rest of his family was already seated when he came out. Susie suppressed a giggle. Andrew suppressed outright laughter. His gawking dad suspended heaping mashed potatoes upon his plate as he suppressed incredulity. His mom suppressed outright consternation but still managed to say, "Billy, this is quite an eye-opener ..." before Billy interrupted, announcing, "I have made a statement, and I don't want to hear a word about it."

His family respected his wishes, and the meal was eaten along with discussion having nothing to do with Billy's stark head. A few times Billy gave an opinion that no one agreed with, but none of them dared to argue.

The next morning, a bare-headed Billy entered the schoolyard, hardly knowing what might go down. It was a bright, sunny morning in Cedar Glen, and light shined on his head, even with the sun still low in the sky. He said to himself, "I don't care what they think. I'm making a statement, and that's all there is to it."

A girl named Sharon, who he recognized as a Suntanner leader, sauntered over. She had the latest hairstyle—well maybe the second latest—and the latest store-bought raggedy jeans with holes. She exclaimed, while staring at Billy's head, "Wow! That's cool! Say, how would you like to come to the barbecue we're having this weekend? It's finally the end of SPF Month, you know."

Along came Peter, a Dreamer, in authentic-from-use raggedy jeans, who said, "That's cool! You must think some deep thoughts with that head. And you've got to be creative to shave yourself like that. Why not join our Creative

Writing Club?"

Garth, a nose tackle on the football team, came by and said, "Hey, man! Your head's cool! From far away it looked like you were wearing a football helmet. Why not try out for the team?"

Later, one of the thick-bespectacled Brains came by. "You appear the coolest of contemporary brainiacs. Our Phrenology Club meets Fridays, and I'd utterly savor running my fingers across your powerful lobes to read your personality. Just ask for Anna Spaghetti. That's me. Anna Spaghetti."

Billy thought her name would be really easy to remember because he had a cousin named Anna.

Tony, a Hoodlum in a black motorcycle jacket, neared him and said, "Man, that's the coolest do I ever saw at this high school. And I've been here six years. We're going to trash some lawns later, and drink some illegal beers. Want to join us?"

Romero, his old Goodie pal, approached. "Billy, you are cool. You look mature beyond your years. Are you interested in joining the service fraternity with me?" Billy considered, then rejected, the possibility Romero was putting him on.

Later, Raw Meat Gus approached, slapped Billy hard on both cheeks, and for good measure butted Billy's forehead with his own. Then he told him, "That's the coolest head in school! I love your scabs! Man, I want to see you at the Mass Massacre concert. Be there!"

Mr. Carlyle, on yard duty, came over and said, "I see you've come to your senses and gotten an acceptable haircut. If you're still interested, show for Cheerleader Squad practice today."

Everybody wanted him. He could be anything he desired. He had his choice of not one, not two, but seven different worlds, or was it six, or eight? It was hard to keep track.

Joannie ambled toward him and spoke with a shy smile, "Hi, Billy." He waited for her comment about his head, but she merely continued on.

"What world does she come from?" he thought.

At first Billy glowed in his mentalized notoriety. But after a while he told himself, "This is all foolishness and folly. I've decided just what I'm going to be. A Nobody. They're the only ones smart enough not to fawn all over me. I don't want to be in any group that cares for me only because I shaved my head. I'm much more level-headed than that. In a manner of speaking."

But he decided to show up at Cheerleader Squad practice later. After all, he still wanted to be the boy who climbed to the top of the Human Pyramid. That was the real Billy Harrington!

And just then, Andrew stormed in the room singing "Death to The Skeletons," the hit song that first took Mass Massacre to stardom. Andrew hadn't realized that Billy, eyes closed, was still having a sweet dream and was now startled awake.

"Sorry, bro," Andrew told him, the 'bro' actually being true in this case.

Billy's sweet dreaming had been close to the surface and vivid. So, Billy could recall much of what he'd been fantasizing. He felt the top of his head, and thankfully his hair was still there.

The school did indeed have a Huckle Buckle team. There was a real girl named Joannie, who'd been nice to him for a few years and was becoming a special friend. There was a Cheerleader team, though their pyramid was three tiers tall, not four.

And some of the types of groups really existed, though not with formal group names. For example, hoodlum-type kids don't want to be known as "Hoodlums," which sounded cheap. Most preferred the term "Undocumented Villains."

And specific group members meeting Billy in his reverie didn't exist, though people *like them* did.

Billy knew his sweet dreaming was so colorful that he might write it down one day, maybe in a Creative Writing class where there'd probably *not* be a girl named Anna Spaghetti.

A Family Affair

Later in the evening, having skipped dinner, I was lying in bed, running through my messed-up mind how I should handle the next morning's meeting with Joannie, when I was interrupted by my dad knocking on the door, then calling my name.

"Uh-oh," I anticipated, wary of his reaction to the news I was virtually certain my mom had delivered to the family. I had hoped he'd wait until at least after I finished my planning for tomorrow, which was taking longer than I figured.

I called, "Come in," in what I thought was a barely hearable voice, but one apparently loud enough, for the door slowly pivoted, and Dad strode in and sat in the chair near the bed.

Stoically, I awaited his stern lecture, his declaration of disappointment in me, his assertion that by not thinking, I'd made a shambles of my life and embarrassed the family.

He reached over, cradled the bowl of his unlit pipe in one hand, a pipe he bought at another yard sale, patted me once hard on the shoulder with the other hand, and to my surprise, broke into a broad smile. So, he was going to laugh at me, that my life was a joke. I wasn't expecting that. A lecture yes, but not an ironic, jokey sermon that victimized me.

"Congratulations, Billy! Well, I guess this makes you a man! You know, it's not every male that can reproduce. Some men just can't do it. That's why there are sperm banks, Billy! Oh! I know it's not quite the timing you might have chosen. But it's something! It's something. I remember how I felt when I first learned your mom was pregnant with Susie, and then with you and Andrew. Each time it was quite a thrill. Of course, we were married then, and we wanted a family. So, it wasn't a Whoopsie-Doopsie. Your timing's off a little, but at least you know you can do it! It runs in the family, Billy. Why I remember your great-uncle Waldo fathered eleven kids, and his dad sired thirteen. Of course, they could use extra hands on the farms they ran. In those days a man and his wife were admired for having large families. It was before the environmentalists started shaming those with more than two kids for depleting the earth's resources. Why, if it wasn't for your mother agreeing with those whiny Democrat earth savers, you might have had six or seven more brothers and sisters, Billy."

I shuddered at the thought of sharing a room full of bunk beds with a slew of siblings.

"How are you coming along?"

"I have a few things to work out, but coping fine."

"That's my boy! Congratulations again."

And as he left the room without a word of censure, he instead informed me, "Passing down the creation of children, as I've done with you and your siblings, far outweighs my being branded a fogey by imbeciles in some circles."

A few minutes after he left, Susie, in a light pink robe and matching slippers, padded through the doorway self-consciously and sat next to my bed, a very unusual occurrence. I couldn't remember the last time she'd visited my room. Her face had a modest flush, taking on the cast of her robe, and she smiled nervously. She balanced her hands on her spread knees and cleared her throat while leaning forward. She was more ill at ease than I was, and I was the one with the problem.

"Hi, Billy. It must be rough, going through this. Can I share something with you? A few years ago, my period was late, and I was certain I was pregnant. I thought I'd go nuts. I felt so ashamed. I wondered if I'd have to quit school, if I'd ruined my life, the whole Whoopsie-Doopsie dance you're probably going through."

"I sort of am, like you," I confessed. "Except about the period part. Boys don't have …"

"I know that. I got an A in biology last term. Billy, I never told anyone in the family about my missing it, and I'm trusting you won't pass this on to Mom and Dad. But you're my little brother, and I wanted to tell you everything will work out okay. It turned out my period showed up a week late, and since then I've sworn off sex without protection. Maybe the same thing will go down with Joannie. Periods can be temperamental. But even if it doesn't and she really is expecting, you're the sort of person who can figure out the right thing to do. Sleep well, brother."

She blew me a little kiss before leaving. If she'd hugged me, I wouldn't have minded, though I think she thought I would've.

Soon Andrew breezed in, exhausted from the latest in a series of Huckle Buckle games, and began to undress. He tossed each piece of clothing into the air, sometimes over his head, sometimes to the side, once behind his back, and yawningly told me, "Heard you knocked up Joannie. Monster Whoopsie-Doopsie! Nice girl. I like her a lot. Tell her I said so. Oh, also, tell her I say hello."

Like, in Andrew's mind, being knocked up was almost an everyday occurrence.

Still in his undershorts, Andrew plopped down into bed, shrouded his body with the sheet and blanket, covered his head with the pillow, and within thirty seconds began to snore. Somehow, Andrew's seemingly random clothes-flinging resulted in their accumulation in a neat pile at the foot of his bed. It always amazed me!

Reviewing the evening, I realized my family was full of encouraging intentions and refreshing surprises.

The Seedy Part of Town

In the cool stillness of his dark bedroom, where the shadows were all familiar, Billy stared upward, perplexed. Just who was that lady with the red rose pinned to her sweater, the heavy woman in the black beret? The answer was so close, but he just couldn't find it.

He saw her on the trip to the seedy part of town he and his family took earlier that sunny autumn Sunday afternoon, one of those educational trips his dad insisted would "broaden experience." Usually, their educational trips meant a visit to the country, a museum, or an art gallery. Like that.

Once, his mom and dad tried to broaden their three kids by having them spend a whole weekend watching only programs on the Public Television channel. But the kids' "I'm so bored" protests were so vehement that his mom and dad knew never to do that again. Billy suspected his parents also had been totally bored, despite his dad being a college professor and his mom a librarian.

This trip was of a different sort—a visit to the not-so-nice … well, he had to admit—the seedy part of Cedar Glen. His dad had pronounced, "We live in a great section of town. We have friendly neighbors, the houses are fine-looking, and we have sufficient funds to pay our bills, thank the Lord. It's important for you children to learn that not everyone lives as well as we do. Today we're going to visit a dingier part of this city so you can develop appreciation for where your mother and I chose to raise you rascals."

Billy thought it was a bit odd, at fifteen, to be called a "little rascal," but decided the minor slander wasn't worth complaining about.

One of the first places they saw was the mission where homeless people stood in line to be served soup. Billy knew that when not in line, the unfortunates drank other sorts of beverages.

"These people drink too much wine," his teetotaler dad pointed out. "Very little for sacramental purposes. Fortunately, the mission provides beverages like good, wholesome soup."

"Soup's a food, dear, not a beverage," corrected his mom.

"That depends," interjected Susie, now in her first year at Cedar Glen College, where her father taught. "Soup with ingredients that can be eaten with a fork is defined as a food. On the other hand, soup without such ingredients comprises a beverage. Vegetable soup, therefore, is a food, while tomato soup is a beverage. So, Mom and Dad, you're both right."

Smug Susie was very pleased with herself. Listening to his sister, Billy pondered, if this is what college students were like, maybe he'd have a career at the gas station. His younger brother Andrew, who also thought his sister ridiculous, asked her, "Did you take a course in Soupology? Maybe you'll become a dietitian one day. Besides, who cares?"

Through the large SUV windows, Billy observed raggedy, sometimes shoeless men and women, often weaving unsteadily. A few were in pairs, but most were alone. Others sat vacantly or slept on the sidewalk. Some people were probably in those tents, although he didn't know for sure since they'd be indoors.

Unlike his own spotless neighborhood, the streets were littered with junk, glass shards, and empty bottles and beer cans. Billy supposed people in this area obviously weren't much for recycling. A derelict pulled beer cans from a trash bin but probably was less interested in saving the planet than in collecting change to buy his next drink.

"This is disgusting," said a repugnant Susie, while wide-eyed Andrew exclaimed, "I've never seen so many drunks in one place in my life."

Billy, expecting a moral tale from the mouth of his father, asked, "Dad, are you going to tell us about one of your relatives who ended up in this part of town?"

"No, Billy. As far as I know, no member of the Harrington clan has ever ended up here. I can't speak for your mother's side of the family, of course. Molly, how about you?"

"No comment," Molly said.

As their vehicle paused at a red light, Billy noticed a heavyset woman with a blotched pink face and squinting eyes standing on the sidewalk, waiting for the light to change. She wore a long black skirt and two sweaters, on the outer of which was pinned a red rose. Straggly long hair drooped listlessly from under her black beret. He couldn't tell her age. Maybe twenty-five. Fifty-five? In between? One smudged hand held tightly to an overloaded shopping cart. Her other hand grasped a pint of some brown substance. She took a swig.

She seemed familiar; he'd seen her before. But he couldn't place her. Just who was she?

Further on, they toured streets where women in very short skirts with lots of makeup walked slowly up and down. They appeared to Billy to be very friendly, as they simply walked up to drivers just to say hello. In fact, one of them came over to their SUV when it was stopped at a light.

"Hello, Professor Harrington," she said to his dad.

She didn't say hello to his mom, though, who sweetly asked his dad, "Who was that, dear?"

"A student doing primary participant observer research for an anthropology class," he replied.

"Seems pretty old for a student," remarked his mom.

Billy, not completely naïve, suspected the woman was more than just a student. He had an inkling of how she knew his dad but tabled it as unlikely. Well ... maybe! He wondered if his mom had the same notion.

Billy's dad must've been distracted by traffic, or something, for just then, he mistakenly put his foot on the gas pedal. The SUV lurched ahead, crashing into a truck waiting to turn. Although no one was hurt, the front of the SUV had a big dent, and for a few minutes the Harrington family, examining the damage, was the subject of curious study by residents of the run-down neighborhood.

Yes, damage to the SUV, but who was the red rose woman?

They left the area soon after, without directly mingling with its inhabitants, the SUV serving as a mobile curtain of division. Billy thought of that woman on the ride home, and the rest of the day, even during dinner, and still now, flat on his back in bed. Did she sleep on the streets, or have a bed? Why was she on his mind? How did he know her?

This bothersome sort of thing had gone down with him before—the teasing elusiveness of being unable to recall a particularly appropriate word, or the name of some person he just knew. He figured that maybe if he didn't think about her, but allowed his subconscious mind to cook, before you knew it the answer would just be there. So, Billy tried to not think about her for a while, wondering instead, "I know there's a word for trying to remember something but can't. But I can't remember that word."

But intentional mental avoidance didn't work either. The woman kept popping up in his mind.

Then he determined what he'd do the very next day and quickly fell asleep.

Classes seemed interminable, and he paid little attention to teachers, as he considered the trek he'd go on later. In math class he thought, "Of what importance is the Pythagorean formula when people are homeless on the streets? Is a hypotenuse really as important as having a bed to lie on?"

In history class he wondered, "Why is it important to know the names of 19th-century presidents, in order, when some people don't have enough to eat?" Who really cared about Millard Fillmore, James Polk, and Abraham Lincoln? Well, maybe people did care about Lincoln, mostly what currency he appeared on. Okay, I suppose also which memorial he sat on, and whose face was on some mountain, and who was named after a city in Nebraska. But not the gosh darn others!

In language class he considered, "How will I ever be able to learn French if my memory is such that I can't remember who that lady is? And why is it even important to learn French with all the misery on the shabby side of town where almost no one speaks that language, aside from knowing that 'Si' means yes in French."

No! "Oui" was correct. But at first, making that mistake unnerved Billy.

After school, Billy called in sick to his convenience store job and hopped on the bus to the run-down area, feeling both the excitement of adventure and a little frightened. He'd never visited such a precarious area by himself.

After taking a moment to ponder why buses didn't have safety belts, Billy felt glad his parents had taken him to the seedy part of Cedar Glen. It felt satisfying, in a way, to feel guilty, something like how muscle stiffness after unfamiliar exercise felt good, except it was his character, not his body, afflicted now. From now on, he'd never leave food on his plate. He'd take smaller portions, so he'd have less to throw in the trash. He'd contribute frequently to food banks. He'd register as a Democrat when he reached voting age.

Leaving the bus, he marched to where he saw her yesterday. At the corner, a derelict approached cars at red lights with a squeezable bottle and a rag, his tools for cleaning windshields. Most drivers shut their windows and ignored him when he advanced for a tip. Billy knew he wouldn't like that window-washing job. He couldn't take the rejection.

While the light was green, Billy reluctantly asked the derelict, and then an old unshaven man sipping from a bottle in a brown bag, about the woman. Neither knew anything about her.

The same woman who said, "Hello, Gordon," to his dad yesterday, stood on the opposite corner. She wore stockings like a net you might see to catch fish, and an even shorter skirt than yesterday. Billy felt himself becoming a bit warmer, probably from all the walking he'd done. He crossed over and introduced himself as Billy Harrington, Gordon Harrington's son.

When he asked if she knew the woman with the black beret, she answered in a low, velvety voice that Billy found intriguing.

"I wish I could help you, Billy," she said. "Your dad's been helping me out with my anthropological research. I'm a working girl making my way through grad school, a participant observer here, integrating into the community. Expect to get my Master's once I've submitted my thesis in a few days. Real sorry I can't help you, Billy. Well, ciao."

Billy thought she sure was flash! Saying "ciao" instead of goodbye! While Billy briefly wondered about his dad helping her, his concentration turned back to the woman he was searching for.

Soon a policeman ambled past. Billy figured he was gazing about for muggers, shoplifters, and other forms of riffraff and law-breaking lowlifes. He wasn't looking for loiterers or passed-out drunks, though. Billy asked him about the woman in the black beret and shopping cart. The policeman referred him to a place a half block down. "Fellow there at the Christian Science Reading Room knows most folks."

"Thanks, officer," offered Billy, thinking, "I'm glad the police are always there when you really need them to give you directions."

A *Christian Science* Reading Room! Billy recognized a good omen when he heard one. A *Christian Science* Reading Room. Not a reading room of some other religion. Actually, though, he'd never heard about reading rooms of other religions. Maybe there were, maybe there weren't.

At the Reading Room, a huge man told Billy his name was Roland. Billy wondered if Roland was the man's first or last name. He thought it unfair when people whose names could either be a first or last name didn't let you know which one it was. Name play reminded him a little, sort of, when he was back in nursery school, where some people working there were called by their first name, like Miss Bonnie, and others called by their last name, like Miss Maplezewski.

"I'm looking for a heavy woman pushing a shopping cart and wearing a black beret. Do you have any idea who she is?"

"With a red rose pinned to her clothing?"

"Yes! Yes!"

"Don't know her name, but I know where you probably can find her. Two blocks down, to the park, at the sandbox."

Suddenly, Billy knew who the lady was! At least he thought he did. If Roland was correct, Billy thought he'd give some thought to returning to the Christian Science fold.

But when he thought more about it, he realized that true devotion to a religion should be based on theological considerations, not just that someone did you a favor.

Anyway, sure enough, she was there, on a park bench, watching children play. The same kindly smile he remembered. Her face still round, she still with a large rump. It was her, all right!

He sat on the other side of the bench. She paid him no attention and giggled when a little boy fell on his butt and laughed. After a few minutes—"Hello, Miss Bonnie," he said softly.

She looked around, startled, and her laughter vanished. Nobody had called her Miss Bonnie for years, ever since … ever since …

"Who are you?" she asked.

"I'm Billy Harrington. I was one of your students. You were the nicest teacher I ever had. You taught me to play fair, to share, to clean up a mess, and put things back where I found them. Neatness counts, you always said. I wouldn't be the same person I am today without you, Miss Bonnie."

She trembled, her eyelids closed, and a tear drifted down her cheek.

"But, Miss Bonnie, why are you here depriving other preschoolers of such a fine teacher?"

"Billy. Billy. Of course. When you graduated you said you'd come back to visit. Lots of my preschoolers said that. But none ever did, except you. When you were in third grade. I was so proud to show you off to my little preschoolers."

"Miss Bonnie, will you have dinner with my family? Come back with me on the bus. I'll pay your fare."

"Oh, I'm not quite dressed for dinner," she smiled nervously.

"Don't worry. The thrift store just around the block is sure to have something. Besides you don't have to be the wife of Pythagoras to eat with the Harringtons," he said, immediately regretting this unnecessary flaunting of knowledge.

"I'd love to. I haven't eaten a home-cooked meal in years, and I would enjoy visiting with you and your family."

Billy sensed she was unsure who Pythagoras was but decided not to ask. After all, nursery school geometry extended only to placing different shaped pegs into holes.

"But I don't think they'll let me take my cart on the bus."

"I have the feeling you won't be needing your shopping cart anymore," he responded, and gave it a push with his foot. It rolled away across the path and clanked to rest against a tree.

The pair walked to the thrift store and bought, for just a few dollars, two new outfits. She threw tattered clothing in the trash. But, at Billy's insistence, she retained the beret, unpinned the rose from her discarded sweater and pinned it on the lapel of her new blazer.

"If you need to shower, you can do it at our house," Billy told her on the way to the bus stop.

"No need for that. I washed at the supermarket restroom this morning."

Neither talked much on the bus. They arrived at the Harringtons just as dinner was to be served. Billy's mom was ready to scold him for being late but held off when she saw he had a guest. Billy asked his family, "Remember, everybody? My preschool teacher—Miss Bonnie!"

In mid-reach his dad stopped spooning mashed potatoes from the serving dish and just stared at her. His mom gasped, then rushed over to give Miss Bonnie a big hug, gushing, "My goodness word. Miss Bonnie. How very nice to see you! You were such a wonderful teacher for Billy, and then Andrew. But when it came time for Andrew to visit you when he was in third grade, you were no longer there. They never would say why, though. I must have asked Miss Maplezewski three times, and each time she changed the subject, denying me an answer."

Andrew strode to Miss Bonnie and gave her a hug, surprising the rest of the family no end. Andrew hadn't hugged anyone for years.

"Billy found me," Miss Bonnie said. Ever since I saw him this afternoon, I just knew things were going to straighten out. It was as if a savior had arrived."

"The only true savior is the Lord, Miss Bonnie. Not Billy, even though he is my son, just like Jesus was the son of God. Still is. But I know what you mean. So, I won't think less of you and damage your reputation, if you get my meaning." That was Billy's dad.

"I'm so glad to see you all. You too, Mr. Harrington."

Billy asked, "Would you like to use the bathroom, Miss Bonnie? We have two. They each have just one toilet, though." He wondered if anyone else would remember the bathroom in Miss Bonnie's classroom held four toilets.

"No, thanks. But I would like to bite into some of that fine roast beef," she said.

"Sit here, Miss Bonnie," his mom said, pointing to Billy's usual seat, then asking him to bring another chair for himself.

Once Miss Bonnie was seated, Billy's dad picked up his wineglass and offered, "Some grape juice, Miss Bonnie? Molly and I partake every evening at dinner. Keeps the blood moving, as they say. We're practicing Christian Scientists, you know, always been quite religious, obeying all the commandments. All of them. We pride ourselves on living a principled life. (Beat) Well, there is no commandment that says 'Thou shalt not drink alcoholic beverages.' But we refrain anyway."

His dad's hand was shaking, and some of the juice spilled onto his mom's lace tablecloth. But he continued, "My great-grandfather's cousin Augustus— everyone just called him Gus—why he ..."

"Thank goodness we're having white grape juice instead of purple grape juice tonight," his mom interrupted, dabbing the mess on the lace with a napkin.

His dad was behaving preposterously, thought Billy. He hardly knew Miss Bonnie. He'd only been to Cedar Glen Nursery a few times, to drop off forms at the office.

Miss Bonnie responded to his dad's grape juice offer. "Thank you, I will, Mr. Harrington," and poured herself a glass from the carafe. Then, after she served herself portions of roast beef, mashed potatoes, and green beans, she informed his mom, "It doesn't surprise me one bit to learn Miss Maplezewski didn't tell you what happened. If you like, I'll tell you now."

"Say, isn't this good roast beef? Where did you buy it, Molly?" interrupted his dad.

"At the market, dear. But Miss Bonnie was about to tell us something."

Miss Bonnie continued, "My problems started when I caught Miss Maplezewski sneaking a kiss with the father of a former student. A married man! I didn't do it intentionally. One morning I opened the supply closet to get glue so my kids could make a color paper pizza, and there they were in the back of the closet, smooching away. I pretended I hadn't seen them and walked away muttering to myself as if I'd forgotten something, but Miss Maplezewski knew I had."

"Who was the married man?" asked his curious mom, ever alert for a juicy scandal.

"That's not important now," Miss Bonnie replied. "A few weeks later I began feeding incoming students food they were allergic to. I couldn't figure out how I made those mistakes. It occasionally happened before, if paperwork was lost. But never three times in one month. After the third time, I was fired. I can't blame the school's owners. Some kids got really sick.

"It was only years later that I caught on. Miss Maplezewski forged Child Description Forms so I'd feed those kids food they were allergic to. She hid the real form, which she pulled out when the kids got sick. The parents complained, and the blame was on me. They let me go.

"I was devastated. I loved being a nursery schoolteacher, stimulating imaginations, helping kids learn, just watching them be cute. And now I lost my job, couldn't find another one, and life became, well, meaningless.

Years later, when I figured out what happened, I told the owner, and he fired Miss Maplezewski but wouldn't rehire me. I didn't blame him. I wouldn't hire someone with a drinking problem. And so, life went on, or rather, didn't. I lost my apartment, my car, my clothes, my savings. For the past I-don't-know-how-many years, I've been living on the streets. And then Billy came along today. Now I feel more alert than I've felt for years.

"Interesting tale, isn't it, Dr. Harrington?" she said, setting her gaze on him.

Almost a week later, in the late afternoon, Billy, not working at the market that day, bused to the university and dropped in to see his dad, figuring they'd have a good chat. There were certain things he wanted to ask about. Definite man-to-man things.

As he got close to his dad's office, Billy saw the participant observer from the rough part of town enter the room. He stood just outside the office listening, peeking in. She handed his dad a document, said she was submitting her anthropological research thesis for his review, and thanked him for being her advisor. They shook hands before she left, and, as she exited the room, she noticed Billy. She just said, "Hi."

Billy saw she wasn't wearing stockings that looked like a net.

And, oh! His dad's new assistant was hard at work at her administrative assistant job in the English Department of Cedar Glen University. She was a former nursery schoolteacher.

Back at the Lake

Hedges and flowers stood tall and lawns glistened in the stillness of early morning, just past dawn. Trees seemed greener, their leaves hanging motionless. More self-assured than I'd been the day before, I honked once, and Joannie promptly marched from her house to the car, haughtier, less waif-like, than a few days ago. Aside from the muted "Hi's" we exchanged when she first got to the car, we were quiet, each intently watching the road directly ahead, until Joannie broke the silence by asking where we were going.

"The lake," I announced. I glanced over and noticed her squinting, quizzically examining me. I intentionally drove faster than I normally did, though not unsafely, given the absence of traffic, imagining I was a NASCAR driver out for a pleasure jaunt. It was important to let Joannie know I was far different from the other day, to present the impression of mastery. My family, and my own consideration of who I was, made me confident that I'd do what needed to be done, said what needed to be said.

We parked. For a while I took her hand, surprising her, and strode off along the path to the lake and then the sinewy trail on the lake bank. When the trail narrowed, I led, occasionally looking back to assure she wasn't lagging far behind. The crunching of shoes against pine needles and pebbles intermingled with harsh chirps of stellar jays. The slanting early-morning sun raised small wisps of steam from dew-beaded rocks and promised a warm day. Finally, we reached the toppled tree we'd stopped at a few days earlier. As if I was in authority, I firmly requested, "Joannie, please sit down. Either on the grass, or if you like, we both can sit on the tree."

Joannie sat, kneecaps raised, in the same grass area she'd been at the last time. Instead of mounting the tree trunk, I sat beside her, a foot or so away. She stared challengingly, chin up, apprehensive of what I seemed eager to say and perhaps wondering whether the person next to her was indeed the same person who sat next to her the last time they were here.

Just before beginning the speech I'd semi-rehearsed, a dragonfly hovered between us. I shooed it away with flicks of my hand and wondered aloud, "Why do insects have to pester you, just when you're ready for an important discussion?"

"This is their domain, Billy. You're the intruder here," she pointed out.

"Sometimes nature doesn't want to cooperate with your life," I philosophized.

"I know," she agreed, patting her belly.

I cleared my throat, wrapped my fingers around her willowy hand, and began.

"Joannie, you were absolutely right about these tree roots. When you said I resolved my problems because they referred me to my own roots, my instinct was that you'd said something astute. But I didn't want to admit it, either to myself or to you. I became jealous because you could think clearly—more than clearly, ingeniously—while I was mixed-up paralyzed. I was angry at myself for being incompetent and took it out on you. I was downright nasty, and you didn't deserve it. I'm sorry.

"I finally told my mom about our problem, and her advice was basically what you told me—follow the guidance of your roots. She used different words than you but said the same thing. Well, I think I've done that. When I ask myself who is Billy Harrington, I say he's grown to be a person, a man, who appreciates beauty, is loyal to his friends, and lives up to his responsibilities, who doesn't shirk from his duty. He also recognizes who will make him a fine companion, and values intelligence. If you can match my mom's wisdom at your age, you're the kind of person who should be the mother of my baby. I think we should have the baby, and if you'd like, I'd be proud to marry you."

I stared down and picked at the dried grass, satisfied with the performance I'd been anxious about, awaiting her response. Joannie nodded and touched my cheek lightly.

She said, "That's a pretty long-winded speech there, Billy."

"Meant every word."

Although, did I?

I reached for her hand and pressed it against the side of my face. She gently released her hand and addressed me softly, "Billy, thank you for apologizing. It's not always easy to apologize. You've told me how wise I am, how perceptive, and how beautiful. You've examined who you are, and you've found, as I've always known, that the true Billy is someone loyal, who lives up to his responsibilities. He's someone sensitive and kind. And I'm honored that you'd consider me to be your wife."

She paused and briefly gazed down. As she picked up her chin, I saw myself reflected in her eyes' glistening moistness. She continued, "But there are two things you haven't told me, either now or the last time we were here. One is that you want the baby. Not out of duty, or because of your religion, but because you want it. The other thing is that you love me. If you did love me, you would've said it already. I'm glad you didn't say either of those things because it wouldn't have been the true Billy speaking. I know that. If some day you do want a child and grow into love for me, I'd be proud to have you as my husband. But for now, I don't think we should get married or make any commitment to each other except to remain friends."

"Friends?"

"Close friends."

Is that all we are? Were?

"I thought it was my duty not to be selfish," I told her.

"Your duty was to be honest with me," she corrected with a smile.

I bowed my head and pawed the wild grass at my feet.

She went on, "I know the true Billy is someone with plans, who wants a college degree, then a graduate degree, and to do something important. He's not someone who deserves to be tied down, especially with a baby who needs to be loved, not resented. And the fact is, Billy, I feel the same way for myself. I too have career plans. When I have a child, I want it to be someone I love, not someone I can't help but feel will be a detour, an imposition."

I was relieved. If I was being selfish by not wanting a baby, I wasn't alone. If I was being selfish, now that I had a partner, it was more acceptable to be selfish. It crossed my mind that if both of us were selfish, then neither was.

It seemed there was a flaw somewhere in that argument, but I didn't have time just then to think it through.

I asked, "You mean, we don't have to get married, and you'll give the baby up for adoption?"

"We don't have to get married. But Billy, I don't want to have the baby at all. And right now, we're not talking about a baby. In fact, it's even wrong to consider what's inside me a baby at all. Right now, all it is is some living tissue. It has no personality, no will, no distinctive appearance."

Did she really mean that? Hmmm. Some instinct told me she didn't. But still, she said it.

As she stared at me in a brief uncomfortable silence I looked away, thinking that soon the growth inside Joannie would be gone, though all traces of the pregnancy would never be eradicated. I'd never forget this conundrum. I'd always think of what Theodore would look like—sort of like me—and coaching him at Huckle Buckle, helping with his homework, teaching how to deal with bullies. What life is like.

When I looked back at Joannie, I noticed a small flinch accompanied by her eyes sliding to the side, movements only someone who knew her well would detect.

But why? Did she notice something about me that only someone knowing me well would detect? Something even I was not aware of. Was she reading my mind about Theodore?

Or, did she notice something about herself, either definite or a suggestion of a possibility?

Something was going on. But what?

I should've been ecstatic. But I wasn't. I felt Joannie withdrawing from my life, a loosening of our connection.

And there was something else. But what?

I told Joannie, "I imagine the scenario. You going to the clinic with your mom, me not coming, all of us uneasy if I was. You trudging toward the entrance of some nondescript medical building, staring ahead with lifeless eyes, your mom's arm draped over your shoulder. The pivoting glass door soundlessly closing behind you, emphasizing the shutting me out. A few hours later, after the surgery, I'd get a call. You'd tell me, 'The procedure was successful. The deed's done. I'm home, resting comfortably. It's gone.'

"Or even worse, emphasizing the isolation, *your mom* doing the telling: 'The procedure was successful. The deed's done. She's home, resting comfortably. It's gone.'"

It's gone? It?

After I told her what I was imagining, she informed me, "That's a strikingly vivid visualization. But I'm not having surgery. I'm having a medication termination, Billy, which means taking certain pills to end the pregnancy. So many these days are done medically. I already have the prescription. I'm taking the pills on a Friday, so I have the weekend."

I suppose this was a relief. The idea of surgery made me uncomfortable. And she seemed so sure the pills would work.

But there was something ...

At any rate, figuring I should be supportive, or at least make me feel a part of things, I offered, "Do you need any money? I've got a few hundred dollars."

Then I was concerned the offer might seem callous by assuming a monetary contribution would somehow absolve me.

"Don't worry about it, Billy," she assured.

"It would make me feel better. I should pay something. No matter the amount. Something."

"You already have paid," she said, and kissed my cheek. I couldn't quite grasp what she meant, but surely she did. Probably.

When our conversation was done, we sat in silence a long while, holding hands, then returned to Jake's Spirit. Trying to lighten the mood, I commented, "Putting together a wedding with you might've been difficult. Where could we ever find an atheistic rabbi who'd officiate at the wedding of a Christian Scientist?"

"Well, if it all pans out, we have years to work on it."

But I was still troubled, dissatisfied with myself, knowing I was not the forthright person she considered me.

And there was that something … that invisible, hiding from me, something.

Our situation was not yet resolved. I didn't know why, but I knew it was true.

I wondered whether I was now just Joannie's good friend, or whether I was destined to marry her. Or both. I was growing up pretty fast. The years were piling up, a number of them having elapsed in the past few days alone.

Feeling the Spirit

Billy was proud of his new car, although it wasn't exactly a new car, being six years old, and recently bought for him as a sixteenth-birthday gift by his dad. Now that he had real wheels, Billy could go almost everywhere. In the past he'd had similar feelings of great freedom. His travel range exploded when he was one year old and learned to walk. Although not too soon after his walks, he was very tired and had to take a nap. At ten, he got his first two-wheeled bike and was thrilled when he could pedal miles away. But at the end of cycling a long trip, he'd be tired. And he was stuck if it rained.

Now, with a car, he could go a lot further, in most any weather, and even take along some buddies, or his younger brother Andrew, or even a girl. Girls loved driving in cars with boys, especially if they didn't have their own car yet, and the boy wasn't their dad. Like Joannie, his really good friend—well, really more than just another friend—the really pretty girl he sort of really liked, who used to be skinny, but now was filled out curvy and firm, and the one who he'd kissed in the sixth grade to pay for her vote in a class election but now was doing a lot more than kissing with him and didn't ask for more in return.

And he didn't get tired after driving. All he had to do was press his foot down to make the car streak faster and move his arms on that wheel, and the car would go just where he wanted it to go. He also could press the brake when he wanted to slow down or stop altogether.

One place Billy drove to was his baseball games. He was the part-time right fielder for the Diablos, an American Legion team. The first time he drove up to the field at Cedar Glen Park, the guys gathered around his new used car (actually, it wasn't a *new* used car since he didn't have *any* used car before). They asked all sorts of questions, about engine displacement, horsepower, and cylinders, as well as how he got it and how much it cost. He was the first on his team to own a car. Everyone else had to be driven to the game by an adult. He felt really special.

His Blue Blaster, as he called it, had two doors, power steering, power brakes, and a 200-horsepower engine. Newly installed, at his own expense, were a music player with power speakers both front and rear. It was recently painted a dark metallic blue.

Twice a week Billy worked on keeping his car clean and shiny, washing and polishing it in the driveway after school and on the weekends. His dad had counseled the importance of caring for his vehicle, but there was no need, since his car was something very special to Billy, who did not need to be convinced about care and maintenance.

Early one Saturday afternoon in late May, he was in the driveway, having just replaced the oil, and beginning a good wash and wax, when he saw an old man saunter down the sidewalk with a mild limp, someone he'd never seen before. The short, skinny man was impeccably jaunty in his brown fedora and white shirt with a handkerchief tidily folded into the pocket. His neatly trimmed white mustache was pointed at the ends. He was, Billy guessed, seventy years old.

The man passed the driveway and admired, "Howdy, young fella. Nice car." And he continued striding on down the street, with the hitch in his step.

"Thanks," Billy said, and continued hosing.

Sometime later, Billy finished buffing the car with his chamois and, noticing his own reflection, admired its shine. He was sure being responsible, though he knew it was just as important to be a responsible *driver* of a car as well as a responsible washer and waxer. Then Billy noticed the same man walking back toward him. "Howdy, young fella. Looks shiny. Good job!"

Billy reached into the car through an open window to turn off the heavy-beated Mass Massacre he'd been listening to. He folded his chamois and responded, "Thanks. It's my new car. I mean it's used, but it's new to me."

"I remember when I had my first car. It was years and years ago. A Mustang. It was blue too. Say, young fella, what's your name? Mine's Jake." He extended his hand, and Billy took it, saying, "Billy. I live here, with my parents and sister and brother."

"Glad to meet you, Billy. I'm new to the neighborhood. Got here a month ago. Live with my daughter and son-in-law three blocks down. Lived in New York my whole life, before that. Had a little heart problem a couple of months ago, nothing bad, then a little stroke. Except for a slight limp, I'm fine, but my daughter insisted I move in with her."

"This is a great neighborhood," Billy told him.

Jake coughed, then took out a handkerchief to cover his mouth. He reported, "My wife's gone many years. Heart attack too. Doctor says take regular exercise. So, I walk the neighborhood every day. If I don't take my walk, I know—poof, I'm gone. Well, so long fella. See you around. And don't park that car under any birds, you hear?"

As the old man strode away, Billy knew he'd never let himself get a limp from a stroke. He was a Christian Scientist, after all, and prevention was the best medicine, and the next best medicine was prayer. Or was it the other way around? Sometimes he forgot what the readers told him.

Billy entered his house, strode to his bedroom, and dressed in his Diablos uniform. When he returned outside, he tossed his glove, cleats, and cap into the front seat, got in, and drove off. He thought about Jake. He'd never *really* known an old person well before. Both sets of grandparents died before he was born. Some of his teachers were old, but not *that* old. Of course, he'd seen old folks shopping, in the streets and parks, and attending parties for their grandchildren. But that wasn't the same as really knowing them.

He knew some old people were crotchety, and some were wise. But he didn't know—were more of them likely to be crotchety than wise, or vice versa? And was it possible for someone to be *both* crotchety and wise? Or neither. The limited and polite contact he'd had thus far suggested neither. But he wasn't at all sure. A few minutes later he reached the ballfield, where some teammates were already taking fielding practice.

As he slid on his cleats, seated on the first row of the grandstand, his coach came over to remind him it was Scott's turn to play today. Neither boy was one of the better players, and they alternated playing right field, the area balls were least likely to be hit. Billy thought he should be playing ahead of Scott every day. "I'm faster, smarter, and field better. I also get on base more often. The only way he's better is he's stronger, and can hit the ball a longer way, if he gets hold of one. But he strikes out so much, and it's rare he gets hold of one. And I hustle. All the time."

A half hour later the game began. Billy's team won in a 19-1 rout, and he got to play the last two innings but didn't get up to bat. He didn't really feel a part of things.

The following Saturday, the old man, as well-kempt as the previous week, gimped to the driveway and got there just as Billy finished checking the oil. "Howdy, Billy. Say, I wonder if you could do me a favor."

"What's that?" Billy offered, turning down Mass Massacre.

"Could you drive me to an apartment complex a couple of minutes' drive away. I've just got to get there, and my daughter can't take me. I'd really appreciate it. I'd drive myself, except I'm not allowed. In case I get another heart attack behind the wheel and crash," he smiled with embarrassment. Then he coughed into his handkerchief.

"How long will you be there?"

"Maybe ten minutes."

"Then, sure," agreed Billy, "But I've got a baseball game in a couple of hours. Hey, since you won't be very long at the complex, like to come to the game?"

Jake's eyes opened wide. "Sure!" he said with delight.

"Come back here in an hour, then. Meanwhile you can tell your daughter where you'll be."

An hour later, when Billy came from his house in his Diablos uniform, Jake was buffing the front hood with the arm of his jacket, informing Billy, "Howdy. You missed a spot."

Billy backed out of the driveway slowly, put the car in drive, and accelerated gradually. He wasn't one of those foolish boys who needed the attention generated by screeching, suddenly accelerating tires. Those kinds of show-off boys often ended up where he didn't want to end up—in manual jobs at the factory, not in a profession requiring a degree. And their cars ended up in the junkyard sooner than not!

Jake gave Billy directions, then told him, "I'm really appreciative, Billy, really am. I've been feeling low, mighty low. It's a shame when you get old. Nobody wants you. Your children, they've got their own lives. I had a fight with my daughter … not the first one. Told her I was going to move out and find an apartment of my own. And I will. Called the manager this morning, and he told me to come down. It's awfully nice of you to take me there, awfully nice."

"No worries," Billy said.

"Shows you're youthful. Most people my age say 'no *problem.*' Thank God I've got health. And I'm going to move out too. I can take care of myself. Maybe I'll move into an apartment with somebody. Have a roommate. You know, just for companionship. Look, I'm seventy-five years old, and I can take care of myself. It's no good for me there with my daughter, just no good. In the month I've been here, they haven't taken me anywhere, except the market, the doctor, and the pharmacy. Not once. He takes the big car to work, and with the kids, there's never enough room for me in the small one.

"Sorry," Billy commiserated.

"Ah! What's the use? I feel low, and it's a shame, a goddamn shame. I can support myself. Got enough money. Worked for fifty-nine years, since I was sixteen years old, until I had to quit. If she doesn't want me, I'll spend it on myself. It helps to talk to someone and get it off my chest. Thanks for driving me. Listening to me. You know, Billy, you'd probably make a good psychiatrist, listening as you do."

It struck Billy a little peculiar, how the old man ran on all about his life without being asked. He himself wouldn't reveal any problems he was having with his family to a virtual stranger. It wouldn't be surprising if Jake knew something about psychiatrists from visiting them in the past.

Billy wondered why the old man thought he'd make a good psychiatrist. A psychiatrist. Hmmm. Last year someone had said he'd make a good sociologist. The trend seemed quite clear. He'd probably end up in a professional occupation ending in "ist." Which left baseball player out. But he already knew he wasn't cut out to be a professional baseball player. If he couldn't start regularly for the Diablos, what chance did he have to make the roster of the Dodgers or Yankees? But still he was better than Scott!

During his long speech, Jake had coughed several times. Billy told him, "You should take care of that cough."

"Allergies," said Jake, as if that explained everything.

Billy parked in the lot of a large apartment complex stretching a whole block. Jake left the car, said he'd be back in just a few minutes. Billy couldn't make up his mind whether or not Jake was crotchety, wise, both, or neither. It's not always easy to size people up. He wondered whether psychiatrists could size people up quickly because they were trained to do so, or if it came naturally to them. Hey, maybe they faked taking a long time to size people up, so patients had to continue paid "treatment" for that long time. Or maybe it actually did take them a long time. Or maybe they never could, over a long period of remunerated visits, and never admitted it.

As Billy buffed his bumper, ruminating about psychiatrists, Jake returned. The two got back in the car, and the old man began speaking again.

"Nice man, the manager. Building for senior citizens. Don't let in anyone with kids. Keep it clean and safe. Reasonable rent. Says most renters are widows. No one ever moves out. The only time there's a vacancy is when somebody dies who doesn't have a roommate. Maybe I could move in with one of the widows. For companionship, you understand. With my prostate that's all it'd be! Manager suggests I come back every week, hang around the pool. If they know me, they might push me ahead on the waiting list. I met a nice lady there, very nice. We talked a minute or two and got along. Who knows, maybe I'll move in with her one day. With my daughter it's just no good, no good at all. Is this the field? Never knew there was a field here. So big. Look at all those other ballfields too."

Billy felt exhausted, even though he hadn't really done anything strenuous to tire out his body recently. Perhaps he wouldn't become a psychiatrist, after all. He parked the car, and the two of them walked to the ballfield.

Billy left Jake in the stands and jogged to the outfield to shag flies. After a while, he noticed Jake leaning back, his face in the air. A few minutes later Billy again peered into the grandstand and saw the old man motionless, unchanged in position, face bent backwards, arms hanging listlessly to the side. Billy raced in worriedly, hoping the inert Jake was still alive! Just when he reached the old man, Jake opened his eyes, stretched, and said, "It's wonderful, just wonderful, being at the ballpark with the sun on your face."

Billy felt kind of silly, but very relieved Jake was all right.

The game soon began, Billy in right field. His team lost, and he went hitless for the day. On the trip home they both were quiet, Jake even drifting off in a brief nap. Billy pulled into the daughter's driveway, and Jake thanked him.

"I really appreciate your driving me around. You're the best chauffeur I ever had, and I'd be happy to be your passenger any time."

"How about the same time next week?" inquired Billy, masking a slight annoyance with being termed a chauffeur, though he knew Jake was kidding. He much preferred being called a psychiatrist than a chauffeur, even though he suspected he'd never be one. At least not the chauffeur.

"I'll be there," Jake asserted.

The following week, a dapper Jake arrived at Billy's driveway a half hour before they were scheduled to leave, a clean towel in hand, a Yankees cap on his head that didn't quite go with his brown slacks, a white shirt, and suspenders. "Brought my tools. Thought I'd help you buff."

"Just in time. I just finished checking the oil and water, and now it's time to wash the Blue Blaster. Don't know if I'll have time to wax her today, though."

The two washed the car, dried her off, and as Billy went in to change into his Diablos uniform, his dad came to his room.

"I see Jake's been helping you with the Blue Blaster. I'm glad you have a friend who's old. I regret your grandparents didn't live long enough to see you and your sister and brother. Your mom and I will be old someday, but by then you'll be all grown up. But Billy, not all old people are the same. Some are wise and some are crotchety, and some are both, and some are neither. Let that be a lesson to you, my boy."

"I already figured that out, Dad," Billy advised his father.

"Now, even though your grandparents didn't make it to being old, your great great-grandparent Cyrus, who never shaved, got so old that his beard ..."

"Can you tell me later? I've got a game to go to."

At the apartment complex, Billy again waited as Jake entered the grounds. Ten minutes later Jake came out, and they motored mindfully to the baseball field.

It was Billy's turn to sit out, and he didn't get in the game at all. On the way home, he tried to act cheery. His team won, but still he didn't quite feel a part of the victory.

When Billy reached dropped off the old man at his daughter's place, Jake told him, "Thanks, Billy. You don't know how much this means to me."

The next week, Jake, spiffily attired in a herringbone sports jacket, dress shirt, and bow tie, but now garnished with a Dodgers cap, arrived with an enthused "Howdy" at Billy's driveway, again a half hour early. Billy, already in his Diablos uniform, told Jake, "I already checked the oil and water, and washed her. Today's a special day. I'm playing right field, and Joannie's coming to watch. After we visit the complex, I've got to pick her up."

The pair parked at the apartment complex, and Jake went inside while Billy waited. And waited. And waited.

Billy checked his phone. Game time was fast creeping up. Shortly he checked again. Still no Jake! He thought about entering the complex in search of Jake, but what if the old man returned to the car while he looked? He anxiously paced, never straying far from the car. Still no Jake! And he still had to pick up Joannie. He was getting angry, but then worried, "What if something's happened to Jake?"

Finally, Jake came out, hobbling quickly on his bad leg. He started talking as soon as he saw Billy, occasionally interrupting himself with his allergic cough. "Sorry I'm a little late. Got into a conversation with the manager. Just couldn't just break it. He kept on talking. I met that lady again. Her name's Rose. Nice lady. Maybe I'll end up moving in with her. Told me the roommate she used to have died two months ago. Forgot to ask if it was a man or a woman. Rose is eighty, though. Don't know if I should be moving in with an older woman. I'd really like this neighborhood. I can walk to the market. Sorry for being so late."

At first relieved to see Jake, Billy was now very upset that Jake had kept him waiting so long. Furious, in fact. He questioned whether to let the old man know he was angry. He decided he should, remembering his mom once told him, "Don't hold things in; the more you do, the more the situation will become inflated, and suddenly burst out in an explosion. Besides, if you don't let people know you're upset and why, how can they be expected to change their behavior?"

Well, he didn't remember the exact words she used, only the general idea.

So, after they attached seat belts and shoulder harnesses, Billy turned on Mass Massacre and upped the volume. He quickly backed up, then put it into drive and gunned the motor, his car lurching out the lot and onto the street. Billy felt certain this variation in his normal driving pattern would let Jake know he was mad, and as to the reason why, Jake could easily figure that out!

He drove fast, coming only to rolling halts at stop signs, until reaching Joannie's house, which, luckily, was on the way to the ballfield. She waited on her porch. He turned down the volume, yelled and waved for her to come to the car, and when she did he hastily apologized for being late. He sped away, but when they finally arrived at the ballfield a few minutes later the game had just begun, and there was Scott, standing out in right field!

The coach informed Billy that if he didn't care enough to get to the game on time, he shouldn't care much about not playing. Billy sat dejectedly in the dugout the whole game and felt even worse when Scott hit a home run in the last inning to win the game for the Diablos.

"Nice team game," Joannie offered kindly after the contest ended.

"Thanks," sighed a resigned, clearly unhappy Billy. "We've got some good players."

No one spoke a word as Billy drove Joannie back to her house. "See you," she told him as he dropped her off. He was very thankful she hadn't said anything about him not playing.

Later, when he dropped off Jake, the old man said, "Sorry, Billy. My fault you didn't play. I shouldn't have stayed so long. An old codger like me should have known better."

"It's okay. You're not an old codger," stated Billy, though he really didn't believe it and thought only an old codger would use the word "codger." He watched the limping Jake shuffle off slowly toward the house.

At dinner, a subdued Billy noticed his mom glancing at him. He wasn't hungry and asked to be excused. A half hour later she went to his room and told him, "I noticed that today you've been withdrawn and quiet. Is there anything you'd like to talk about?"

Billy spilled everything.

She commiserated, "You must have felt terrible, after planning to play in that game all week."

"Yep," Billy agreed.

"You must've been embarrassed when you asked Joannie to come, and here you sat on the bench the whole game," she empathized.

"Sure was."

"You must have been furious with Jake! I mean really angry," she affirmed.

"Absolutely."

"Just like the time you were angry at Andrew for breaking your piggy bank, and the time you were so upset at Susie for forgetting to tell you that girl called and wanted you to come to her house and help her with homework. What's her name, the one whose parents both work at night, leaving the poor girl alone?"

"Rachel, Mom."

"You're such a terrific person. You really are," she added before leaving the room. Suddenly Billy felt better. His mom so often gave him a lift and new perspective.

By then he'd spent his anger and, thinking more on it, realized that taking Jake around had made him feel good about himself. He was a better citizen of the world, helping others, a mature being, not a selfish, hot-rodding kid.

Jake didn't show up at Billy's driveway the next Saturday, nor the one after that. Billy wondered where Jake was. Were his feelings badly hurt by Billy not talking to him on the ride home that day? Was he so upset that he decided not to bother Billy anymore?

To find the answer, Billy drove to Jake's daughter's house after his baseball game and rang the doorbell. A tall woman about his mom's age opened the door. Billy said, "Hi, are you Jake's daughter?"

"Yes?" she answered, as if asking a question.

He was introducing himself, "I'm Billy Harrington, and ..." when she interrupted.

"I know who you are. My dad told me you drove him to your baseball games. He had so much fun. It was all he would talk about. The Diablos, and the green field, and whether you'd won or lost. Except for the last time. He was so quiet that night. I couldn't figure it out.

"Anyway, you should be proud of yourself for doing that man so much good. But I guess no one told you. Dad had a heart attack. The doctor told us before it could happen at any time. It was the day after you last drove him to a game. And he didn't make it. He passed that night."

Billy's arms shook in small tremors. He was unable to speak.

The daughter, sensing Billy's paralysis, kept talking. "The funeral was the next day. I guess we should have told you about it, but we were so upset we just forgot. I want to thank you for being so nice to my dad, for being his friend."

He'd never had a real friend die before. Jake wasn't a typical friend, but he was someone whose life he shared, for at least a short while. He told Jake's daughter he was very sorry, thanked her for telling him, and trudged to his car with moist eyes. He'd never see or hear Jake again.

As he got in the car, Billy recalled Jake sitting beside him, debonair and talkative. He could almost feel Jake's presence, his new, but gone, older friend, who wanted, like everyone, to belong. He regretted not treating Jake nicer the last time he saw him. He wished he had a chance to apologize for being silently furious in a way Jake must have noticed. He wished he hadn't gotten so angry. He'd remember Jake!

Shortly after leaving the driveway, Billy heard a thumping. Then he felt a lurching, the car dropping slightly, then rising, then falling again in a regular pattern. Thump-athump-athump. Like it had a limp. He'd heard the symptoms enough times in his parents' cars to know he'd have to be dealing with a flat tire.

Then, just before he reached home, he heard the engine sputter, first intermittently then regularly until it turned into a constant cough. Unless his dad could figure out what was wrong with the engine, Billy knew they'd have to bring the car to the mechanic. He wondered why it was okay, even desirable, to take a malfunctioning car to a mechanic, but not permissible for a sick Christian Scientist to visit a doctor.

At first Billy got angry at his misbehaving car. Limping flat tire. Coughing engine. Why was all this going down? And why just now?

Suddenly Billy thought he understood. It could all be coincidence, but ...

He patted his dashboard, as he himself was patted on the head in the past when someone wanted to display affection. He said aloud, "Howdy, Jake! I know you're with me."

Then he gazed up to the skies, honked his horn, and said, "Thank you, Lord."

When he arrived home, he told his dad about the flat and the engine noise, but surprised his father by asking, "Can we wait until tomorrow before making any repairs?"

A short while later, he went to the driveway and gave Jake's Spirit, his new name for the car, a good wash and wax, even though he'd done these jobs just a few hours before.

The Final Decision

I should've been buoyed by knowing I'd soon escape the trap of premature fatherhood. My life could resume, though it would never be the same. Tautness in my neck and shoulders should've diminished. But didn't.

As I drove us from the park toward school I noticed some flowers at the side of the road, so totally lush days before, had lost petals, leaving only the floret. They were probably much the same back then, but I looked at them more honestly now.

As we rode, silently, I was disturbed by a dilemma I hadn't anticipated. I reflected on the conversation we'd had at the lake, and I realized I hadn't said everything I needed to say. I'd been unfair to her, my best friend. I'd been manipulative and deceptive, to myself as well. I had to confess now. Missing first period wouldn't turn us into truants, although the dutiful allegiance to school I'd grown up with had greater importance than one might think.

I pulled Jake's Spirit to the side of the road, shut the motor. Joannie was surprised and about to say something, but held off. I got out and sat in the dirt under a fir tree, motionless, obviously upset. She joined me, said nothing, though by sitting so close to me she was saying something.

I reached and held her wrists. "I'm sorry, Joannie. I'm sorry," I said. Then, I muffled my head in her shoulder to conceal embarrassing tears.

"Billy, there's nothing to cry about. We've decided to do the right thing. It's best for both of us," she admonished. She stroked my hair, reminiscent of the comforting mother of a perfectionistic child who'd erred slightly in building models and threw a self-loathing tantrum.

I raised my head, sniffled, and looked directly at her, confessing, "No! No! You don't understand! I spent hours struggling to decide what to say to you, until I concluded what my responsibilities were, what I thought you really wanted, and what was best for both of us. But I knew if I made it seem I wanted you to terminate, you'd think I was ... was ruthless and self-centered, I ... I manipulated you into not wanting to get married and agreeing to terminating. I knew if I didn't say I loved you, and didn't talk about wanting the baby, you wouldn't want to have it. So, I intentionally didn't say them."

Even after this admission I sensed that there was another admission I hadn't made. But what? How could I admit something I was unaware of?

She stroked my hair. "Billy, I know you better than you give me credit for, and you're the finest boy I've ever met. But you are not the hardest person to see through. I knew you intentionally didn't say you loved me and wanted the baby. And I knew you were aware of how I'd react when you didn't say them. You would've said those things, if you truly felt them. You didn't deceive me, Billy. You didn't even deceive yourself. You did the right thing."

A tear ran down my cheek. I raised my head. My stare penetrated her tender eyes, into her depths as if she deserved worship.

She added, "Billy, one more thing. You spoke of deceiving me. I can say the same about myself. When I alluded to the roots the other day, it was just something I made up. I saw how indecisive you were, not like the take-charge person you normally are. So, I said something, anything, I thought might give you direction. In the past you probably never even noticed the roots to that tree. Who would notice roots, the trunk is so huge and glorious? I could've just as well said something about branches reaching out, or sap circulating, but just then I happened to think of the roots. It turned out that what I said worked, but it was an accident."

I shook my head, smiled, "I don't at all think it was an accident. There was a reason you said what you did and not something else."

She continued her apology, "Instead of opening my yap, I should have let you sit by that tree. You'd've figured everything out by yourself."

"Maybe. But probably not."

"Am I still your blanket?" she inquired.

"Only if I'm still your pillow."

We hugged, her head now buried in my shoulder. She whispered, "You need to wipe off your new loafers—Swazis? They're covered with dust."

And then it hit me! Why I was still uneasy. That something! What had been unconsciously troubling me. The invisible had appeared. It felt … spiritual. Only rarely do matters hit me as a feeding of my soul.

I knew what I had to admit. Well, maybe not 'admit' per se, but divulge.

"Joannie, at the lake, just before, at the lake, I thought of Theodore."

"Theodore?"

"Who I mentioned for the first time before. A vision materialized. Of Theodore, the name I gave to the boy inside you. Before, he was just a boy. Now, with a name, he seemed a real person.

Not a bunch of random cells, but a live person. I can see him now — his eyes sparkling with excitement after he scored his first bangle at Huckle Buckle. Hugging me after the game, thanking me for being his coach."

"You'd be a great coach. Huckle Buckle's your sport."

"But even if he botched the shot in the last quintum and his team lost, I'd put my arm around him, consoling, so he didn't lose his love for the game. And we'd go for pizza."

"You don't care that much for pizza."

"No, but he does. … I mean would. He wouldn't always mirror me."

"It wouldn't be so bad if he did."

"I picture you and me looking in the distance, admiring how many friends he had."

"Your vision includes me?"

"Of course. I imagine him delivering the valedictory speech at his high school graduation, and thanking both of us, his 'devoted parents', for our example and encouragement."

"What does he look like?"

"Not a miniature me. Taller. Though there'd be some similarity, he'd be his own person. Most people would call him 'Teddy'. But he'd always be my Theodore. The son I never had."

She thought a moment, then — "Maybe at the same time at the lake I was thinking of Rebecca."

"Rebecca?"

"The name I'd give her. Who looked a lot like me. But like with you, not a mirror."

"Any of my features?"

"Maybe those dreamy eyes… I can imagine her excitement when first meeting that frisky little puppy at the rescue pound. Or, the two of us skipping in a downpour, laughing and stomping on puddles."

"Seeing who could make the water jump the highest."

"Consoling her when she didn't win the third-grade spelling bee."

"As I recall that loss happened to you as well, didn't it?"

"Yeah, Showoff!"

"Sorry, I couldn't help it."

"We'd probably end up calling her 'Becky'. Who'd be the high school valedictorian."

Maybe that's what Joannie's flinching was about there at the lake. Like me, she'd named the baby, visualized what Becky would be like, not consciously realizing its import.

"Is Becky as strong in your creative mind as Theodore is in mine?"

"Becky is strikingly vivid in my imagination."

"Do you think Theodore — or Becky — would like it if you took those pills?"

"Doubtful."

"Joannie, do you think we should, you should …"

"Reconsider?"

"There's no rush to make a final decision now."

She was quick to agree.

So, would the fate of Theodore and Becky be decided another day? Or had it already been decided, and waiting for us to realize it?

"Billy, do you have courage?"

"Think so. And able to overcome even huge obstacles."

"Me too."

I blurted, "Joannie, if we were really courageous, we'd have the baby."

"And Theodore or Rebecca would be a product of our courage."

"Of course, we could put the baby up for adoption."

"Billy, I can't imagine someone else raising her, even with open adoption where we stayed in touch with who adopted her."

"Or him… We have dreams for our future lives. But what would our dreams be like if we … took the other option? Or if we didn't raise him or her by ourselves?"

"Nightmares."

"We'd need to figure out, at least in the beginning — who we'd live with …"

"And, what about those future career plans?"

"We'd still have plans, Joannie. Just new ones. Which could include the old ones. We'd figure it out. After all, we'd be parents of a valedictorian who got their smarts from us."

"So, is that the final decision – raise the baby ourselves? Based on what our unreal imaginations have conjured up?

"Imaginations are not unreal. They exist. They can tell us what we truly want. Or what our true emotions are… Let's take a vote. I vote "Aye".

"Aye."

"We should take a day off from school today. To celebrate our courage."

She told me, "I love you, Billy."

Meaningfully and genuinely — "I love you, Joannie."

"And I'll also love Theodore or Becky."

"Our child."

"We won't be making a mistake, Billy."

"No way. This time, this decision — no 'Whoopsie-Doopsie.'"

Discussion Questions

The Problem

1. The decision choices: What did you think about the decision choices Billy and Joannie had? Are the pro-choice and pro-life arguments presented equally and fairly, or is one favored? Were there any other arguments that could have been made on either side?
2. If you were Joannie (or Billy), what decision would you have made? Why?
3. Have you ever been in some sort of unpleasant situation where you had to make a difficult decision, like Billy and Joannie needed to make? What happened?

Overall Reaction

1. Likability: Would you recommend *The Billy Chronicles* to your book-reading friends? Why/why not?
2. Are there any chapters you particularly liked? Didn't care for? Why?
3. Future books: The book was written from Billy's point of view. Would you now be interested in reading a book from Joannie's point of view? Would you be interested in reading about Billy and/or Joannie at an older age?
4. Billy's introspection: What did you think of the book organization in terms of having alternate chapters? Of Billy's introspection, and stories that happened in his life at different ages? Was Billy's introspection believable? Did the stories about Billy at different ages relate to the

introspection chapters?

5. What did you think about how the book ended?

6. Did you find the book humorous? Satirical? Discuss the humor.

7. Connections with the content: Did the book evoke any memories for you? What?

8. Are there any particular messages or lessons you took from the book? What?

Characters and Relationships

1. What did you think of Billy as a person? Joannie? Did you like them? Were they believable?

2. Specific relationships: What do you think of the relationship between Billy and Joannie? Was it believable? What did you think of Billy's relationships with the various members of his family: Mom, Dad, Andrew, Susie? What about Joannie's relationship with her mom?

3. Aside from Billy and Joannie, which other significant characters did you most like reading about?

About the Author

Art Shulman graduated with a Ph.D. in psychology and was called professor for the 20 years he taught at California State University, Northridge. A native of Brooklyn, he lives in Los Angeles with his wife, Rebecca.

Art is a sports nut, and he does stand-up comedy. He has had more than 100 produced plays—dramas, comedies, and dramadies.

His other books include:

A Kid Grows in Brooklyn: Memories of a Magical Time
 A memoir about growing up in the most magical place—Brooklyn

I'm Wrong, I'm Sorry, I Love You!
 Getting along with your mate after a squabble: A survival manual for men

Tyrus Carson's Ride
 A Western coming-of-age story

Barnaby Brain
 An illustrated children's book about a brain who transforms into a whole boy